Books by Eileen Watkins

THE PERSIAN ALWAYS MEOWS TWICE

THE BENGAL IDENTITY

FERAL ATTRACTION

GONE, KITTY, GONE

CLAW & DISORDER

Published by Kensington Publishing Corp.

CLAW & DISORDER

EILEEN WATKINS

KENSINGTON
PUBLISHING CORP.

www.kensingtonbooks.com

KENSINGTON BOOKS are published by

Kensington Publishing Corp.
119 West 40th Street
New York, NY 10018

Copyright © 2021 by Eileen Watkins

All Kensington titles, imprints, and distributed lines are available at special quantity discounts for bulk purchases for sales promotion, premiums, fund-raising, educational, or institutional use.

Special book excerpts or customized printings can also be created to fit specific needs. For details, write or phone the office of the Kensington Sales Manager: Kensington Publishing Corp., 119 West 40th Street, New York, NY 10018. Attn. Sales Department. Phone: 1-800-221-2647.

The K logo is a trademark of Kensington Publishing Corp.

ISBN-13: 978-1-4967-2301-7 (ebook)
ISBN-10: 1-4967-2301-5 (ebook)

ISBN-13: 978-1-4967-2298-0
ISBN-10: 1-4967-2298-1
First Kensington Trade Paperback Printing: February 2021

10 9 8 7 6 5 4 3 2 1

Printed in the United States of America

Acknowledgments

Once again, I must thank my critique partners, Nicki Montaperto, Lew Preschel, and Jo-Ann Lamon Reccoppa, all members of Sisters in Crime Central Jersey.

Thanks also to my agent, Evan Marshall, and my Kensington editor, John Scognamiglio.

My friend-since-college Anne-Marie Cottone accompanied me to several jazz events, so I could get a better feel for Mark Coccia's new hobby, and helped with other research questions.

Thanks also to Matt Chylak for info on the University of Pennsylvania, and to Pat Marinelli for her insights on small-town police operations.

Chapter 1

Gillian Foster removed her tortoiseshell-framed sunglasses and tucked them into her small Coach crossbody bag. Her cool hazel eyes swept over what she could see of the front of my store. "Hmph. I expected this place to be bigger."

"It's deceptive," I assured her. "The building lot is pretty deep."

She frowned at my hot-pink sales counter and the screened wall just behind it. "What's all of this . . . wire mesh?"

"That's the playroom, where we let the cats out for exercise. Would you like to see—?"

Just then, my assistant, Sarah Wilcox, entered through the wood-framed door in the screen, and I introduced her to our prospective customer. Again, I got the impression that Gillian did not totally approve. To give her the benefit of the doubt, I didn't think she objected to Sarah's dusky complexion as much as to her sturdy figure and unglamorous, graying hair. Her bib apron, branded with the shop name, CASSIE'S COMFY CATS, still sported a few wisps of pale fur from the last Persian we had groomed.

So did mine, and I also wasn't looking my best in other respects. Some of us actually worked for a living, and I found myself wondering if Gillian Foster would know anything about that.

Despite the warmth of the June morning outside—and the fact that it was Saturday, a dress-down time for most residents of Chadwick, New Jersey—our visitor remained crisp and cool in a pressed white cotton blouse, pale-gray ankle-length slacks and low-heeled sandals. I judged her to be at least in her mid-forties. The blond streak at the front of her classic page-boy haircut probably camouflaged some silver, and those appraising eyes tilted up at their outer corners in a way that suggested surgical help.

I tried to maintain a pleasantly professional demeanor. "How did you hear about us? From our website?"

"Not initially. I was picking up a few things this morning at Towne Antiques, down on Center Street? I mentioned that I needed to find a place to board my cat, Leya, for a week or so, and Philip recommended you. He told me, 'Cassie Mc-Glone's just been here a couple of years, but everyone says great things about her.' Thought I might as well stop by while I was still downtown. It's a good thing he described the building to me, though, or I might have driven right on by."

I found this a little hard to believe. Though my business is in an older, converted two-story house, I'd stenciled the name in large purple letters across the front window, to make sure it stood out among its neighbors.

The counter phone rang and Sarah picked it up. Cheerfully, she assured the caller that we handled cats only. We did not accept ferals, she explained, but yes, we would take cranky household pets, as long as they were fixed and vaccinated.

Gillian asked me, "Was this place a private home?"

I nodded. "And then a beauty salon, for a while. You could say it's serving a similar purpose now, but for felines."

That inspired the faintest of smiles. "You've got room to board here, too?"

"We make optimal use of the space we have. Can I show you around?"

Leaving Sarah to take over in front, I opened the door in the screened wall and escorted Gillian through.

Meanwhile, my prospective client raked me again with a critical eye. Did she expect someone who boarded and groomed cats for a living to maintain an appearance as meticulous as hers? At least I'd tied back my shoulder-length brown hair and wore my own "CCC" apron over a T-shirt and jeans. More likely Gillian was wondering, *How old are you, anyway?* I was still a couple of years shy of thirty but didn't usually wear makeup on the job. People sometimes told me that without it I looked younger—though not necessarily in a good way.

Instead, Gillian asked, "How long have you been in business?"

"A little over two years. People around here say we're really filling a need. Many pet groomers won't even deal with cats, and the cats often get upset if they're kept in a kennel near dogs."

"That is true. The first time I boarded Leya, when Donald and I went to Cancun, it was in a facility about ten miles from here with a very good reputation. But still, the other wing had a lot of barking dogs, and I could tell she hadn't been happy. She'd lost a whole pound and even had a bald patch on one leg. The fur grew back as soon as she settled in again at home."

"Yes, I hear stories like that a lot." My opinion of Gillian rebounded a little. At least she'd cared enough about her pet to notice these signs of stress. "Is she a longhair?"

"Himalayan, purebred."

Of course she was.

In the cat playroom, I began pointing out all of the carpeted tunnels and towers, sisal scratching posts and wall shelves that our boarders could use for exercise. Meanwhile, I saw Gillian mentally count the three felines perched at various spots around the room.

"You turn several cats out at the same time?" she accused me. "That's unacceptable! They could fight and injure each other, or pass germs . . ."

"We only do this with animals that come from the same home, with the permission of the owner." I went on to explain that, except under emergency circumstances, I took only altered cats. Each owner also had to sign a release stating their pets did not have any diseases that could easily spread to others.

That calmed Gillian somewhat, though I still wasn't a hundred percent sure she trusted me. "My husband's folks live in upstate New York," she said, "and when we visit them we put Leya in a wonderful place—a cat hotel, really. They have several different play areas, and you can choose an 'activity package' including your pet's favorite types of play."

I thought fast. "We don't have any structured arrangement, but if Leya prefers certain activities, we can try to provide those. When the cats are turned out here, Sarah plays with them most of the time, and I help when I can."

"You've only got one assistant to exercise . . . what, a dozen boarders? And there must be other cats that come in just to be groomed."

Although the implied criticism annoyed me, I had to admit the woman was observant. It was true, I did feel the crunch at times. Still, I told her, "It works out. Lately, since our business has been growing, I've taken on another part-time helper who comes with me on house calls."

Gillian wrinkled her nose again over my cute pink and black grooming studio, which I'm sure did not compare to the spa-like accommodations of the upstate New York "hotel." Neither, I guessed, did the baker's dozen of cat condos, ten of them currently occupied. Each was the size of a broom closet and featured two wide shelves, with a litter box at the bottom, dishes for food and water at midlevel, and a cat bed on the top.

She told me wistfully, "The New York place had a choice of condo size, and some 'luxury suites' had their own exercise areas."

"As you can see, ours are very democratic. We did add this larger one, set off by itself, in case we have to take a cat who's ill or not neutered, and needs to be kept apart from the others."

Gillian glanced toward the white-painted tin ceiling. "What's upstairs?"

"My living quarters." I certainly hoped she didn't ask to see those. But from her disappointed air, she'd probably hoped that I might be hiding the luxury suites on the second floor.

I attempted to steer the conversation in a more positive direction. "Are you and your husband taking another vacation?"

"No, but we're renovating our house. Well, we've *been* renovating it for the past two years, but next week the designer is putting the final touches on the décor. While it was just construction work, I usually could shut Leya up in a room somewhere out of the way. But next week will be complete chaos, with furniture getting moved around in all the spaces. I can't risk her slipping out through an open door."

"Very smart." I was a firm believer in keeping cats inside, especially pampered pets who lived in suburban neighborhoods. "Are you near a busy street?"

"We're on Cooper's Mill Road. The Ramsford-Cooper house." My blank expression seemed to shock her. "I'm so surprised that you haven't heard of it! John Ramsford was one of this town's most prominent citizens, going back to Revolutionary times. He owned one of the most productive iron mines in the area. Some people think Chadwick really should have been named after him, instead of that milquetoast of a general."

I felt ill-equipped to argue local history with her. "I've only lived here two years, so I guess I'm not up on all of the town's lore. Is your house a historic site?"

"Yes, although it's not on the register . . . yet. The main part dates back to the early 1800s. The last owners had no taste at all, so we've had to do a lot of work on the place."

"To modernize it?"

Gillian recoiled at the idea. "No, to restore it! We modernized the utilities, of course. But the living spaces have been taken back, as far as possible, to what they might have been like in Ramsford's day. That's why I've gotten so many things lately from Philip—he carries a good assortment of Early American redware, fireplace tools and even primitive art."

I nodded. On my visits to Towne Antiques, I mostly had to window-shop. I could afford some fun, retro items, but those treasures from the 1800s were priced far beyond my budget. Good thing they really weren't my taste, anyway.

"The town historical society is very interested," Gillian went on. "At the end of next week, when everything's perfect, I'm holding a reception so they can see what we've done."

"Sounds very exciting," I said.

As we traveled back through the playroom, Gillian took a final glance around and sighed. "Well, I suppose this will do for Leya. I *am* in a bind, and Philip did say he's heard good things about your services."

I made a mental note to thank him. Philip had done me a

favor, whether or not Ms. Foster turned out to be a difficult client.

We passed back through the door in the screened wall to the front sales area. Sarah watched us return with a questioning look.

Stepping to the customers' side of the counter, Gillian whipped a business card out of her small bag. "Here's my address. I'll need you to pick Leya up on Tuesday. Eight a.m., or even earlier if possible—that's when the design crew will be starting work. I'll give you a week's worth of her food and a list of her play and grooming needs. Plan on keeping her until Friday morning. If anything changes before then, I'll let you know."

While I bristled at the sense that she was barking orders at me, Sarah calmly opened our appointment book and jotted down the information. "Your cat's name is Leia?" She smiled at Gillian. "Like the princess in *Star Wars*?"

Our new client rolled those hazel eyes, though still the corners never drooped. "No, L-E-Y-A. It's Hindi. It means 'lioness.'"

I set my jaw. Disrespect me and I can shrug it off. But disrespect my assistant—a former high school math teacher who toiled for decades in inner-city schools before retiring to take on our fractious feline customers—and you're treading on dangerous ground.

Sarah herself remained unflappable. "Oh, that's nice, too. And she's a Himalayan? I guess Hindi is close enough to Nepali, eh?"

She spoke in a gentle, joking tone, but a flush crept up Gillian's cheek.

Nice burn, Sarah. She's thinks she's so sophisticated!

I handed Gillian the standard form I required all owners to fill out for their boarding pets. I expected more complaints, but she dutifully entered all of the cat's known medical history. The bottom of the form listed our rates per day and per service, and she checked boxes for two groomings and one claw clipping during her pet's stay. The cost for all of this plus board amounted to a tidy sum, but I guessed it was still cheaper than the posh cat hotel in upstate New York.

Gillian was about to pass the sheet back to me, when I quoted her an additional cost for the pick-up and drop-off service. She accepted that, too, with merely a nod.

"Thanks," I told her. "See you at eight on Tuesday."

After our self-important customer left, Sarah grinned at me. "You charged her five dollars more each way for the pick-up and drop-off than you do for our other customers. How come?"

"So far, no other customer has asked me to pick up before standard work hours. Anyhow, I have a feeling I'm going to earn that extra ten dollars with this lady."

"We probably shouldn't discourage clients with deep pockets, even if they are a little demanding." Sarah read the form that Gillian had filled out. "At least in the space that asks if her cat has any 'temperamental issues,' she marked 'no.' "

"That's good. Guess Leya doesn't take after her owner."

Not expecting any more customers that morning, Sarah and I rounded up the playroom's three cats, put them back in their condos, and turned out Mia, a sleek Siamese who came in to board a couple of times a year. Meanwhile, my assistant rather hesitantly requested a favor.

"You know I do some work, through my church, with some of the poorer families in the county," she said. "We've got an older couple in our parish, Bernice and Chester Tillman, who are in a bad way. Both have health issues, and their living situation doesn't help. They're in a small house that's pretty run-down, and they've been hoarding stuff for years and years. It's almost as bad as one of those reality TV shows. Along with the piles of newspapers, broken appliances and gadgets, and kids' toys and games, they've got cats. I mean, cats outdoors and indoors!"

"Oh, dear." I had a sense of where this was going and tried to tactfully distance myself. "You'd better call the SPCA."

"We did, but you know how they are. They'll take 'em all to the county shelter, and any that don't get adopted right away will be put to sleep. Bernice and Chester know that and are afraid to let any of them go. She'll break down in tears just talking about it."

I thought of our local no-kill shelter, the Friends of Chadwick Animals. "FOCA might be able to help, but they're small and can only take so many."

"I know, and they usually accept them only from here in town. The Tillmans live over in Dalton. Could you possibly talk to FOCA, though, and see if they'd make an exception?" Sarah's large dark eyes behind her wire-rimmed glasses pleaded with me.

"Any idea how many cats they've got, in all?"

Sarah shook her head of short salt-and-pepper curls. "Hard to say. Some pretty much stay indoors and others run in and out. There are maybe half a dozen that might be tame enough to go to other homes." My assistant brightened, because I'm sure she could tell I was weakening. "If you want to see for yourself, I'm going there after church tomorrow. I'll give you the address and you can meet me there."

A visit to the house of two ailing hoarders did not sound like the most cheerful way to spend my scarce time off, but I figured I owed Sarah. She'd become much more than just an extra pair of hands to me over the past two years. She occasionally ran outside errands and pulled extra hours—with pay—on short notice. But mainly she'd been a good friend, listening to my troubles and offering sound advice. She'd even brainstormed with me about the criminal cases involving our customers that I'd sometimes helped to investigate.

In return, she didn't ask a lot of favors, so I wouldn't deny her this one.

"Okay," I agreed. "I'll have a look at the situation. Maybe I'll think of an angle to pitch their case to FOCA."

Sarah patted my arm in thanks. "I wouldn't ask you to get mixed up in their problems, but you're an expert; Bernice and Chester might listen to you more than to the rest of us. And though we're trying to help them to clean up the clutter, I think it's even more urgent that they part with some of the cats. Bernice has asthma, which all that fur and dander isn't helping. And Chester's eyes are bad, so a cat could dash in front of him and trip him." Half joking, she added, "I'm scared that, one of these days, their pets might be the death of them!"

Chapter 2

In theory, I close my shop at noon on Saturdays, and I always
let Sarah leave at that time. If things were busy, or someone
had to drop off or pick up a cat in the afternoon, I could always stay on and handle things alone. But it was June, and
while we had a fairly full house in terms of boarders—their
owners on vacation, or traveling to graduations or wed-
dings—no one was coming that day just for grooming. I had
the sunny spring afternoon to myself.

I cleaned up, shook my hair loose from its coated elastic
band, and phoned my friend Dawn. She operated a natural-
foods store a couple of blocks down from me, Nature's Way,
and usually worked a full shift on Saturday. "Are you busy?
Okay if I visit for a few minutes?"

She wailed, "Please do, it's *dead* here today. Everybody
must have taken off for the lake or the shore. Have you had
any customers?"

"Just one drop-in." I told her, briefly, about Gillian Foster. "In fact, I think on my way to your place I'll stop by
Towne Antiques and thank Philip for the referral."

"Yeah, that was nice of him. I love his shop and I haven't

been in for a long time. Maybe I'll play hooky for a little while and meet you there."

Philip Russell worked Wednesday through Sunday, because the weekend was his prime time to attract the well-heeled tourists who'd started to discover Chadwick over the past few years. Dawn had come to know him fairly well, thanks to her Bohemian style of dressing and decorating. At Towne Antiques, she could find clothing and other textiles that actually came from the 1970s, for better prices than modern knockoffs. I dressed in a sportier, more conventional style, though when I'd first moved into the second floor of my building I'd also picked up a few "shabby chic" furniture pieces from Philip.

Today, as Dawn and I stepped beneath the shop's overhanging roof, a middle-aged man in a T-shirt and jeans blustered out the front door. He carried a tote bag and, with eyes cast down, didn't even appear to see us. The doorway of Philip's shop was flanked by a pair of decorative columns, and the stranger almost pushed me into one of them.

"Rude!" Dawn called him, under her breath, but by then he was too far down the sidewalk to hear.

Inside, we found Philip standing at attention behind his solid mahogany sales desk. Tall and slim, with wavy silver hair, he'd dressed today in a checked, button-front shirt with the sleeves rolled up and dark-washed jeans. Though long and narrow, his face usually wore a good-natured expression, and he greeted me and Dawn with a smile.

When I wondered aloud about the man with the tote bag who had almost knocked me off the curb, Philip apologized.

"He was annoyed because I wasn't interested in buying some 1980s video games. People often come in here trying to sell me things that they think must be extremely valuable," he said. "When I have to burst that bubble, sometimes they don't take it so well!"

The shop consisted of several rooms, with furniture and artwork from different eras dispersed throughout. The front rooms tended to display higher-quality pieces such as McCoy and Roseville pottery, good midcentury furniture, and art deco light fixtures. The paintings on the walls ranged from decent oils of still lifes and landscapes to kitschy, heavily textured abstracts. I knew that one space farther back held older toys and electronics, and another offered vintage clothes and accessories.

Dawn gravitated toward the last area, as usual. Soon she spotted a long, rayon hippie skirt, black with a sinuous pattern of coral daylilies, that she *had* to try on. You need to understand, my best friend stands about five-ten, slim below and statuesque above, with a strong profile and long, wavy auburn hair. She can carry off dramatic looks that would swallow me whole. Philip pointed her to an alcove with a folding screen, where she could step out of her fringed bell-bottoms in privacy.

While we waited for her to return, I thanked him for referring Gillian Foster to me. "She stopped by this morning and arranged to board her cat next week."

"Did she? Oh, I'm so glad. She was going on about how she couldn't find anyone she could trust with Leya, and I told her she couldn't do better than you. I said you always go the extra mile for any cat in your care, and have a great reputation around town." He leaned toward me with an air of conspiracy and whispered, "I didn't mention any of that business with the police over the years, of course. If she hasn't read about it in the papers, no need to call her attention to it."

"No need at all. I appreciate both what you did and didn't say to her. She told me she bought some Early American pieces from you."

He nodded. "Some redware pottery, some hand-painted boxes, and a couple of American primitive oils. You might have noticed, I don't keep many things from that period here in the shop—no large pieces of furniture, for example. For security reasons, I sell most of that through my website."

That made sense to me. "I guess the older something is, the more valuable it is, right?"

Philip chuckled. "Of course, that depends on the condition and the rarity of the piece. Some older items are pretty commonplace, and some newer things are worth more than you'd think—certain types of costume jewelry, toys, or ephemera. There's a particular edition of the Beatles' *White Album* that's worth a fortune. Some early comic books, too. Collectors will pay a lot for baseball cards from the early 1900s and other kinds of sports memorabilia."

He broke off when Dawn returned from the back of the shop with the flowered skirt over her arm. I could tell from her satisfied smile that it was going home with her.

"Gee, you aren't going to model it for us?" Philip teased.

"Not now, I should get back to my shop. But I'll drop by some other time when I have it on." While Philip folded the long garment and tucked it into one of the store's branded bags, Dawn counted out the payment in cash. She never used credit cards for small, everyday purchases, she'd once told me, because cash kept her more conscious of how much she was spending.

"You and Mark have any plans for the evening?" she asked me as we headed back toward Nature's Way.

"Only dinner at his place . . . that I know of," I said.

"That sounds intriguing. Just what are you expecting?" I

had been dating Mark Coccia, the local veterinarian, for more than a year now, so Dawn knew that our spending the night together would not be a novel occurrence.

"He said he has a surprise in store for me. It's not my birthday or any other special occasion, so I really don't know what to expect. He sounded a bit nervous about it, too."

Dawn halted abruptly on the sidewalk, her amber-brown eyes widening. "Oh, my gosh. You don't think he's going to—"

I shook my head. "I really *don't* think so. I hope he wouldn't spring something like that on me!"

She giggled. "He'd better not, if that's your attitude."

"I don't mean it like that, but he and I have had The Discussion. If and when we decide to get married, we'll make the decision together. I wouldn't want to be blindsided or pressured, and he knows that. At least, I hope he does."

Dawn shifted her approach to calming me down. "It's probably nothing so major. Maybe he got a dog. Brought one home from the clinic that was abandoned by its owner."

I relaxed. "That, I could almost imagine. Though I don't know why he'd be nervous—he knows I like all kinds of animals."

"Maybe it's a big, ugly dog that sniffs crotches, and jumps up on you, and bays like the Hound of the Baskervilles."

"Small chance. Mark lives in a condo, remember? His HOA board would come down on him like a ton of bricks."

We reached Nature's Way, also in a converted, turn-of-the-century structure. Unlike my shop, though, it had started life as a feed store patronized by local farmers; now it stocked organic fodder for humans. Dawn had the exterior painted in two coordinating shades of soft green, to play up the architectural details and emphasize the wholesomeness of her merchandise.

As usual, her adolescent tabby cat, Tigger, romped up to us when we entered. I scooped him into my arms as I followed Dawn across the scarred wooden floors toward the showpiece of her store, an antique carved-oak display counter. She set the bag containing her "new" skirt on the glass top.

"Mark's been acting strange lately, in general," I admitted. "Last week I dropped by the clinic around closing time, hoping to catch him on his way out, but the receptionist said he'd left early. I mean, he's so dedicated, he hardly ever does that."

Dawn shrugged. "Maybe he had an important errand to run."

"That's what I figured. But I texted him and he didn't reply until about an hour later. Then he was really vague about what he'd been doing, totally skirted the issue."

"Buying the ring!" she suggested with a sly grin.

I swatted her arm. "It's happened a couple more times, that I tried to make plans with him on a weeknight and he made some kind of excuse, then practically contradicted himself the next time I talked to him."

"Well, he's a smart guy. If he was seeing somebody else, he'd probably put more effort into his alibis."

"And he probably wouldn't give me all this buildup about having a 'surprise' for me tonight. At least that doesn't sound like he wants to break up!"

"Though that *would* be a surprise." When I looked daggers at her, Dawn laughed. "Is he very religious? Maybe he's decided to become a priest."

"You are not helping!"

Mark was a better cook than I was, and specialized in Italian dishes he'd learned from his father. About six feet and slim, he reflected his Mediterranean heritage in his dark hair and great bone structure, everything except possibly his deep blue eyes. On the drive across town to his condo building, I hoped maybe he just planned to try out a new dish on me that evening.

When he opened the door and kissed me hello, from the kitchen I caught a whiff of garlic . . . but mixed with ginger. Chinese food? Granted, Mark could have decided to branch out, but as soon as I stepped inside his small kitchen I saw takeout bags on the counter from a new highway place, Hunan House.

He noticed my glance and must have thought I was disappointed. "Sorry—I've been super busy lately, as you know. Anyway, when we tried this place last month we both liked it, so I got Szechuan shrimp for me and lo mein for you. Okay?"

"Just fine." I actually felt a bit relieved. If he was going to "pop the question," wouldn't he have cooked something fancy?

On the other hand, the big surprise obviously would be something besides dinner.

Mark poured us both glasses of wine and scooped the food onto everyday-nice ceramic dishes. We ate in the dining alcove right off his kitchen. No candles or anything super romantic, though. He used chopsticks fairly well; I'd never gotten the knack and still opted for a knife and fork.

I told him about the visit from Gillian Foster. Unlike me, he at least had heard of the Ramsford-Cooper house, but didn't know much about its history, either. He agreed that Gillian sounded like she might be a witch to deal with, though I'd survived worse.

The elderly hoarders in Dalton rang more of a bell with him. "Yeah, I know a vet over there, Ronnie Martin, who's had some dealings with them. He spayed a couple of their cats pro bono, because the neighbors were complaining. That kind of situation always is rough to deal with. The people tend to really love their animals, but when the number gets out of control they aren't doing them any favors."

"Guess I'll see just how bad it is when I go there tomorrow." My suspense had been building all through our dinner, but when I finally asked, I tried to sound casual. "So, what's this big surprise you have in store for me tonight?"

Mark's chuckle sounded edgy. "Oh, it's coming. Let's just . . . open our fortune cookies first."

That didn't reassure me too much, but I played along. We both cracked the thin cookies open at the same time. I unfolded my tiny strip of paper and swallowed hard.

No vinegar tastes so bitter as love turned to hate.

Well, *that* was a cheerful sentiment! I looked across the table at Mark. Even if he could possibly have arranged to have a particular message put in my cookie, I certainly hoped he wouldn't have picked this one.

It probably was random, though, because he seemed a bit distressed by his fortune, too. "Gee, thanks a lot!" he muttered to the crisp shards left on his plate.

That made me laugh. "I'll show you mine if you show me yours."

We swapped slips of paper and he whooped over my dire warning. "Yikes! Whatever this means, I promise it has nothing to do with me."

His read:

Life is like grass—don't spread yourself too thin.

"That isn't so bad," I said. "You have been putting in pretty long hours at the clinic lately." *And at whatever else has been occupying your time on weeknights.*

"Yeah, that's probably what it means." He popped the bits of cookie into his mouth and crunched in defiance. Then he stood up rather sharply, avoiding my eyes, and took his plate to the sink. "Coffee?"

"Sure, thanks." *Or would another glass of wine better prepare me for whatever was coming?*

I brought my coffee into the living room and settled on the navy-blue sectional sofa. So far, Mark had resisted the urge to take in any roommates who might sully that dark chenille surface with shed fur. Maybe, in his line of work, he'd become all too aware of the ailments and injuries that could afflict even a well-cared-for pet, and of the heartbreak involved in losing one.

Still, he must have been tempted, now and then, to do as Dawn had suggested and rescue a stray. Did Mark's pet-free life show a fear of commitment? I didn't dare accuse him of such a thing, though. I had three cats, but still remained a little wary about sharing my home full-time with another human being.

I knew that Mark's last girlfriend, someone named Diane, had helped him decorate this room. It might be sexist, but I assumed she had chosen the sofa's collection of throw pillows; their assorted geometric patterns of navy, tan and red coordinated perfectly with the Cubist-style print of a jazz combo that hung just above. At first it had bothered me a bit that Mark didn't toss out the pillows along with Diane, after she cheated on him with a mutual friend.

But now, as I listened to him scraping the leftover Chinese food back into the cartons, to refrigerate for another time, I understood. He did not keep the décor as it was out of any lingering feelings for his ex, just out of frugal good sense. He liked the way it looked, so why change? Even a successful veterinarian—and Mark's clinic was pretty busy these days—did not usually rake in big bucks. Plus, he did a fair amount of work cut-rate or free, for emergency cases and the local shelter.

Near the chamois-colored armchair/recliner, his guitar from his college years stood on a stand, the case closed as usual. Mark sometimes complained that his work schedule didn't allow him to keep up with his old hobby of learning to play jazz. On past visits I'd sometimes even noticed a thin layer of dust on the case; at least tonight it seemed like he'd recently wiped it down.

These days, the dark, contemporary coffee and side tables displayed one flattering head shot of me, taken by Mark, and a photo of us both, in work clothes, snapped by a friend during a local cat expo that spring. The dark wood entertainment center held a Christmas photo of his Philadelphia-based family, including his sister, his two brothers and his mother . . . but not his dad, from whom she was divorced.

When Mark finally emerged from the kitchen, I shifted over on the sofa so he could join me. Instead, he chose to sit in the recliner, several feet away.

Oh, dear, I thought, *this can't be good. Worried as I was that he might propose, there could always be worse things!*

I remembered Dawn's wild speculations. Mark might be an upstanding, ethical guy, but judging from our romantic history over the past year and a half, I doubted he had the makings of a priest. But what the heck *did* he plan to spring on me?

He hunched forward nervously, hands clasped on his knees, and his intense blue eyes met mine. "I know you've had trouble reaching me after hours lately, and I never gave you much of an explanation. Sorry to be so secretive, but I didn't want to say anything too soon . . . not until I had a better idea of how things were going to turn out."

He's been recruited by some big veterinary clinic in the Midwest and the money's too good to turn down. Or his mother has developed a serious health problem, and he's moving back to Philly to help take care of her.

"I wanted to be sure I wouldn't be making a complete fool of myself . . ."

Yow, maybe it is a ring, after all! What can I say? Do?

I was almost hyperventilating by the time he unsnapped the nearby guitar case and lifted out the instrument. I had seen it only once before, when he hadn't even bothered to take it out, and the full view impressed me. Wood grain with a cherry finish, it seemed a kind of cross between acoustic and electric; it had two pickups at the base of the fretboard and four control knobs, but also an elongated S-shaped cutout on either side. Mark had told me at the time that it was a "semi-hollowbody" and could be played with or without an amplifier.

He drew it onto his lap tonight with a new air of confidence. I exhaled, finally reassured that his surprise was more likely to be pleasant than scary.

Unless, of course, he was terrible!

But as he'd already suggested, Dr. Coccia would never have tortured my ears with any clumsy fumbling on the frets. Without any misstep that I could hear, he rendered a very credible version of "'Round Midnight," an old, minor-key jazz standard we both loved. Occasionally he added an unexpected note or strum, but mainly it was his phrasing that gave the number just the right cool, melancholy tone. I stopped feeling anxious for him and was able to sit back and enjoy his performance.

With the last note still hanging in the air, Mark kept his eyes on the guitar for a beat. Then he sneaked a glance at me, as if half-prepared for a scathing review.

"That was amazing!" I told him. "And I'm *so* glad your surprise didn't involve taking a new job, somewhere like Michigan."

"What?" He reddened a little. "You thought that? Hey, I didn't mean to actually worry you."

"Let's just say, this was much better than some of the possible alternatives." I got up and hugged him. "But not long ago you told me you hadn't touched this baby in many years, because you had no time. You said you were so out of practice, it hurt your fingers to push down the strings."

"All that was true," Mark admitted. "But when we went to that Eddie Broom concert in January—my Christmas gift from you, so thanks again—I remembered how I used to listen to his CDs in college and try to imitate his style. I realized I was becoming 'all work and no play,' and maybe I needed that creative outlet again."

"I know you've hired more help lately, since the clinic's been doing so well," I filled in.

"Yeah, I'm not quite as harried anymore. So I found a local guy who's played with a combo for years and gives lessons. That's where I've been going, Mondays and Thursdays after work. He helped me get my chops back . . . or start to, anyway."

"Sounds to me like you've gotten them back all the way," I told him.

He blushed a bit again; I liked the way it warmed his pale-olive complexion. "I still have a lot to learn. Jazz uses different scales than other types of music, and that part's still a challenge. I'll have to understand all of that before I can really improvise. But at least now I can play a tune."

I egged him on. "What else you got?"

Mark demonstrated that he could also do justice to an up-tempo number, with a lively version of "Sunny." He then confessed those were the only two he'd practiced enough to show off. "I've only been back at it for a month."

"For only a month, I think that's damned good," I assured him. "When are you going to learn 'Stray Cat Strut'?"

Knowing it was the ringtone for my cell phone, he laughed. "I'll make that next on my list. So, you don't think by taking guitar lessons I'll be 'spreading myself too thin'?"

"Not at all." I smiled to myself—so that's why his fortune cookie message had annoyed him!

Mark put the guitar away and I took its place on his lap. "Gee, I thought I was lucky to be dating a hot veterinarian, but now I can also have a cool jazzman on the side."

After we'd necked for a minute, he asked, "Speaking of cats, are all of yours settled for the night?"

I understood the coded message. "All on automatic feeders. They won't miss me until tomorrow morning. I do have to get back fairly early, though, because I'm meeting Sarah in Dalton at eleven."

"Oh, right, the hoarders' house." He ruffled my hair at the nape, giving me chills. "Use bug repellent all over before you go. They might have fleas, and you don't want to bring those back to your place."

"Ugh, I hadn't thought of that. You think it'll be bad?"

Mark shrugged. "Ronnie said he's been to some places where the ammonia was so thick in the air, everybody on his team wore respirators. I don't suppose this house could be so far gone, though, or Sarah would have warned you. Let's hope not, right?"

I swallowed my apprehension. "Yeah, let's hope not."

Chapter 3

Thanks to my GPS, I didn't have too much trouble finding the Tillman house on the outskirts of Dalton.

That small, semirural town had not yet begun to attract first-time homebuyers looking for bargain properties, a trend that had benefitted Chadwick in recent years. And even if a young couple was seeking a modest place at a rock-bottom price, they might run through the realtors' whole list before considering this sad-looking ranch home. Its beige aluminum siding not only screamed 1970s, it didn't look as if it had even been power-washed since that era. From the road I could spot missing shingles on the roof, and the front bay window revealed a row of vertical blinds with several slats broken or twisted, like a mouth with long, crooked teeth. A black-and-white tuxedo cat sat on the inside sill and peered out through one of the gaps.

The only sight that encouraged me was Sarah's well-kept navy-blue Camry parked in the fissured blacktop driveway. I knew she and a friend from her Baptist church must already be inside, paying their weekly visit to check on the couple.

When I peeked through the window of the closed garage door, I thought I could make out another vehicle in there. It was hard to tell, though, through the window grime . . . and the junk piled on all sides.

I climbed the dingy cement steps to the small front porch, waking a scruffy ginger cat from his nap on the doormat. He hesitated only a second before slipping away through the wrought-iron railing and bounding off toward some nearby woods. Possibly the Tillmans fed him, but he still seemed semiferal.

I rang the gilded plastic doorbell, chipped with age, and was relieved when it actually sounded inside. After a minute, Sarah opened the door and welcomed me with a broad smile. "Cassie, so glad you could make it. C'mon in . . . watch your step."

Though I'm pretty agile and have good eyesight, her advice was necessary. The home's front corridor was stacked on both sides with magazines and newspapers, so that Sarah and I had to sidle our way in between.

"Our church group is hauling this stuff to the recycling center next week," she confided in a low voice. "Took us a month to convince Chester that he was never going to read any of these articles again, and that they've already started crumbling to dust. Terrible for his wife's asthma, too."

The yellowing magazines probably weren't the only thing contributing to the woman's health issues. The air also carried the scent of multiple litter boxes, though not as bad as I would have expected. Maybe the First Baptist volunteers were also helping to keep those clean.

"Let me introduce you to Mr. Tillman," said Sarah as cheerfully as if we were at a cocktail party, and led me into the living room.

That space still wore brown '70s paneling on its walls, and the sofa and two chairs all seemed to be upholstered in beige tweed or stripes—what I could see of them.

A thin, elderly black man had found just enough space to sit on the couch, and appeared almost out of place with his neat attire of a short-sleeved, pale-yellow shirt and chino pants. He wore bedroom slippers, but the closed kind that looked like loafers. It was his dignified air that contrasted the most; he sat very erect, hands resting on his thighs, and looked straight ahead. He squinted in spite of his glasses, and I remembered Sarah telling me Chester had become very farsighted and badly needed a change of prescription.

"Chester, this is my friend Cassie," she told him.

I held out my hand, and he grazed knuckles with me once before he found it to shake it. He said softly, "How d'you do? Are you from social services?"

"No, no," I told him. "Just a friend of Sarah's."

"Cassie's my boss, I told you about her," she said. "We run the grooming place over in Chadwick. She's a cat lover, like you and Bernice."

"Oh, that's nice." He finally smiled, then looked back over his shoulder at the window with the wrecked vertical blinds. "Did you meet Minnie-Mouse? She oughta be around here somewhere."

I guessed he meant the tuxedo cat who had watched me come up the front walk. "I saw her through the window. Maybe she just got scared when I rang the bell."

I cast around for a spot to sit near him. Plastic milk crates and open shoeboxes, overflowing with mail and other papers, occupied the sofa's other cushion. Sarah urged me to shift some of them to the floor, though there was barely room for them there, either.

I surveyed the rest of the room in disbelief. An old, boxy

TV set rested on a console table opposite the sofa, and stacked next to it I saw plastic organizing drawers filled with videotapes and DVDs, mixed in with vintage video games. Just inside the room's doorway, a pipe rack held coats and jackets in both men's and women's styles, probably the overflow from a jammed hall closet. Shelves on the wall sagged beneath the weight of countless sentimental knickknacks. Beyond that, there were items almost too abundant and diverse to categorize—cat scratching posts, family photos, old LP records, fleece throws, kids' toys. Other stuff had been crammed into see-through trash bags, as if someone from the church group hoped to ease them out the door and into the garbage.

A tall, slim woman of about forty entered, also carefully, from the nearby kitchen. She wore her hair in a short Afro, and her stretch pants and top would have looked stylish in an exercise class. But the empty black garbage bag she toted and her bright-pink rubber gloves told me that she'd come to the house that day to work.

She smiled and took off her right glove to shake my hand. "Hi, I'm Robin. You must be the cat whisperer."

I laughed. "Is that what Sarah's been calling me? She speaks highly of you, too. You work as a nurse at the same high school where she used to teach, right?"

"I do. Luckily, that gives me summers off, so I've had a chance to help out the Tillmans. In addition to all of this"— she gestured with the full trash bag—"Chester and his wife both have some health problems that need looking after."

"Do you have family of your own?" I wondered if they would mind her spending so much time helping out the hoarders.

"I'm divorced, but I have two sons, eighteen and twenty." She smiled again. "They're good boys, but the less I'm into their business these days, the better they like it!"

Another feline—not Minnie, but a calico—sprang from somewhere in back of the sofa onto its arm, near Chester. I also saw a mostly white one scoot down the hall. With the ginger cat outside, that made four. I wondered how many more lurked in the other rooms.

Chester reached out to absently stroke the calico, who purred loudly. She looked in decent condition, not too skinny and her coat fairly lush. I saw no sign of fleas, though I'd followed Mark's advice and sprayed repellent on my clothes. Chester murmured to the cat and called her Candy.

Robin pulled a semi-comic frown. "Sarah and I, and a couple of the other folks from First Baptist, have been taking turns getting things under control here. Not easy, though."

Across the room from me, my assistant sat down on a stack of crates, packed so solidly that they could easily support her. "We've even been cooking meals in the church's kitchen and bringing them over. Things Chester and Bernice can microwave, because their oven's full of pots and pans."

Robin studied one of the plastic wall shelves, bowing under the weight of its burden, and shook open her trash bag. "Chester, one day this stuff is going to come down on somebody's head. It's just old video games, collecting dust. I'm going to get rid of them, okay?"

"What?" He glanced around, as if agitated that he couldn't clearly see what she was removing. "Naw, don't do that. Those're your brother Jimmy's games. I promised I'd keep them for him."

I glanced at Robin in question, but she shook her head.

Meanwhile, Sarah told him, "Chester, this isn't your daughter. This is Robin, from the church, remember?"

Possibly annoyed at the mistaken identity, Robin chided him further. "And Jimmy is how old now? In his forties? He doesn't care about those games, Chester. Besides, you have to play them on a VCR."

"We got one," he insisted.

"Bernice said it doesn't work anymore. Please, you've *got* to get rid of some of this."

Maybe to spare Chester an audience for his confusion, Sarah rose and beckoned to me. "Why don't you come say hello to Bernice? She's the real cat fanatic."

As we picked our way down another crowded corridor, she told me that a healthcare worker visited once a month to check on Bernice and give her an injection of a new anti-asthma medication. "But she still uses an inhaler, once in a while, when it gets too bad," Sarah added. "Her doctor says she won't really improve until she either gets out of this house or they clean out all the junk, and at least some of the animals. But neither of them will listen."

Bernice Tillman sat propped up by pillows on her bed, watching a talk show on a small, portable TV that she'd parked on a folding table. In spite of the warm day, a colorful afghan lay over her lap. When she saw Sarah and me, she used her remote to mute the TV, and greeted us. Her wispy gray hair waved back from a strong-featured face, but the circles under her eyes testified to her health problems.

Three cats kept her company—a mostly white one with a red spot on his hip, a longhaired tortoiseshell and a pale-gray tabby. Only the last of these looked up when Sarah and I entered; the other two dozed on, cuddled tight against Bernice's hip on top of the afghan.

The bedroom would have been a decent size, but numerous small pieces of furniture packed against the walls on all sides made it feel claustrophobic. The tops of the dresser and the chest of drawers were cluttered with costume jewelry, knickknacks and bottles of medications; a pile of paperback books teetered on the nightstand, and clothes from the half-open closet had spilled out onto a nearby chair. I spotted a covered litter box in one corner and wondered how often the cats even bothered to make their way through the trash to visit it. At least this room had an air conditioner, droning away in a window by the bed.

Sarah told Bernice, "This is my boss, Cassie. She's the cat expert I told you about."

"A cat expert?" She rumpled the fur on the head of the mostly white shorthair. "How about that, Sugarman? This lady *studies* you guys!"

I laughed. "Well, in a way." In case Sarah hadn't done so before, I explained our business. Meanwhile, I stroked the tortoiseshell female cat and could tell that she hadn't been adequately groomed in a while.

"Her name is Autumn," Bernice said in a fond voice.

I told Autumn what a beautiful coat she had, and she ate up the praise, blinking at me happily. "You've got a few knots, though, don't you? Want me to get them out for you, real quick?" A workaholic, I travel with a small pet brush. With Bernice's permission, I gently worked some of the mats out of the tortie's coat, as if it was just a casual demonstration of my service. "There, all pretty again."

"We called her Autumn because her color's like the woods in the fall," Bernice told me. "She belonged to a neighbor, and when he moved away ten years ago we took her in. Sugarman, he's been with us so long, I don't even remember how we got him. Winky, the gray one, is Minnie's son from her last litter, about two years ago. He was crazy as a kitten, but he's settled down now." Bernice also went on to explain which of the other cats these three did and didn't get along with, and their various idiosyncrasies.

This was more information than I needed, but it did tell me something important—and heartbreaking. These animals were family to Bernice, and probably to Chester, as well. It would be hard to persuade them to give up any of their pets, at least the indoor ones. And unfortunately, those were the ones affecting Bernice's health.

Even as she talked to me, gaining energy and enthusiasm from the subject, she began to punctuate every third or fourth sentence with a cough. When she finally paused for breath, Sarah interrupted, "Bernice, do you need your inhaler? Is it nearby?"

The older woman scanned the bedding, the afghan, the cats and the top of the nightstand, as if trying to remember. Then she opened the nightstand drawer to rummage through many small items inside. Finally she pulled out the bright-yellow, L-shaped device, shook it in a practiced way, put one end in her mouth and breathed deeply.

I didn't know a lot about asthma, but I had heard that the sufferers weren't supposed to rely on inhalers too heavily. This was only a temporary fix; Bernice couldn't go on living in these conditions much longer.

"Have all of your cats been spayed or neutered?" I asked her. "It's really important that they don't go on having kittens."

The woman on the bed shrugged. "The house cats are. We got 'em done a couple of years ago. The ones that go in and out, though, you can't catch 'em long enough to get 'em to a vet."

That's where FOCA might be able to help, I thought. "I know some people who are really good at trapping feral cats and getting them fixed," I told her.

Bernice's eyes narrowed suspiciously. "And then they'll take them away."

"No, they can bring them back here. They did it a couple of months ago at a condo community. It's called trap-neuter-return. The only difference would be that the colony wouldn't get out of control."

For confirmation, Bernice glanced at Sarah, who nodded. "It's true. They're good people. They have a shelter in Chadwick, and Cassie and I work with them a lot."

"Do you want me to talk to them about it?" I prodded.

Bernice gathered Winky protectively against her bosom, even though his anatomy no longer required altering. "I'll . . . think about it."

"Good." While she was making up her mind, I'd run the idea by my two FOCA buddies, Becky Newmeyer and Chris Eberhardt, to make sure they could take on the project. Maybe if Bernice and Chester got to know them, I eventually might bring up the subject of taking some of the indoor animals to the shelter.

For the next half hour or so, I helped Robin and Sarah in their Herculean task of de-junking the Tillman house. The hardest part was convincing the owners that their endless "treasures" had no real value to anyone. Sarah took on the thankless job of going through the plastic file boxes of audiotapes and videotapes with Chester, and trying to get him to dispose of some of them. Once I overheard him arguing with her that those things were "his past."

I asked Robin, toiling near me in the kitchen, what he meant by that.

"Chester had a local radio show for a while—he was a sportscaster. He interviewed some baseball and basketball stars, and I guess some of his shows may be on those tapes. But they can't all be that memorable, and anyway, who plays cassettes these days?" She paused beneath a half-emptied upper cabinet. "He had a very interesting career. Started out as an equipment manager for some baseball team, made connections, became an announcer and worked his way into radio."

"He told you all of this?" I felt just a little skeptical that a guy with so much energy and talent would end up living in his present conditions.

"One of their neighbors, Bob Smiley, told me. He's one of the only friends who still visits them. He was here once when I came by, and got Chester talking about his past. I guess that's how Chester got most of this memorabilia—from his connection with sports figures." Robin sighed. "He must have had a lot on the ball, in those days. Such a shame, when someone's mind goes like that."

I agreed. "Does he often get you confused with his daughter?"

"It happens now and then. Maybe I do resemble her a little, who knows? Sylvia lives in Chicago now, and he hasn't seen her in maybe six or seven years, so it's no wonder if he forgets exactly what she looks like." Robin checked the expiration date on a jar of peanut butter, grimaced and consigned it to the trash bag. "Can't say I have a very high opinion of either of their kids. Jimmy's in Florida, has a family, runs a construction company. They send money, but they don't want to get their hands dirty, I guess. Really, they should be dealing with this situation, not us at First Baptist."

I dampened a paper towel and used it to clean up some flour that had spilled onto the kitchen counter. "Chester made it sound as if social services has been by. Do they help at all?"

"The county offers a meal program, and they arranged for a doctor to see Bernice about her medical problems. I took Chester to the optometrist last week, and I'll be picking up his new glasses for him tomorrow. Beyond that, though, it's hard to help people who don't really want help. If there were more neighbors nearby, and the house got so bad that they complained to the town, I guess that might be different—the county might see it as more urgent."

Around three, Robin, Sarah and I decided we had accomplished as much as we could for the present. We reminded both of the Tillmans of the meals stockpiled in their refrigerator and made sure we left a clear path to the microwave. Finally we said goodbye to Bernice, Chester, and any cats that happened to be present at the time.

Sarah turned the lock on the front door before pulling it shut behind us. "A lot of good this will do. Chester will probably leave the back door propped open for the strays. He thinks they should be able to get in out of the rain."

That sounded risky to me, too—for an elderly and disabled couple to leave their house open to anyone who might be passing by. On the other hand, they were off the beaten path, and it wasn't as if they lived in a McMansion.

Robin pretty much voiced the same thoughts. "I guess as long as a raccoon or a skunk doesn't get in, it won't do any harm. After all, the way this place looks from the outside, who'd break in? It sure doesn't look like there's anything to steal!"

Chapter 4

Early Tuesday morning, I drove up to a much different residence, not far from downtown Chadwick. Set close to the road, it was built of brown bricks, irregular and weathered-looking on one half and newer and more uniform on the other. Even I could tell, with my limited knowledge of architecture, that the smaller, plainer section must date back to around 1800, and the newer one closer to the mid-nineteenth century. Thick gray shingles on the steeply slanting roof, and white trim around the main entry and the many small windows, added to the antique character.

I parked my six-year-old Honda CR-V at the curb. That day I hadn't brought my grooming van, since I was picking up only one cat and bringing her right back to my shop. Just as well, because another white van already occupied the driveway. It faced the street, with the back doors open toward the house. As I watched, a slim young man with collar-length brown hair lifted out two large, rustic-looking jars. He hustled them toward the propped-open front door, as if they might explode before he got them into the house.

The side of the van bore a logo with the initials *LF*,

framed in a lacy green border, above the cursive words *Linda Freeman, Interior Design.*

Well, Gillian had warned me that the process of refurnishing the house for the reception would already be underway when I arrived. I just hoped she had corralled Leya someplace safe in the meantime.

I climbed a couple of steps onto the low front porch and paused there. From somewhere inside, a woman called out, "Robert, those vases go in the dining room. The dried plants are already on the table—can you put them in for me?"

I detected a note of banked hysteria and didn't want to get in their way. On the other hand, I needed someone to point me toward the cat I was supposed to pick up. While I loitered in confusion, a figure in a white T-shirt and black yoga pants backed out of a doorway to my right, her gaze still fixed on something in that room. We collided, and she wheeled around with a look of terror. It faded as soon as she saw my face.

"Oh, sorry!" She laughed in relief. "I didn't know anyone else was . . ."

"That's okay," I assured her. "I can see you're very busy."

"Very," she admitted, but with a small smile. "Can I help you?"

I introduced myself and explained my presence. "I guess you're Linda Freeman?"

"I am." The woman's pretty, oval face relaxed a bit. She looked in her mid-thirties and wore no makeup. But the way she'd pulled her dark hair into an artsy, practical topknot, and rattled off instructions to the young man toting the vases, suggested professional expertise.

"I'm afraid I don't know anything about the cat," she told me with a shrug. "You'd have to ask Gillian. Or maybe her daughter, Whitney, if she's around . . ."

The young man returned and hovered near Linda's elbow, awaiting further instructions. Linda introduced him as her assistant, Robert. Crisply, she told him, "Get the quilt. That goes in the living room. The rod's already mounted." She nodded toward the doorway from which she had just come. Through it, I could glimpse a brick fireplace with an aged-looking wooden surround, a faded Oriental carpet and a couple of mismatched wing chairs.

Robert headed outside again at a brisk clip.

I told Linda, "It's like watching a stage crew set up for a play."

"Yes, and almost that crazy. We put so many of the Fosters' things in storage, while the walls and floors were being redone. Now we have to move them all back in."

The floors were impressive, I had to admit. Wide oak planks, no doubt original, had been expertly refinished to show off the fine grain and knotholes.

"We'll bring most of the big pieces back today, and tomorrow we'll add the accessories—Gillian has a *lot* of those," Linda continued. "It's going to look wonderful when it's all together, though. I hope the historical society folks will be impressed."

"They're coming to the reception Friday?"

"Yes, along with some other bigwigs from the town."

I decided I liked Linda. On the one hand, she seemed to take her design work seriously. On the other, from the way she tossed off this comment, I sensed she wasn't as overawed by the local officials as her client seemed to be.

Finally, I saw Gillian heading our way from the rear of the house, most likely the kitchen. She wore navy-blue cropped pants this time, with a navy-and-white striped tee and white Top-Sider shoes; the outfit would have been perfect on a yacht. Her stern expression, though, made me hesitate to ask where I might find Leya. Linda, next to me, also stiffened her spine, and I suddenly understood why she'd overreacted earlier when she'd bumped into me.

Robert picked that unlucky moment to come in the front door carrying a large, clear-plastic blanket bag.

Gillian dove at him like a hawk. "Don't tell me you've had that antique quilt stored for all of these weeks in *plastic*. What on earth were you thinking?" She grabbed the package from his hands.

Linda tried to mediate. "Gillian, it's okay. It was in a climate-controlled environment, so it wasn't exposed to any moisture."

Her client rudely turned her back, brought the bag to a chair near a sunny window, unzipped it, and began to examine the quilt inch by inch for signs of damage.

Linda rejoined me and Robert near the doorway. She let out a puff of breath and, while Gillian was so intensely occupied, threw us a secret, apologetic glance.

I didn't think she was the one who needed to apologize, but it wasn't my place to interfere. Now I wanted even more desperately to get Leya and whisk us both out of Gillian's orbit; at the same time, I didn't have the nerve to interrupt her at the moment.

Apparently the star-patterned quilt was fine—big surprise—so Gillian turned her attention to micromanaging the way Robert draped it over the wooden dowel, already fastened horizontally to one wall. ("Fold it over a *third* of the way. That will keep it in place, but you'll still be able to see three rows of the stars.") Meanwhile I lingered in suspense, telling myself that Sarah would have opened our shop by now. She knew I was running this errand, but might wonder why it was taking so long. A little hard to explain that I'd been too afraid of our client to ask where I could find her cat.

Or maybe not. After all, Sarah *had* met Gillian.

"Can I help you?" asked a quiet voice behind me.

I turned to face a teenaged girl whose blond head came just a little past my shoulder. She had wide gray eyes, a slightly chunky figure, and wore casual riding clothes—a pink polo shirt, buff breeches and short brown boots.

"Hi, I'm Cassie McGlone." *Linda mentioned the daughter's name . . . What was it?* "Are you Whitney?"

When she nodded, I explained my dilemma.

"Yeah, Mom told me to keep an eye out for you. C'mon back. Leya's in the guest bedroom."

I followed Whitney past a small family room, also only half-furnished. The *Little House on the Prairie* clan might consider it the height of luxury, but it looked pretty Spartan for a modern, upscale family living in suburban New Jersey. The floor was herringbone brick, with a handwoven colonial rug spread in front of the soot-blackened fireplace; a wooden rocker with what looked like a hard-carved back stood nearby. Of course, some more furniture might still be coming, but I didn't see any likely spot to hang a big-screen TV.

Trying to be tactful, I commented to Whitney, "Your mother has certainly gone to a lot of trouble to restore the house authentically, hasn't she?"

The girl snorted. "You could say that. It's been, like, our whole *lives* the past couple of years."

She stopped before a door on our left and cautiously cracked it open a couple of inches. "Le-ya," she singsonged, "somebody's here to see you! She's gonna take you away from all this craziness."

We eased into the room so the cat couldn't sprint past us, but she was nowhere in sight. In the meantime, I took in the home's guest accommodations, the strangest spectacle so far.

The room was small, with sage-green wainscoting around

the lower walls; above hung some framed needlework of old-time adages. The sentiments included: *He is the happiest, be he king or peasant, who finds peace in his home,* by Goethe, and *A guest has not to thank the host, but the host the guest,* uncredited. The top of a scarred black chest of drawers displayed a collection of antique, ankle-high shoes, most of them child size.

But most extremely authentic was the guest bed—single size, with a rope mattress! I could tell this because the thick ropes threaded through the sides of the frame. Another patchwork quilt had been partially turned down to reveal linens that might have been tea-dyed, for a sense of age, but just looked stained. And against the pillows rested the saddest-looking doll I'd ever seen—hand-stitched together from homespun cloth, its stuffed head just a beige, blank egg shape.

I've heard people joke that they didn't want their guest room too comfortable, or visitors might stay too long. But this is ridiculous!

Whitney didn't notice my appalled reaction, since she had dropped to her knees next to the bed. I knew she'd found Leya because she baby-talked for a few more minutes before pulling her out of hiding. One advantage to a bed that narrow, I supposed—the cat could never get too far out of reach.

I spotted a large, hard-sided pet carrier near the window and brought it over. Although Leya squirmed and complained a bit while we loaded her in, I could see she was a stunning animal. A Himalayan basically has a Persian body with Siamese coloring, and she was cream with chocolate-brown points (legs, tail, face mask and ears). Her abundant fur looked in good condition, in spite of how long she might have been cowering under the bed.

"I'll miss you, sweetie," Whitney cooed through the front grill of the carrier. Straightening up again, she asked me about my business and seemed intrigued by the idea of working with animals for a living. "How long are you supposed to keep Leya?"

"Only a few days. Your mother told me to bring her back for the reception."

"Of course. Mom'll want to show her off, even if the poor cat would probably be happier hiding in here." The girl chuckled under her breath. "Probably the only creature who ever *would* be comfortable in here."

I hesitated to criticize my client's taste, even to her daughter. "I guess beds like this were good enough for people for hundreds of years."

"Centuries of backaches—that's why somebody invented actual mattresses. And wouldn't you just expect that creepy doll to come alive some night and kill you in your sleep?" Whitney shuddered. "Those shoes, too! I call them the Dead Orphans Memorial. Makes Mom furious, but Dad had a laugh over it."

"Only four kids. Maybe it was a family." I pointed to one larger pair of lace-ups at the end of the row. "Those belonged to the Nanny."

"I still say it's ghoulish. She didn't do *my* room like this. I wouldn't have it, so mine won't be on Friday's tour. I've got one antique print, of a lady jumping sidesaddle in a hunt, but that's it."

With a glance at her outfit, I said, "You ride, I presume."

Her round face brightened for the first time. "I've got a thoroughbred mare, Glory Days. I board her at a hunter-jumper stable just a couple of miles down the road. She's doing real well; we'll probably be in a couple of shows this summer."

Whitney reminded me to take along a few cans of Leya's food, plus Gillian's list of demands—er, recommendations—

for the cat's care, and we made our way back to the kitchen. I was relieved to see at least one concession to modern convenience in that area: the high-end AGA range almost looked colonial, but probably could launch a spaceship. I didn't spot either a refrigerator or a dishwasher, but no doubt those lurked behind some of the cream-painted, expertly distressed cabinetry.

As instructed, Robert had placed the two brown stoneware vases at each end of the dining table and filled them with dried grasses and flowers, artistically arranged. As we entered that space, a nice-looking man with brown hair graying at the temples, and a full, trimmed beard, rose from one of the caned chairs and took a plate and a coffee mug to the sink. He wore a striped dress shirt and dark slacks, so I presumed this was Mr. Foster, even before Whitney made the introductions.

"Thought you were going to blow off work today!" she teased him, with a glint in her eye.

"Well, as you can see, I'm getting a late start," he answered, in the same light vein. "But I might as well go in. I can do more good there than here." About to leave, Donald Foster noticed something above his head and frowned. "Uh-oh. This cabinet door still doesn't shut right."

"Sshh!" Whitney warned him. "Let's all get out of here, before—"

"Oh Lord, is that door *still* out of line?" Too late. Gillian had joined us and spotted the flaw.

Which was more than I'd been able to do. Shifting my angle, I finally could see that one of the upper cabinets hung open by maybe a quarter inch, instead of closing completely. I had a couple like that in my apartment; I'd fixed them with stick-on patches of Velcro tape.

Donald inched toward the back door, his body language

deliberately calm—the way you'd move around an unpredictable wild animal. "Better get the contractor back here." His mild tone indicated that he couldn't care less, but knew that until the error was repaired there would be no peace.

"I can't! I already called him about that wobble in the porch railing, and he said the earliest he can come back is next week. That won't do—everything's got to be perfect for the reception."

Her mention of a wobbly railing touched off a memory in my brain, about a similar problem I'd had repaired not long ago. Should I open my mouth?

"Actually, I know someone who might be able to help," I said. "Nick Janos, my handyman. He's right here in town."

Gillian's cool glance conveyed her skepticism about anyone I might suggest, especially a mere handyman. But Donald and Whitney looked willing to hear me out.

"Carpentry is his main thing," I went on. "He built all of those cat condos at my shop, and repaired and stabilized my back steps last year. And he usually can come on short notice—at least, he does for me."

"Sounds perfect!" said Donald, obviously eager to give his wife one less issue to complain about. Finally, she also gave me the nod.

I checked my phone and read off Nick's number, while Gillian wrote it with a ballpoint pen on a scrap of paper. Meanwhile, I hoped I wasn't condemning my friend and favorite handyman to the Job from Hell.

"Thank you, Cassie," Gillian deigned to say.

"You're very welcome. Now I'd better get Leya back to my shop so she can settle in. Good luck with the decorating!"

Gillian just rolled her eyes—not at me, I sensed, but at the monumental task that lay before her. Then her phone rang, and she started an equally urgent conversation with someone named Michael. The three of us, counting Leya, took the opportunity to slip out the back door.

"The contractor?" I asked Donald, hopefully.

"Nope, that's the caterer. At least he hasn't quit on us yet."

"He might, when he hears about that awful porridge thing she wants them to serve." Whitney grimaced. "Who cares if the people ate that stuff back in colonial days? They had to, they were *poor*. They didn't even have, like, grocery stores."

I couldn't help smiling, and Donald noticed. "Anyway, thanks for recommending the handyman, Cassie," he said. "If he works out, that will be one more 'crisis' averted."

He slid behind the wheel of his silver BMW sedan and backed down the long driveway. Whitney detoured up to the front porch to get her bicycle. Meanwhile, Linda stepped out the front door, and as Donald drove past her van, they waved to each other.

Still toting the cat carrier, I stopped to say goodbye to the harried designer.

Linda's eyes still followed the departing BMW. "There goes a very patient man."

"He sure seems to be," I agreed. "I guess he knows how to handle her by now. Are all of your clients so demanding?"

"Most are fussy about one thing or another, but Gillian's in a class by herself. She can't bear the slightest flaw—everything has to be perfect! And in this house, that means exactly right for the period, too."

"In this house? You mean, you've worked for her before?"

"Ooooh, yes." A rueful smile, as if she should have known better. "I did her last place, a midcentury modern ranch in Somerset County. Apparently, she also once had a Victorian over in Montclair. I'm sure she put that designer through the same routine."

"And her family, too?"

"No doubt."

I glanced toward the house, to make sure the subject of our discussion was nowhere near. "Does Gillian work, at all?"

"She does. Want to take a guess?" When I shrugged, Linda said, "She's an independent efficiency consultant. Must be damned good at it, right?"

The designer got back to work then, and I continued toward my car with cat carrier in hand. Whitney rolled her bicycle past me and I wished her a good ride on her horse.

"I hope it will be." She laughed. "Glory's in season, so she'll be skittish and cranky. But I'd still rather take my chances with her."

Chapter 5

I parked in the lot behind my shop and brought Leya in the back door. I called out to Sarah to let her know I'd returned, but there was no answer. Finding the largest cat condo empty and already prepared, I settled the fluffy Himalayan inside and gave her a dish of her personal, expensive food. She ignored it, but that didn't surprise me—many of our boarders were hesitant, at first, about eating in a strange environment.

I'd just started through the playroom, toward the front of the shop, when Sarah met me halfway. My normally steady, stalwart assistant looked as if she'd been crying.

"Oh, my God, what's wrong?" I asked.

"Bernice Tillman . . . she died last night. I just got off the phone with Robin."

I put my arm around Sarah's shoulders. "I'm so sorry. She didn't seem that badly off when we saw her on Sunday, did she? Was it her asthma?"

"They don't know. She died in her sleep, and the Dalton cops don't seem concerned. But Robin and I still think it sounds suspicious."

With no customers requiring our immediate attention, we

sat down on some of playroom's sturdier, carpeted cat furniture. Might sound odd, but we'd gotten into the habit of doing that. I told myself I really should get some regular, human-size chairs for the space, one of these days.

"Why do you think so?" I asked.

Sarah fished a tissue out of her apron pocket to dab at the tears. "The M.E. found signs that she suffocated, and Robin says that's not exactly what would happen, even with a bad asthma attack."

"Was Chester with her?"

"They didn't share a room anymore, not since her health got so bad. He sleeps across the hall, in what used to be his son's room. He says he didn't know she had passed until he checked on her this morning."

"So, how could she have suffocated?" I couldn't help trying to unravel the mystery. "Maybe tangled in the bed-clothes—?"

Sarah sighed heavily. "She does sleep with all those cats. She had three on the bed when we visited her, and she's told me one or two others often join them at night."

I felt sick. It was true that cats sometimes liked to sleep right next to their owners' faces, even on top of their heads. I supposed it was possible that, in a crowd of four or five, one of them might have rolled onto Bernice's face and blocked her breathing. A well person should have felt that happening and woken up, but she *was* ill and on medication. Maybe she even took sleeping pills.

In all my training and experience with cats, though, I'd never heard of such a thing happening.

"Robin said they'll probably know more later today, after the autopsy," Sarah continued. "Meanwhile, we're both wondering where this leaves Chester. You saw how vague he is about things. He was physically in better shape than Bernice, except for his eyesight, but she took care of the household business. She kept track of their Social Security deposits and paid the bills. She always knew what time it was and what day of the week."

"Oh, dear." I saw the problem. "So he may not be able to stay in that house by himself."

"Or else he's going to need a full-time caregiver. We'll have to see if his insurance would cover an arrangement like that." Sarah attempted to ease off this gloomy topic and smiled. "So, did you pick up Her Highness's cat, Princess Leya?"

I laughed. "Come back and meet her. She's in her condo, but still a little shaken up. Frankly, so am I."

While we checked on the newcomer, who finally had begun to nibble at her food, I summarized my experiences of that morning at the Foster house.

"Wow, Gillian sounds like a real piece of work," Sarah said. "You got lucky, being able to just grab the cat and ske-daddle out of there. I feel sorry for that designer and her er-rand boy."

"I even feel sorry for Gillian's husband and daughter, in spite of all their money," I told her. "Can you imagine mov-ing to one old house after another, then living with renova-tions most of the time? And it sounds like, in each of these places, everything had to follow a certain theme!"

"Maybe she's flipping the houses, to increase their value?" Sarah suggested.

"That would make some sense, but you should see what she's doing with this place. Except for the kitchen and the bathrooms, where you'd *have* to have modern conveniences, it really looks like this John Ramsford—whoever he was—could still be living there. *Not* something that would appeal to a lot of buyers."

We chuckled over that, and I was glad I'd been able to distract my assistant, a least for a while, from her sad news. While we turned out a pair of Devon Rex brothers in the playroom, she brought me up to speed about any calls the shop had received in my absence.

During our lunch break, I nibbled at a sliced-turkey sandwich while I used my laptop to do a little nosy research on Gillian Foster. I soon found a website for her business, WORK SMARTER. The flattering, three-quarter headshot of Ms. Foster proved she could indeed smile, if necessary. The slogan for her services came as no surprise: *Excellence is doing ordinary things extraordinarily well.*

The copy below gave her impressive educational and corporate background, and stated that she specialized in "strategy consulting" and "business process reengineering." I didn't understand the jargon well enough to even speculate how Gillian might "improve processes" and "leverage innovation" at Cassie's Comfy Cats. I suspected she'd be happy to give me loads of destructive criticism, but even if she offered it free of charge, I didn't intend to request her help.

After lunch, Sarah and I groomed the Devon Rexes, who were being picked up by their owner the next morning. These guys required special care, because their thin, curly coats were easily damaged. They also needed a bath every few weeks, so their owner had requested we give them one during their stay.

Because of all this, Sarah and I spent a couple of hours sprucing up the feline brothers for their return home the next day. Toward the end of the session I heard my phone's ringtone play, but I couldn't answer it for about twenty minutes.

It surprised me a bit to see Mark's cell number and hear his voice.

"I know this is really last-minute," he said, "but are you free tonight? I thought about going to the Firehouse for dinner."

Now, I won't say Mark is a creature of routine, but he wasn't usually that spontaneous. Especially since the demands of his job often keep him at the clinic after hours. Once Sarah and I had returned the Rexes to their shared condo, I returned the call.

"Sure, I don't have anything going on," I told Mark. "But dinner out on a Tuesday? What's the occasion?"

"Nothing too much, but there's a combo playing that I'd like to hear."

Ah, that explained it. Mark and I dropped into the Firehouse from time to time to hear the jazz or rock bands; in fact, we'd had our first date there a little over two years ago. It sounded as if he was getting serious enough about his guitar lessons to want to check out the competition. "What's the group?"

"Quintessence," he said, but offered no more details.

I thought I'd seen an ad for them somewhere, maybe in the online version of the local paper, but otherwise I knew nothing about them. "Okay. You're not planning another 'surprise' for me, are you?"

He laughed. "Maybe just a little one. Pick you up at six thirty?"

"Sounds fine. I'll try to be ready for anything."

The Firehouse had started out in about 1900 as just that, a brick two-story building with limestone trim. Its corner turret used to house the firemen's pole. The three large front bays that once opened for hook-and-ladder trucks had become oak-trimmed double doors with deep windows. That night the weather was so mellow that they stood open to the street. The chalkboard sign on the sidewalk bore the announcement:

TONITE—QUINTESSENCE

Because it was a Tuesday and early in the evening, the restaurant was not too crowded, though a half-dozen working folks lined the bentwood stools at the bar. Hip, industrial-style fans spun slowly to cool the interior.

Mark asked for a table close to the stage, confirming my suspicions that he wanted to watch as well as listen to the musicians. At least the jazz groups that played here tended not to amp it up as much as the rock bands. The original pressed-tin ceilings looked very cool but boosted the volume a bit, as did the exposed-brick wall behind the stage.

Familiar with the spicy menu, we ordered watermelon salsa salads, and Mark went for the lemon chicken while I ordered the sweet-potato casserole. Neither of us is strictly vegetarian, but we both knew enough about the horrors of factory farming to bypass—most of the time—beef, lamb and pork, and to opt for either seafood or free-range poultry.

While waiting for our dinners, we nursed a couple of glasses of white wine and caught up on each other's news. Mark deals with a fair number of crises on his job, but was pleased to report that so far this week his clinic had seen no dogs recently hit by cars or cats wasting away from kidney disease. Maybe that was why he felt like celebrating? I both entertained and horrified him with my stories about the drama at the Foster house. (I don't normally gossip about my clients, but with Mark, Sarah and Dawn, I know the information will go no further.)

"Boy, I had a teacher in vet school like Gillian," he reminisced. "Of course, perfectionism runs rampant in any type of medicine, because you're under a lot of pressure to be precise and get things exactly right. But he was compulsive even about unimportant things. Surgical instruments had to be lined up in order of use and size, and all the medicine bottles in the cabinets had to be stored not only by type, alphabeti-

cally, and with the labels facing out, but by the size of the bottle! He also gave us strict rules about how to behave that did-
n't allow for any flexibility or any adapting to the situation."

"Sounds tough," I said. "Did he completely freak out if a
cabinet door closed just a millimeter out of line?"

Mark laughed. "I don't remember that ever happening,
but he might have—he was that hyper. Even in medicine,
some things have to be done as perfectly as possible, and others
not so much. If you don't have a sense of priorities, you'll
make yourself a nervous wreck."

I sipped my wine. "From what I saw at the Foster house,
Gillian's already a wreck and won't be satisfied until everyone
around her is in the same condition. At the same time, I'm
dealing with another situation that's practically the opposite."

"Those hoarders you told me about?"

I explained that, since my visit to the Tillmans on Sunday,
Bernice had died under mysterious circumstances. Mark listened with a sober expression.

"It should be easy enough for the M.E. to tell whether it
was accidental or foul play," he said. "If she did smother in her
sleep, she would have gone fairly peacefully. But if she actually struggled with someone, there should be signs of that,
such as hemorrhaging in the eyes."

The waiter picked this awkward time to set our dinners in
front of us. Fortunately, because of our animal-related jobs
and my tendency to get involved in murder investigations, we
both have strong stomachs. We continued to speculate about
the Tillmans' hoarding habits when Mark came up with a
keen insight.

"It's interesting," he said. "Both of your situations involve
people obsessed with *stuff*, but in different ways. Don't they?
Chester can't let go of his possessions because he's living in the
past, when he was young and successful. And Gillian needs

her house to be a perfect replica of the past, though who knows why?"

"I can't imagine," I said, "especially since it sounds as if she's done this kind of thing at least twice before. Maybe she just thinks she'd be happier living in another time? But meanwhile, she's alienating her husband and her daughter in the process."

"Well, once you return her cat you never have to see her again," Mark reminded me with a smile.

At that point, Quintessence took the stage. Only a modest platform with a set of drums and a couple of microphone stands, it rose not very far above the audience. As often seemed to be the case with jazz combos, most of the guys looked a bit older. The keyboard man resembled an accountant, with a rapidly receding hairline and owlish round glasses; his black pants and short-sleeved black shirt struggled to counter this image. The guitarist also had specs, plus a head of bushy white hair, and camouflaged a thickening waist beneath a blue Hawaiian-flowered shirt. The tall double-bass player sported a vertically striped bowling shirt and a shadow of beard, his graying brown hair moussed high in front. The drummer looked youngest to me, his sleeves rolled up to show off his well-developed "guns" and his hair a helmet of tight cornrows.

Their entrance drew applause, but much of it could have been for their singer. She sashayed onto the small stage like a retro pinup girl, in a cherry-printed halter top, tight black Capri pants and red platform sandals. She must have been around my age, but had styled her hair like a forties vamp, in platinum waves that cascaded to her shoulders. Her eye makeup could have been seen from space, and her scarlet lipstick matched her shoes.

At the microphone, she introduced the band by their first

names—Kenny, Herb, Nash and Stan—and herself as Tracy, all in a breathy, Marilyn Monroe voice. They began their first number, "I've Got You Under My Skin," which started out slow and dreamy but then shifted to up-tempo. I was relieved to hear that Tracy actually held in reserve a stronger, earthier tone that came through when she sang.

Then I stole a glance at Mark, who leaned forward in his seat, bright blue eyes riveted to the small stage. What the heck was going on here? Could sexy Tracy have been the reason he was so intent on coming out tonight to see Quintessence?

We finished our dinners while listening to the group's first set. To me, all of the musicians sounded very good, and different numbers gave each of them some solo time. Tracy had a decent voice, too, but when she went into that breathy mode it got on my nerves. I also didn't care for her suggestive patter with the two younger guys in the band, and occasionally even comments about men seated at the front of the audience. The feminist in me wondered why she couldn't concentrate on the music, instead of falling back on some trite sex-kitten act.

Quintessence took a short break just as our college-age waiter removed our empty plates and took our orders for coffee. After he'd left, Mark asked me, "So, how do you like the band?"

I opted for honesty with a dash of tact. "I think the guys sound great, and they've got a nice, versatile repertoire. The singer's talented, but she seems to be trying too hard."

He grinned. "Well, I understand she's only been working with them for a couple of months, so maybe she's still finding her stride. She's the niece of the keyboard guy." Before I could ask how he knew all of this, he posed another question. "What did you think of the guitarist?"

That confused me a bit. "He's good. I really liked his solo

on 'My Favorite Things.' He's got kind of a Wes Montgomery style." When I spotted a twinkle in Mark's eye, things finally came together for me. "He's the one giving you lessons, right?"

"Ah, you guessed!"

The waiter brought our coffees and tried to interest us in dessert. We passed on any of the flaming Firehouse specialties, Mark ordering a slice of cheesecake and I the flan. Satisfied, the waiter bustled off again.

Mark added milk to his coffee and stirred it thoughtfully. "Think I'll ever be able to play like that?"

This time I needed an even more skillful blend of tact and candor. Mark's playing was fine, for someone who'd only been back at the guitar for a little over a month. Bushy-haired Stan obviously had developed his finesse over the better part of a lifetime.

"I don't think he got to sound like that in just a few months, or even a few years," I said gently, "so I wouldn't expect you to, either. I think you've made a fine start, though, and he must be a good teacher."

Basically a realist, Mark nodded, with a self-deprecating smile. "Maybe after *I've* been at it for another twenty years or so?"

"Well, I'm sure this is his life's work. If it's any consolation, I doubt that Stan could pin together a broken leg on a Great Dane, either."

"Probably not."

When Quintessence finally took a break, Stan chugged from a bottle of water and gave Mark a little wave. Then he left the platform to say hi to both of us. Mark introduced me, mentioning what I did for a living. Stan enthused about the cleverness and charm of cats in general, and reminisced about a few he'd had as pets.

"Mark surprised me just a few days ago by playing a couple of songs," I told Stan. "He was always too self-conscious before, but he must have learned a lot from his lessons with you."

The older man clapped his student on the shoulder. "He's coming along fast, for somebody who was so rusty."

Mark dropped his gaze modestly. "Hearing you guys tonight reminded me how much further I have to go!"

"Ah, not really. Once you get the basics down, you'll just have to learn to riff and improvise. That's a matter of personal style, and it takes time to develop."

"I tried to remind him that you've probably been at it for a long while," I said, then hoped Stan didn't think I was calling him an old fossil.

"I have," he agreed. "And even though when I first started gigging I also held down other jobs, they weren't very demanding ones. Mark's a partner in a busy clinic, where sometimes he has to work late and even has emergencies. I'm sure that doesn't give him a lot of spare time to practice."

"True," Mark admitted, with a disheartened air.

"But you're also a smart guy, and you're motivated. It shouldn't be too long before you're ready for prime time, as they say." Stan gulped the last of his water. "Let's see where you are in another month or two. You might even be ready to sit in with us for a couple of numbers."

Mark's chiseled jaw dropped in panic. "Oh, I don't know. . . ."

"Well, we'll see. Meanwhile, gives you something to shoot for, right?" With a broad wink, the older man bid us goodbye and headed back to the stage.

The rest of the band members had been relaxing and chatting up there, and now I noticed that Tracy had fixed her bedroom eyes on my boyfriend. When he watched Stan return to the platform, she intercepted Mark's gaze with a wink of her own. He quickly broke the connection, and I also shot her an icy glare that I hoped would freeze Tracy's libido in its tracks.

Much as I'd have liked to see Mark fulfill his dream of playing with a real jazz combo, did it have to be this one? I didn't relish the idea of him spending any time in closer proximity to the flashy blonde, especially if she acted like a sexpot offstage as well as on.

During the music and our conversation with Stan, I had silenced my phone but felt it buzz. Now I checked the screen and was surprised that Sarah had called. She usually didn't contact me on my cell after hours unless it was important. I explained this to Mark before I listened to her message.

"Cassie, I'm sorry to bother you after hours, but I just got off the phone with Robin. The M.E. finished the preliminary autopsy on Bernice. Sounds like she didn't die just from the asthma, though I'm sure that didn't help. They found cat hairs in her lungs—no big surprise—and also pillow fibers. The Dalton police think Chester smothered her!"

Mark must have heard me gasp, because he shot me a concerned look. Briefly, I explained the situation. "I should call her back. Do you mind?"

He patted the air. "No, no. Go ahead."

I hit speed dial for her number. When Sarah heard the background noise on my end, she caught on that I must be in a public place. "Oh, dear, are you out with Mark? I didn't mean to interrupt."

"That's okay. I won't be able to talk too long, though, because we're at the Firehouse and the music will be starting again. What makes the cops think Chester killed Bernice?"

"She definitely suffocated. The only other explanation might be that one of the pillows fell over her face while she slept, and maybe a cat or two laid on top of it. But I think that would be kind of a long shot, don't you?"

"It's no crazier than the idea of Chester murdering her. Why would he do that?"

"I can't imagine. She was his lifeline to the world, almost—he depended on her to survive." Sarah sighed deeply. "But Robin said the M.E. found signs that she struggled. Something about her eyes . . ."

My heart sank. "Hemorrhaging? Yes, Mark also said that would be present, if she tried to fight someone off."

"Really? Oh, dear." Sarah fell silent for a few seconds. "And you know how cops are, hardheaded and practical. When they came to the house and talked to Chester, they could tell he was kind of confused. Robin says they think maybe he didn't realize what he was doing. That Bernice was snoring too loud, or something, and he was just trying to keep her quiet."

"They didn't arrest him, did they?"

"Not yet. Guess they don't have any real evidence so far. But they took the bed linens and all of her medications for analysis. I still don't know what that will prove. Even if Chester's prints or his DNA are on the pillow, he could have touched it at some other time, for another reason."

True enough, I thought. "How can I help?"

"I don't know. Robin's planning to go over there again tomorrow, hoping Chester may have calmed down a little. But she doesn't know how to handle the police—she gets angry, and that's not the best approach—and she's never dealt with a situation like this before. She knows you have, and . . ."

I filled the pause. "And she wants me to sleuth around a little? I don't know what good it'll do, but I can try."

"Would you? I know we have a light schedule at the shop tomorrow, so I can cover it for the half day. Robin plans to go to Chester's around ten."

"Okay, tell her I'll meet her there."

By the time I hung up, I could feel Mark's look of alarm even before I met his eyes. "You're going over there tonight?"

"No, no, of course not." I rested a hand on his arm. "Tomorrow morning . . . and not too early."

He gave his head a slow shake. "Cassie, what are you getting into now?"

"Just trying to help a harmless old man beat a murder rap that I'm sure he doesn't deserve. Nothing remotely dangerous, unless I get crushed by a falling stack of old newspapers."

"Um-hmm," Mark commented, skeptically. "I've heard *that* song before."

Chapter 6

The next morning, I arrived at Chester's house to find him and Robin attempting to feed the five indoor cats. Chester wore a faded green T-shirt with his chinos and slippers, and different eyeglasses—maybe the new ones she'd picked up for him? He smoothed out a long, crumpled strip of paper with his shaky hands and squinted to make out the handwriting, probably his late wife's.

"No, wait, wait!" he ordered Robin.

Dressed in biking shorts and a T-back top, which hugged her slim figure while no doubt keeping her cool, Robin paused; she held an open can of cat food in midair.

Chester read directions from his list. "Minnie and Candy can eat together, 'cause they're both gobblers. Sugarman has to go in a room by himself, 'cause he's poky. Otherwise, the fast ones will eat all their food and then his, and he'll get nothin'."

After waving hello to me, Robin split a five-ounce can of food into two bowls. Most of the cats already were winding around our legs and singing for their breakfast. She asked me,

"Cassie, can you grab the black-and-white one and the calico?"

I did this without too much trouble. We parked them in Bernice's bedroom, put their bowls on the floor, and shut the door.

Chester nodded, as if impressed by our efficiency. "Sugarman eats the senior feed . . . if we still got any."

I found one last can in their cupboard, and made a mental note to pick some up the next time I swung by the PetMart out on the highway. I scooped some into a dish for the mostly white cat and enticed him toward the hall bathroom. Using my foot to gently stave off the three others, I closed Sugarman in with his meal. Meanwhile I heard Robin ask Chester, "Which one gets urinary care?"

"That's Autumn," he said. "We put her stuff up on the island, to keep it away from Winky. She'll jump up there, but he won't."

Returning to the kitchen, I marveled that any cat would be brave enough to jump onto that island; even from the floor, Autumn had to be able to see that it was cluttered with junk. But she leaped up gracefully, landing in the one spot about five inches square that could accommodate all of her paws. Robin shoved some more things out of the way and set a dish in front of the tortoiseshell longhair.

Winky, the silver tabby, watched all of this activity with wistful patience, so I asked what food he ate.

Chester didn't even have to check the list. "He's young, got no problems yet. Regular dry kibble."

Finally, all the indoor cats were happily chomping away in their respective spaces. For the time being, I didn't ask Chester if he and Bernice normally put out any provisions for the ferals.

I turned to see him slowly stroking Winky as the cat ate. A tear rolled down the older man's dark cheek.

"Chester . . ." I touched his sleeve.

"She knew all about them," he murmured, a tremor in his voice. "All their little tricks and habits, who got along with who. If she didn't leave this list, I might not know how to feed them. Maybe once I would have, but these days?" He shrugged helplessly.

This man couldn't have killed his wife, I thought, *unless he absolutely had no idea what he was doing. And was that even possible?*

Robin washed up some used, dirty cat dishes at the sink, dried her hands with a paper towel, and rejoined us. "Chester, Cassie's real good at solving mysteries. Why don't you tell her what you told me and the police? About what you heard the night Bernice died?"

He sank into one of the chairs that went with the sturdy, colonial-style kitchen table; it almost looked like a mass-produced, 1980s version of one of Gillian Foster's antiques. I removed a bag of cat food from one of the other chairs to sit opposite him.

"I dunno . . ." he began. "I might've been dreaming."

"The cops put that idea in your head," Robin reminded him. "Go on, explain to Cassie."

His eyes met mine, behind their thick glasses. "Bernice and I had taken to sleeping in different bedrooms. Partly because she had trouble breathing at night, but also because of the cats. Sugarman, Autumn, Winky and sometimes even Candy would pile on the bed toward evening, while she was reading or watching TV. Took up as much space as I would have! Even if she put them out of the room and shut the door, they'd whine and scratch all night to get in. Got so it wasn't worth the trouble to keep 'em out." His slight smile showed amusement, rather than annoyance. "At our age, though, that wasn't a big deal. The cats kept her company, and I was right across the hall, in Jimmy's room."

Robin leaned against a nearby wall that still held a landline telephone. "And you heard something, right?"

"I heard her get up during the night. But that wasn't unusual. The bathroom's down the hall, and once in a while she goes to the kitchen at night, too. She's got some medicine she's supposed to take with food, so she'll eat some crackers. The thing is, that night she was real quiet about it."

I cocked my head and waited for him to explain.

"Bernice usually makes . . . made . . . some noise when she got up. Sometimes brushed against the boxes and bags in the hall. Lately I could hear her breathing when she passed by, too, from the asthma. That night I heard steps, but they were quiet, careful. No breathing, either." He glanced up at Robin. "But you been clearing a lot of stuff out of the hall, so I guess there wasn't as much for her to brush against."

"You heard something else, though, didn't you?" Robin reminded him.

Chester pursed his lips in thought. "I heard one of the cats in her room yowl, angry-like. But that doesn't mean too much, either. Sometimes they squabbled with each other on the bed, all wanting . . . to be next to her."

"Do you think someone from outside could have gotten into the house?" I asked gently.

"They could have, easy," he said. "I always leave that back door propped open so these cats can go out, and the strays can come inside if it rains. It's not wide open, but I stick a little rock in there. That morning, though, the door was still just the way I left it."

Robin and I made eye contact. A clever intruder might have thought of that—putting everything back in place to cover his or her tracks.

"Bernice usually gets up . . . got up . . . earlier than me," he went on, "so I was surprised she didn't that morning. I looked in on her, but I didn't see anything wrong. I thought she was just sleeping in. Autumn and Sugarman, though, came right up to me, meowed and pawed my legs. I figured they was just hungry." Chester straightened in his chair, as if struck by a sudden insight, and glanced toward Robin. "You know how that doctor said she must've had a pillow over her face? Wasn't any sign of that when I looked in! She was on her side, facing the window. Had one pillow under her head and the other next to her. I think Winky was lying on it."

That would be something, I thought, if Chester's memory was reliable. And, of course, if he were telling the truth. If he'd killed her accidentally, then felt guilty, he could have re-arranged the pillows before the paramedics arrived. Or if he'd been half-asleep, he might have done all that and not even re-membered.

"How long after that did you realize . . ."

His posture sagged again. "Not too long. I made myself some cereal and went to ask Bernice if she wanted any. When I shook her shoulder, she was cold. So I called her doctor—his number was on her medicine bottle. Good thing I got these new glasses, or I might not've been able to read it."

"The doctor was in his office?"

Chester nodded. "By then it was about nine, I guess. He sent the ambulance."

Robin stepped behind his chair and put a hand on his thin shoulder. "That must have been awful for you, Chester. I'm so sorry."

"Y'know what's awful?" His voice rose in anger. "If somebody did come in and hurt Bernice, it's still my fault. I left that door open, didn't I? An' when I heard somebody in the hall that didn't sound like her, I should've checked. Some husband I am, half-blind and muzzy-headed. Couldn't even protect my wife!"

We tried for a few minutes to console him, and Robin suggested he go lie down and rest for a while. After he retired to his room and closed the door, she and I stayed in the kitchen to talk, keeping our voices low.

"Our pastor has been in touch with a local agency that can send an aide here a few days a week," Robin told me. "Someone who can make sure Chester has food and help him with anything else he needs. There will be a cost, but he does get Social Security checks and has an IRA. I'll try to help him sort out the financial stuff."

"What about his children?" I asked.

"Jim's down in Florida, and Sylvia lives in Chicago. Pastor Gerald did notify them both that the funeral is Saturday, so I'm sure they'll be coming for that. If they've got any class at all, maybe they'll pay for the burial. But as for getting more involved with looking after their father . . ." She frowned in disapproval. "They left both him and Bernice on their own for all these years, so I'm not expecting much from them now."

My gaze drifted to the back door, which still stood open about four inches, held in place by a fist-size gray stone. I wandered over to pick up and study the makeshift doorstop. "Y'know, even though Chester got upset just now, he sounded pretty lucid today. Do you think there's anything to what he said? That someone could have found the door ajar, sneaked into the house and murdered Bernice?"

Robin joined me at the door and peered out across the Tillmans' yard. "It *could* have happened, but why would anyone do that? As far as I know, she had no enemies."

We both stepped out onto the small, shabby back porch,

leaving behind the stuffiness of the house. I reminded Robin, "You said their neighbor, Bob something, visited the Tillmans sometimes. Where does he live?"

She pointed to another modest ranch house, pale blue with black shutters, just visible through the trees. At least from a distance it seemed better maintained than the Tillman place, but of course, most of the neighborhood's other homes were. A dusty red pickup truck stood in the driveway.

"Sounds like he got along well with both of them," I noted.

"I think he did. And it's not as if Bernice had any great inheritance to leave Chester or even their kids. I mean, this place?" She spread her arms to span the rear wall with its peeling beige paint. "The cops already have talked by phone with Jimmy and Sylvia. Besides living so far away, I think they both have alibis for that night."

"Chester said the back door was still propped open in the morning, just the way he'd left it the night before," I reminded her. "He remembered that detail well enough."

"And he said there was no pillow over his wife's face when he looked in on her. That's something he certainly would have noticed!"

We had to raise our voices slightly to compensate for staccato hammering and the whine of a saw in the distance. Leaning over the porch's shaky railing, I saw a larger house rising, maybe a quarter mile down the road. Construction vehicles lined up in the driveway. It looked as if the place had started out about the size of the Tillmans' single-story home, but the workers already had added skeletal framework for a first-floor extension and a second level.

I mentioned this to Robin.

"Yeah, Bob was talking with Chester about that place," she said. "The family who rented there let it get run-down, so the landlord booted them out and sold it to a flipper. With all the work he's doing, it'll probably sell for three times what he paid for it."

I reflected that a chance to snap up the Tillman house cheaply might give even someone who barely knew Bernice a motive to do away with her. "Chester owns this house outright, doesn't he?"

"Oh, yeah. I imagine the mortgage was paid off long ago, back when he was making good money as a sportscaster."

The feral cats had spotted us now and began gathering below the porch, hoping for an easier meal than they could catch in the woods. Robin and I poured some dry food into a half-dozen plastic dishes. This time, we couldn't worry about each animal getting his fair share; we let them sort that out among themselves.

Robin reminded me that Sarah probably would want to go to Bernice's funeral Saturday morning, though normally she'd be working a half day for me.

"Of course, she can have the day off," I said. "We haven't even been that busy—I can handle the shop by myself."

Back indoors, we reflected that Chester didn't need the financial burden of five indoor cats, especially if some were old enough to need special diets and veterinary care.

"Next time I come back, I'll bring my friends from FOCA," I told her. "They're nice kids, and they probably can talk him into parting at with with at least a few animals. Maybe he'll feel better once they assure him it's a no-kill shelter."

"That's a good idea," Robin agreed.

I glanced around the living room. "We've got an antiques shop in Chadwick, too. Maybe I'll ask the proprietor if he'd have any interest in these old toys and memorabilia. That might give Chester some extra cash to pay for the home aide and other expenses."

"Worth a try, I guess," she said.

I stole a look at my phone, since the many clocks in the Tillman house all offered different opinions on the time of day. "If you've got things under control here, Robin, I'd better get back to work. It's not fair of me to leave Sarah there by herself for too long."

That brought a smile to her friend's face. "She always talks about what a considerate boss you are. I think she even enjoys getting mixed up in all of the outside excitement with your clients."

I laughed. "Even though she keeps warning me to stay out of trouble!"

I peeked into Chester's room to say goodbye, but he was fast asleep, still fully clothed and on top of his bedspread.

Robin saw me to the front door, a less hazardous journey now that she had thinned out some of the trash. "Thanks, Cassie, for everything."

"Glad to do it. I hope you can get Chester the help he needs to go on living here safely."

"I hope so, too." She sighed. "Even though he's technically a murder suspect, at least for now he's still a free man. I pray to God he stays that way."

Chapter 7

The next day, Becky Newmeyer and I traveled in my grooming van to make one of our occasional house calls.

I'd first acquired the vehicle as an ugly, matte-black panel truck, but some FOCA volunteers and a company that specialized in van makeovers helped me turn it into a rolling extension of my business. Now it was glossy white with a raised roof; both sides advertised Cassie's Comfy Cats, along with a two-foot-tall cartoon of a smug, prancing Persian. I had used it so far to promote my services at events and to do grooming at the homes of some customers.

Nancy Whyte, who owned two show-quality Maine Coon cats, lived in Sparta, about half an hour away. Her male Coon, named King (for Stephen, the famous Maine resident), weighed in at twenty-five pounds. His sister, Jessie, was only slightly smaller, at about eighteen. And neither were obese—that weight was mostly bone, muscle and fur.

Not overly tall, a bit plump and in her fifties, Nancy brushed both cats herself a couple of times a week. But to keep mats from forming in their thick coats, and even between their toes, they needed a more intensive grooming session about once a month. King and Jessie were so large that when Nancy took them to shows, she used rolling pet carriers intended for medium-size dogs. Rather than make her bring them to my shop, though, it made more sense for me to go to her.

Becky might have looked like a strange choice to help me wrestle with these burly beasts. The petite woman with the boyish cap of platinum hair was stronger than she looked, though, and she'd done a fine job last month, on our first visit to Nancy's place. A recent college grad who spent much of her time volunteering at FOCA, Becky still lived in Chadwick with her parents. Since graduation, she'd been pet-sitting for extra money, and I'd recently started employing her to help me when I needed to make a house call. It expanded my customer base and left Sarah free to mind our shop.

On the drive out to Nancy's place, I filled Becky in on Chester's whole story, including his cat situation. "The first priority, I think, is to reduce the number running around his house. His eyesight isn't great, especially at night, and at some point they're liable to trip him. Once he gets to like and trust you and Chris—which I'm sure he will—you may be able to talk him into parting with at least a few of them."

"We can certainly give it a shot," Becky said. "Even Chris can be charming, when animal lives are at stake!"

I laughed. I'd always gotten along well with Chris Eberhardt, another recent college grad and Becky's boyfriend. But I knew he could get a little intense sometimes about humane issues.

We pulled up in front of Nancy's Tudor-style home, its entrance flanked by rose bushes in full bloom. She escorted us into her living room with a big smile. A scarf covered most of her curly blond hair, and her T-shirt read: BIG MEWS. Nancy had used that name for her cattery, when she'd still been breeding Coons. She had given up the business since her husband's death a couple of years ago, sold off all her animals except King and Jessie, and had them both neutered. But they were such impressive specimens of their breed that she still brought them to a show occasionally.

She led out the massive brown tabby male on a retractable leash, fastened to his padded harness.

My helper, who saw a wide variety of animals pass through the FOCA shelter, shook her head in awe. "This guy is incredible. He's as big as a collie!"

Nancy laughed, obviously enjoying the shock value. "Well, maybe a small one. And he's *almost* as friendly."

"Lucky for us," I said.

While Becky tousled his amber-and-black neck ruff, King looked down his doglike snout at us but maintained his regal composure. His obedience also more canine than feline, he allowed her to lead him out to the van and hopped inside. Nancy obviously walked him this way often, since for her it would have been impossible to carry him.

For the next forty-five minutes or so, my helper and I gently worked any mats out of his double coat—both the long, silky "guard hairs" that give him his tabby coloring, and the thicker, softer fur of his undercoat. The latter functioned almost like a layer of down and had developed to keep Maine Coons comfortable outdoors during the harshest winter weather. He'd probably started losing some of this hair earlier in the spring, but I helped the process along with a shedding comb. I didn't usually trim the coats of longhaired cats unless they were impossibly matted, but in King's case, I used scissors to also take a little off his outer coat, just to help him get through the summer more comfortably.

Becky and I finished by clipping his claws, something I dreaded to undertake even with my own cats. King had been groomed for showing since kittenhood, though, and gave us no trouble. A good thing, too—with his talons, and all the muscle behind them, he could have mauled us badly. I had offered to bathe him, which helps to keep Coons' coats more manageable, but Nancy had told me that was the one job she could manage herself. These cats tolerated water better than most other breeds, and hers would cheerfully jump into an empty bathtub and let her fill it partway, to soap and rinse them.

We returned King, in all his glory, to his owner, then put his sister through the same treatment. As I worked on the silky tufts that gave Jessie's ears such a long, pointed look, Becky asked me, "Is it true that Maine Coons are part Lynx?"

"Nope, though some people think so," I said. "They do look similar because of the ears, neck ruffs and big, furry paws. Probably the domestic cats developed those for the same reasons Lynxes did, to keep them warm and help them walk over snow. Maine Coons don't have any of that 'wild' nature, though—in fact, they're usually very calm and gentle."

When we brought Jessie back into the house, Nancy enthused about how trimming both cats' coats had made them look fuller but feel lighter. "Cassie, would you have a talk with my hairdresser?" she joked. "He could learn some of your techniques!"

She sent us off with a generous check, which I would split in half with Becky. I knew she'd been saving up to get out of her parents' house and into a place of her own. I suspected that she might want to move in with Chris, or at least have the privacy to spend more time alone with him.

I drove to Chadwick, to let Becky off at the shelter before I went back to my shop. "I'll ask Chester Tillman what day might be good for me, you and Chris to stop by," I told her. "You two can spend some time chatting with him. Explain what FOCA does, and that it's a no-kill shelter. Then maybe he'll agree to at least let you take Bernice's three favorite cats off his hands."

Becky nodded, but with a sad expression. "Are those the ones that the cops think smothered her? I guess he might be glad to have them out of the house!"

"Don't be too sure," I said. "I really don't think Chester blames the cats for Bernice's death. He suspects there was a human culprit involved. And after some of the things he told me and Robin, I'm inclined to agree."

Friday afternoon, Sarah and I combed and fluffed Princess Leya to a perfection that should satisfy even her owner. Around four, as specified, we loaded her into the carrier for her trip home. Despite her dazzling blue eyes, the pampered Himalayan wore a gloomy expression, almost as if she would have preferred to stay at our shop rather than return to the Fosters. All right, maybe I was projecting; she'd probably be happy enough to see Whitney again, and maybe even Donald.

Sarah planted her hands on her hips and reviewed the duties we'd been assigned. "Well, we gave her a half hour in the playroom every day. I played with her for two short sessions each time, one with a feather/wand toy and one with a jingly ball, as requested. We groomed her twice and clipped her nails, and kept her in the roomiest condo, away from any of the other cats. Did we forget anything?"

I pointed to a couple of cans of food that I would be returning along with Leya. "Gasp—we have some left over! Think Gillian will accuse me of starving her?"

My assistant laughed. "I'm just glad it's you bringing her back there, not me."

I slipped the can into my shoulder bag and hefted the carrier. "Can't imagine what it'll be like over there today. It was crazy enough when they were just decorating, but now that Gillian's getting ready for the reception—"

"My advice? Get in and out as fast as you can. Just don't forget the check."

This time, a catering truck occupied the Fosters' driveway. Behind it stood a smaller, older, light-blue panel truck branded JANOS HOME REPAIR. So Nick was still here? I thought he would have made short work of fixing that cabinet door and fled the scene as soon as possible.

Maybe Gillian is insisting that he make endless adjustments to suit her stratospheric standards. If so, he won't thank me for recommending him!

The front door was closed this time, so I rang the bell. After a minute, an older, well-rounded blond woman in a starched white apron answered it. I held up Leya's carrier, explained my mission and was admitted. Instantly, I could hear that all the frantic activity today was concentrated in the kitchen.

The aproned woman glanced at the cat and shrugged in confusion. "I don't know where you should take him," she said, obviously not well acquainted with Princess Leya. "I'm sure Mrs. Foster won't want him underfoot . . ."

"I was told that they keep her in the guest room," I said.

Relief dawned on the woman's plain face. "Oh, good. It's down that hall to the left."

Though I remembered, I thanked her for the directions. She might be a new hire. I could imagine that cooks and housekeepers didn't last very long at the Fosters'.

Gillian's clearly enunciated, piercing voice still reached me all the way down the passage. At least Leya should find some peace shut away in the odd little bedroom, and unlike a human, she probably didn't mind the saggy antique bed or the blank stares of the faceless dolls. Of course, a pan with clean litter and a dish of water already had been set out for her. Maybe Gillian's fetish for organization did have some good points. Or had Whitney seen to the cat's creature comforts? Released from her carrier, Leya immediately dove under the low-slung bed. I felt sorry for her, but that was typical cat behavior. She'd just begun to adjust to life boarding at my shop and suddenly found herself back in the spooky guest room. With the familiar smells, though, she would probably feel at home again by evening.

I couldn't easily reach Leya to pet her, so with a few encouraging words I left her alone and closed the room's door. After that, I peeked into the kitchen to see if the bodies were piling up. As I drew nearer, I noticed that Gillian's affected voice had taken on a lilt that almost sounded . . . cheerful! In fact, she actually seemed to be praising somebody! When I peered through the doorway, I realized with a shock that it was Nick.

"Mr. Janos, you have saved the day. That crooked door has been driving me insane, and you fixed it with one turn of a screw!"

The stocky handyman turned pink, all the way from his trim gray beard up to his balding pate. "Aw, thanks. It was a little more than that, but after all my years in this business, at least I know which screw to turn."

"That girl from the cat shop was right, you are a gem. I'll probably have more jobs for you in the future."

She spotted me over Nick's shoulder, and he turned also.

"Hi, Cassie," he hailed me. "Speak of the devil."

Yes, it's me, I thought. *The "girl" from the cat shop.* But at least Nick sounded elated rather than browbeaten. With a glance at the repaired cabinet, I asked, "Everything worked out okay?"

"With Mr. Janos, anyway," Gillian said, her long-suffering air resurfacing. "Would you believe this all has to be pulled together in less than an hour? I gave the caterers recipes and directions weeks ago, but they're still getting some things wrong."

"I'm sure everything will be delicious," I tried to reassure her. I might have told her a child's finger painting would look just fine over her authentic 1824 camelback sofa.

"Of course, but that's not the point," she fretted. "Everything on the menu is authentic to the period. We'll be sampling foods that would have been served in a home like this in the early 1800s. I can't expect a modern caterer to know how to prepare such things, which is why I researched and gave them most of the recipes. Their job is to follow my orders, not just *ignore* them."

Nick and I both nodded soberly, but I suspected we shared a much different thought: *Jeez, major control freak!*

Whitney sneaked in through the back door, carefully dodging around the catering staff, who were chopping vegetables and opening oven doors to check on various dishes. She again wore her riding clothes, along with a bored expression. When she spotted me, she grinned, but mainly because of my connection to the family pet. "Hi, Cassie. Did you bring Leya back?"

"Yep, she's in the guest room, just chilling out," I said.

The girl started in that direction, but her mother's voice halted her. "Leave the cat for now. Go change your clothes, then come help out in the kitchen. Herta is setting the buffet table and I have to get dressed."

Whitney's pale brows drew together, as if she might have liked to hear a "please" tucked in among all of those orders. "Is Daddy coming home for the reception?"

"He wasn't sure. Depends on what's happening at work." Gillian shooed her daughter with a hand. "Go on, hurry!"

The blond girl lingered with a sly smile. "I don't need to change. And I rinsed my hands with the barn hose, right after I picked out Glory's hooves." When Gillian curled a lip in disgust, Whitney giggled and headed down the hall, presumably to her room. The only one in the house that her mother had not completely "colonized"?

Nick and I lingered out of the kitchen's flow of traffic until Gillian finally remembered us. "Oh, goodness, I need to pay you both, don't I?" She located her purse, produced a checkbook, confirmed the amounts she owed each of us, and wrote the checks. "Thanks again, Cassie, for suggesting I contact Nick."

"I've never seen a repair problem he couldn't solve," I told her, while he demurred modestly. Hey, if this lady was willing to give him more work and pay him promptly, I'd gladly encourage her.

Since Nick and I both had parked out front, we were headed down the hall in that direction when Donald Foster came in the front door. He greeted me with a sunny smile, and I confirmed that I had brought Leya back home. Introducing Nick, I also noted that the cabinet door now hung in perfect alignment.

"Oh, boy, you don't know how glad I am to hear that!" Donald stage-whispered, as he clapped the handyman on the shoulder. "The state of the union is safe, eh?"

"Piece o' cake." Nick smiled, obviously hesitant to join in any mockery of Gillian's compulsive nature. He still had her fat check in his pocket, after all.

Donald glanced into the dining room, where the rough-hewn oak table had been draped with a handwoven runner. A weathered, two-handled copper cooking vessel served as the centerpiece. Herta, the blonde in the apron, had begun setting out stacks of colonial yellow ware dishes and a ceramic tureen, probably also antique. The cutlery must have been new but looked as simple in design as possible.

"Speaking of cake," said Donald, "you two should stay for the reception. It's a buffet, so I'm sure there will be plenty to eat. Unless you have other plans?"

I started to say that I needed to get back to my shop, but Nick subtly elbowed me. "Sure, that'd be great. I'd like to hear more about the house. I'm always fascinated by the way these old places were put together."

The two men began chatting happily about joists, framing and footings. Although I had the impression Donald worked for an advertising firm, he sounded as if he'd picked up a lot of knowledge about home improvement. Not too surprising, if he and Gillian also had renovated two other houses.

"The one area we haven't touched yet is the cellar," he told Nick. "That's going to be a bear of a project—dirt floor, wooden posts and beams. Someone actually did put electricity down there, at one time, but the wiring's all knob-and-tube."

Nick hissed and shook his head. "Ah, you can't have that, not with today's currents! It's a fire hazard."

"Don't I know it. Luckily my dad was an electrician, so I learned a lot from him. I already upgraded most of the main floor wiring myself, though it wasn't as old as the stuff in the cellar."

Gillian called to her husband then. He lifted his chin, squared his broad shoulders and joined her in the kitchen.

Left alone with Nick, I asked him, "You really want to stay around? It'll probably be just a bunch of stiffs from the historical society, and Gillian blathering on and on."

He threw me a sly look. "Hey, it's not often that I get paid whatever I ask on the spot, no haggling, just for an easy, fifteen-minute job. If the Fosters wanna sing my praises to their rich friends, I can make nice and get myself more work. You should think like that, too, Cassie. How many folks around here can afford to bring in their cats to be groomed and boarded? But you might find a whole bunch of those people in this room today."

He made a good point. I shouldn't let my aversion to Gillian and the Foster family drama blind me to this marketing opportunity. "Nick, you're not only a 'gem' of a carpenter, but a very shrewd businessman."

Chapter 8

I pulled out my cell phone to tell Sarah I'd be getting back a little later than planned, so she could close the shop for the day. She reminded me with a laugh that she'd warned me not to linger at the Foster house. I pointed out that, as Nick had said, "It could be good for business."

"I know you have Bernice's funeral tomorrow," I added.

"Yes, thanks again for giving me the day off. See you Monday."

After that, Nick and I loitered in the front hall, killing time before the reception officially began. We watched Herta transport various appetizers into the nearby dining room—raw carrots and celery, a dish of walnuts, a plate of small sausages with a dip. Knowing how particular Gillian was, I presumed all of those things would have been available to a prosperous farm family in the early 1800s.

On one of her trips, the maid must have heard my stomach growl, because she took pity on me and Nick. "Grab a couple of those little plates and help yourself to some hors d'oeuvres," she said. "Plenty more where they came from.

And would you like some cider?" She nodded toward a punch bowl, filled with a pale-gold brew, and winked. "It's not *really* hard, but it's got a little kick."

When I accepted the offer, Nick did, too. "I got nothing else lined up 'til later this afternoon," he admitted to me, "and I only got to drive a few blocks home."

I had just as short a distance back to my shop, and surely I'd be sobered up by the time I had to tackle the next cat with a matted coat. Besides, a glass of cider might help to make the next hour or so of historical chitchat more entertaining; I suspected Nick was thinking the same thing.

I'd just plucked a carrot stick from the crudités tray—with a glance over my shoulder in case Gillian should sweep in and scold me for ruining the symmetry of the presentation—when the front bell rang. Herta had her hands full with a big salad bowl, so I told her I'd get the door.

At first I could not identify the person who stood on the stoop, until Linda Freeman peeked out from behind a bouquet of summer wildflowers. She looked surprised but pleased to see me again. I introduced her to Nick, and we stepped aside to let her bring the flowers into the dining room, where she deftly arranged them in the antique copper vessel. When Linda had finished, the daylilies, sunflowers and snapdragons, along with other blooms I couldn't name as easily, formed a sunny array of yellows accented by some soft peach and lavender-blue. They echoed the colors that appeared in the table's patterned dinnerware, which surely was no accident.

"Robert didn't come with you today?" I asked Linda.

She straightened and smoothed the lines of her trim, teal-green skirt suit, short-sleeved in a nod to the warm weather. Her dark updo also looked more controlled and chic than when I'd met her last time. "I gave him the afternoon off," she said with a diplomatic smile. "He works hard enough as it is."

I heard the subtext. If I'd been Robert, I wouldn't have wanted to come back to this house, either, after the way he'd been treated on his last visit.

Just then Gillian appeared, having changed into her hostess garb—a midcalf skirt in a dark floral print and a white gauze blouse with a scooped, gathered neckline. I figured this was her nod to country-colonial fashion. She'd also softened her practical pageboy hairstyle with a few waves around her face, and her tasteful makeup played up the feline slant of her eyes. Gillian would have been a very pretty woman, I thought, if not for the defiant set of her chin and the tense lines that bracketed her thin mouth.

"Oh, good, the flowers are here," she said without directly acknowledging Linda. Of course, she had to fiddle with the already perfect arrangement and move a stalk or two. Then she noticed that Nick and I held plates of hors d'oeuvres, and arched her neatly penciled eyebrows.

The handyman spoke up first. "Mr. Foster invited us to stay for the reception. Hope that's okay."

Gillian almost swallowed her tongue, which told me Donald had not cleared the invitation with her. But she must still have felt grateful for the emergency repair of her cabinet. "Did he? Yes, why not. Help yourselves. Of course, you may not want to stay for the whole reception. There probably will be a lot of boooring speeches."

"That's okay," Nick said with an easygoing shrug. "I'm kind of a history buff."

Gillian had no more time to discourage us, because the doorbell rang again. She glanced around, as if irritated that Herta was not available, before answering the summons herself. In delighted tones, she welcomed the first members of the historical society to arrive. She had no choice but to introduce them to her only other guests, Linda, Nick and me.

"This is Bill and Nona Stafford," she said. "He's the society's president and Nona is VP of membership."

We shook hands with the tall, white-haired man in the open-necked shirt and seersucker jacket, and the much shorter blond woman in the lime-green sleeveless shirt dress. I wondered if she'd chosen the color to keep from being overlooked; at least it actually worked on her.

Knowing I'd be coming to the house in advance of a fancy occasion, I'd dressed a little better than for my usual workday. Still, I felt self-conscious now in my "good" dark-washed jeans and a knit top with a tan-on-white zebra pattern (or, as Sarah had once pointed out, more like tabby stripes in my case). Nick also was pretty dressed down, in denim pants and a chambray work shirt. I wondered if I should explain to the other guests that our invitation had been last minute.

Herta bustled in, a bit breathless, as if aware that she'd made a blunder by not being in two places at once. While Gillian made small talk with the Staffords, the doorbell rang again, and the maid let in another couple. Nick and I introduced ourselves to them, Adele and Jack Dugan. Reed-thin Adele, tastefully casual in beige linen pants and an aqua camp shirt, was the group's vice president of Events; her portly banker husband, in a white shirt and tie but no jacket, merely volunteered with the historical group.

Before long we had almost a dozen pillars of Chadwick society hovering around the hors d'oeuvres and quizzing Gillian about her venerable home. Better late than never, Donald joined us to explain the construction challenges of the renovation. Linda occasionally slipped in a comment to make sure the guests understood that she had a hand in creating the authentic color scheme and styling the rooms.

Kay Lombardi, the group's secretary, asked how Leya had weathered all the excitement. I saw my chance, and explained that the Himalayan had boarded with me for a few days.

"Kay's a great cat lover," Gillian told me, and once more cast an impatient glance toward the kitchen. "If I knew where Whitney was, I'd ask her to bring Leya out . . ."

"Want me to go get her?" I asked. "The cat, I mean."

Another surprised look, as Gillian realized that I knew where Leya was stashed and could handle her at least as well as any family member. "Oh . . . yes, would you?"

On my way down the hall, I stole a glance into the kitchen. Whitney appeared to be helping Herta get the main dishes ready. Despite her threat to stay in her riding clothes, the girl had changed into a dotted sundress and freed her long, straight hair from its ponytail. I didn't bother to interrupt her—bringing the cat out myself would give me a chance to talk up my business, after all.

The Himalayan had recovered from her nerves and lay sprawled on the rope bed, more comfortably, I was sure, than any human would. She even greeted me with a meow.

"Hi, sweetie," I said. "Would you like to go out and see the people? Just for a couple of minutes, then I'll bring you back here. Okay?"

As if she understood, Leya let me scoop her up and carry her from the room. She made quite an armful, though much of it was fur. When we entered the dining room, the guests all made admiring sounds, though you could quickly spot the ones who preferred to appreciate her from afar. Bill Stafford made the excuse of a mild cat allergy, so I kept at a distance from him. But Adele, Jack and Kay approached by turns to stroke the fluffy coat and exclaim over Leya's Siamese coloring and blue eyes. I stayed alert for any sign that the Himalayan was growing cranky and might strike out at someone, but she bore all the attention with good grace.

Meanwhile, I did get to talk up my shop and services. Jack owned a cat that he said sometimes needed boarding, and Kay knew a neighbor who had been struggling to groom a Persian mix on her own. Once I had returned Leya to the guest room, I fished a couple of business cards from my purse and gave them to anyone who was interested. I overheard Nick promoting his handyman business with a few people, too.

After the hors d'oeuvres and cider, Bill Stafford gave a brief talk on the home's original owner, John Ramsford. He explained that, although the property originally had encompassed several acres and a working farm, Ramsford made his fortune primarily from an iron mine and forge located a few miles away. One of the earliest in the area, it helped supply troops during the Revolution, and continued to thrive through the dawn of railroad travel.

"As most of you know, the Ramsford mine has become a historic, educational site today," Stafford added.

The Fosters then led all of us on a brief tour of the house. First, Donald took us around the outside and told how they had preserved most of the original brickwork and the proportions of the doors and windows. He pointed out such details as an old hitching post, a stone-walled well, and a weathervane on the garage roof. Indoors, Gillian took over to explain which seating pieces and tables were authentic antiques. Linda finally got a word in edgewise to talk about the "primitive" American artworks, weavings and quilts they'd used as accessories.

I still marveled at how a modern, well-to-do family could live comfortably in this home, which almost resembled a museum. The army of toy soldiers lined up in that hutch, for ex-

ample—who would have collected those? Whitney? Her father? And those picturesque stacks of hand-painted, oval
boxes—could you actually store anything in them and ever
hope to find it again?

The master bedroom looked most livable, because it had
been enlarged to accommodate a four-poster king-size bed.
But around its fireplace, on tiny chairs and clad in little calico
dresses, sat more of those eerie, faceless dolls. Not an audience
that would put me in the mood for romance, or even a good
night's sleep!

We did not venture into Whitney's room, presumably because she had refused to go along with the historic scheme.
Donald did allow us a peek into the cellar from the wooden
staircase. True to his description, it was pretty rough, with
timbered walls and a dirt-and-stone floor. When he switched
on the lights, they even flickered a bit. He and Nick discussed
possible renovations as we all retreated back to the dining
room.

There, the table had been reset buffet-style with an assortment of unusual foods, although everything smelled wonderful. The caterers had left, but Herta and Whitney brought in
the last few items. The historical society folks made a game of
guessing what the dishes were, until Gillian helped them out.
"There are two different types of meat pastries, beef and pork.
The tureen has a barley-and-vegetable soup."

Adele surveyed the whole spread with a wary eye. I heard
her quietly ask Gillian, "Do you have anything that's gluten-
free?"

"Absolutely," her hostess responded. "I made sure of that,
because I have a problem with gluten myself." She gestured
toward a large serving bowl that held some kind of thick yellow concoction.

"Hummus?" Jack Dugan asked, peering more closely. "I didn't think they had that in Colonial America."

"No, it's pease pudding. Just split yellow peas, boiled down into a porridge, with spices and a little ham." She assured Adele, "No flour of any kind. I tested the recipe last week, just to be sure. And believe me, if it had gluten, I would have known." She laid a hand on her flat stomach and made a face.

"I appreciate it." Smiling, Adele took a generous helping.

"And we have fresh summer berries for dessert, with cream if you want it," Gillian announced to everyone. "I think you'll agree that our ancestors in Colonial New Jersey ate pretty well."

Starving at this point, I went for a couple of the pastries, even though the fillings were meats I normally avoided. Nick did the same, and also took a little of the pease pudding and a big chunk of the rustic-looking bread.

"I get so sick of all that 'gluten-free' business, don't you?" he asked me, his whisper a bit too loud for the small gathering. "People been eating bread for centuries. If it was that bad for us, we'd never have survived this long."

I saw Gillian glance in our direction, and tried to modify his opinion. "Well, some folks have a real allergy to it, called celiac disease. As for whether it's more common these days, I've heard different explanations. Maybe some people always have gotten sick, but didn't know it was because of bread. Farmers also have 'enriched' today's wheat, so it has more gluten than the kind our ancestors baked with."

He didn't argue any further, but made a point of using his bread to mop up all of the pudding. "This porridge stuff looks kind of weird, but y'know, it's pretty tasty."

The reception, I noticed, seemed to be going well. The

society officers reminisced about events they'd held for Christmas, harvest season and Chadwick Founder's Day at various sites around town.

"Maybe we could host something here," Nora Stafford suggested.

"Halloween," her husband joked. "In the cellar."

Donald laughed. "I'll have to make it safe for human habitation first."

"Well, you should at least be on the Christmas tour this year," Nora told Gillian. "I'm sure with his electrical skills, Donald could do some nice outdoor lighting."

"I'll try to rise to the occasion," he said with a smile.

During this exchange, Gillian's face took on an almost giddy glow. I had to give her credit, she'd made the impression that she'd hoped to. Good, now maybe she could chill out a bit and stop nagging and criticizing.

"Excuse me," said a hushed female voice behind me.

I turned to see Adele Dugan looking rather pale. "Do you know where the nearest powder room is?" she asked.

I'd seen one . . . where? "Down the hall, I think, next to the guest bedroom."

She thanked me and walked in that direction at a brisk clip.

The group migrated then to the nearby living room, and Bill Stafford stepped into a central spot in front of the fireplace. I had a sense that the boring speeches, about which Gillian had warned us, would soon begin. Maybe I'd ask Nick if he wanted to slip away. We both had jobs to get back to, and the hostess herself *had* given us permission to leave.

Jack Dugan looked around. "Adele? Now where did she go . . . ?"

I discreetly explained that I'd directed his wife to the guest bathroom. "That was a while ago, though."

"I hope she's okay." He ducked into the hall to check.

Stafford, meanwhile, noticed that he had lost some of his audience, and held off on whatever pronouncement he intended to make. Concerned, I stepped into the hallway myself. I heard muffled voices from the bathroom and edged closer.

Jack emerged minus his wife. I saw panic in his eyes as they met mine. "She's sick," he said. "I need to drive her to the medical center."

Linda, Kay and the Fosters all had drifted out of the living room to ask what was going on. Jack returned to his wife's side, and a few seconds later helped Adele, her linen clothes showing wrinkles now, out of the restroom. She leaned on his shoulder, but looked ready to pass out at any minute.

"You can't drive her like that, Jack." Grim-faced, Donald pulled out his phone. "I'll call nine-one-one."

Dugan didn't argue, and only asked, "Can someone get her a glass of water?"

Whitney, who had made herself scarce for most of the afternoon, appeared in the kitchen doorway with a shocked expression. She heard this request and ran to fill it. Adele drank the tumbler of water slowly, with some effort.

A few minutes later, Officers Mel Jacoby and Steve Baylock of the Chadwick PD arrived. They checked on Adele and questioned us about what had happened.

"She has pretty serious celiac disease," Jack told them. "This happens sometimes, when she accidentally eats the wrong thing."

"Any idea what could have made her sick?" Baylock asked.

"She was being careful, she ate hardly anything," Gillian said. "I know she didn't take any of the pastries."

"There was barley in the soup," Linda said.

"Did you eat any of that, sweetheart?" Jack asked.

Eyelids drooping, Adele shook her head. "Just . . . the dish with the peas."

After some more discussion, Jacoby said they'd need to take samples of some of the food. Gillian sent Herta into the kitchen to fetch a few small containers they could use. Whitney mainly kept out of the way. She pulled her long blond hair forward over one shoulder and twisted it into a rope, as she watched the activity in the front hall.

Meanwhile, an ambulance rolled up outside. Two EMTs tramped in, gave Adele a quick look-over and put her on a gurney. Her husband went along with her.

She was whisked away, with sirens in full cry. The two cops finished taking short statements and contact information from the rest of us; then they also left.

"You had some of the pudding, too, didn't you?" Donald Foster asked his wife.

"Yes, but only a little."

Gillian's shell-shocked face made me actually feel sorry for her. Despite her efforts to control all of the variables at her reception, something had gone very wrong. A key member of the Chadwick Historical Society had eaten something that, in effect, had poisoned her.

Gillian had been so meticulous, though, that I couldn't imagine how such an accident could have happened.

Unless it hadn't been an accident . . .

Chapter 9

By the time Nick and I were free to go, it was early evening. I didn't want to imagine the conversations that would take place among the Fosters, and even their maid, after the rest of us left. Gillian might take out her embarrassment and disappointment on everyone within earshot.

As we walked down the driveway, Nick half joked, "Just hope you and I don't end up on the suspects list. We'll have to alibi each other."

"We can," I pointed out. "We were together during the whole reception, and neither one of us went back into the kitchen. I think we're safe."

He sprang behind the wheel of his blue panel truck with an energy that belied his sixty years, wished me a quiet rest of the evening, and pulled away. I have rarely been so glad to slip into my own older-model CR-V and escape to the relative sanity of my shop.

At least, because it was almost midsummer, the sky remained light when I reached home. Downstairs, Sarah had left things in good order, and I found no urgent messages on the shop answering machine. I checked and fed my four remaining boarders, then climbed the stairs to my apartment. Naturally my own three felines mobbed me as if I'd been gone for a week, and as if I hadn't left them with plenty of dry food for the duration. I gave them a dinner of high-quality canned fare, then collapsed on my slipcovered living room sofa.

On the one hand, I felt emotionally drained from all the tensions of the afternoon. On the other, questions about Adele's mishap kept skittering through my mind. Everyone was assuming she'd suffered a celiac attack, but what if it had been something else? Some illness totally unrelated to what she'd eaten? At least that would let everyone at the reception off the hook. Good thing, anyway, that she'd gone to the hospital. Whatever the problem, I hoped she recovered soon, and completely.

Mark had gone to Philadelphia for the weekend, planning to get together with some old college buddies from UPenn. They had tickets to a Phillies game tomorrow. He'd invited me as a courtesy, but I'm not into many team sports and figured he needed some time to just hang with the guys. I glanced at the clock; they'd probably have gone out to eat by now, so I wasn't going to bother Mark with my story of the ill-fated reception.

I wouldn't disturb Sarah, either, because she might be helping Chester and his family prepare for tomorrow's funeral. Still, I felt like discussing the mysterious incident with someone. Guess I'd just have to suppress that urge for a while.

It was time for a real dinner, but the odd mixture of foods at the reception, plus all the talk about digestive upsets, had blunted my appetite. For the time being, I sat at my kitchen's yellow Formica table—a find from an antiques mall—and made do with a carton of organic yogurt from Nature's Way. This involved fending off sneak attacks from my calico, Matisse, the only one of my trio who adores milk in any form.

The yogurt reminded me of Dawn. She would probably just be closing up her shop and might have time to talk. Bouncing ideas off her was usually productive, especially when I was trying to make sense of a weird and suspicious situation. Before I could even punch in her number, though, the phone in my hand played my ringtone, "Stray Cat Strut." I recognized the caller as Detective Angela Bonelli of the Chadwick PD. Not surprising, really, after the cops had shown up at the reception fiasco.

Her dry contralto voice didn't bother with a hello. "I guess you had a pretty exciting afternoon over at the Fosters' house."

"Not the dignified event everyone was expecting, for sure," I told her. "I'm starting to think I'm some kind of jinx—mayhem finds me wherever I go."

"Well, you haven't been involved in any local crises for a couple of months now, so I guess you were due." Her tone turned serious. "So, what's your take on this, Cassie? Anything about it smell fishy?"

"No fish was served." Bad joke on my part. "The chief suspect seems to have been the pease pudding."

"The hospitalized woman"—Bonelli sounded as if she were checking a written report—"Adele Dugan, told them she couldn't tolerate wheat and ate something that supposedly was gluten-free. Then she had a negative reaction similar to what she usually experiences from wheat."

"Did the doctors confirm that?"

"She had her stomach pumped and was given IV fluids. The latest word is that she's recovering. But they're running tests on her and the food samples to rule out anything else."

I presumed the hospital would find out if Adele had, say, appendicitis, or consumed anything that actually was spoiled or poisoned. "Gillian Foster, the hostess, swore she gave the caterers a gluten-free recipe. When I arrived, I heard her per-sonally making sure they followed her directions to the letter."

"Mmm. My guys said she acted pretty upset."

"She's a bit high-strung, anyway. But she was hoping to impress the historical society folks with her 'authentic' buffet, as well as her house. Instead, one of them gets rushed to the emergency room, and the rest of us spend an hour being questioned by the cops. By the time it was all over, she looked like she wished the floor would open up and swallow her."

"So if anybody played a mean trick on Adele Dugan, I'm guessing it wouldn't have been Gillian."

Yikes, it sounded as if Bonelli really did suspect foul play! "From what I could see, she had absolutely nothing to gain by that. Also, I got the impression most of the people there liked Adele pretty well. I'd never suspect her husband—he seemed horrified, and wanted to drive her to the hospital on his own, before Donald Foster insisted on calling nine-one-one."

Bonelli asked me to describe the pease pudding, and I did my best.

"Did anybody else eat the stuff?"

"I passed because it looked kind of yucky, but Nick had some, and when he headed for home later he was fine. Gillian herself had a bit with no ill effects, even though she also claimed to have a gluten problem."

Angela fell silent for a second. "The people at this recep-tion—they're Gillian's friends? Would they all know about her allergy?"

"She was acquainted with them, but how closely, I don't know. She talked very openly with Adele about how she got sick when she ate wheat, so maybe she's told other people in the past."

"In that case . . . maybe Adele wasn't the intended target of the prank."

I hadn't considered that; but after all, there was a reason why Angela had climbed to the rank of detective. "You think someone was out to get Gillian."

"From what little you observed, could anyone have had a grudge against her?"

I laughed, then gave her a quick summary of what I'd seen and heard on my two visits to the Foster home. "I don't know about the historical society, but between people working on her house and even her family members, that definitely opens up a wide field of suspects."

Bonelli sounded satisfied with my inside info. "Thanks, Cassie. Get some rest—you sound like you need it. By tomorrow we should have some more information from her doctors that could help clarify things."

"I hope so," I said.

Maybe Bonelli suspected that I couldn't wait to share this juicy information with Dawn or Mark, because she added, "Meanwhile, I'd appreciate it if you didn't talk about the details of this case with anyone else. Even if it was just a nasty prank, it might be a crime. And at worst, if the target *was* Adele, it could be attempted murder."

It was no hardship to keep my shop open Saturday morning, on my own, while Sarah went to Bernice's funeral. Still, it reminded me of the first couple of months that I'd been in operation, handling everything solo. It had taken me more than a month just to hire an assistant. I ran ads mostly in the local papers and even posted notices with businesses around town, because I wanted someone who lived fairly nearby. Young kids just out of school, and a couple of women who'd never held another paying job, tried out with me simply because they liked cats. Unfortunately, that didn't qualify most of them for the challenges of handling a customer that could hiss, bite and twist around in your hands like a cobra, with claws front and back that could slash like razors.

Of course, most of our feline clients were reasonably well behaved, and by now I'd learned several tricks and acquired a few devices to keep the testy ones under control. But still, I'd been hampered in my job until Sarah had come along. I hadn't expected that a woman around sixty, with a background in teaching high school math, would work out so much better than any of the other candidates. But she had nerves of steel, a strong work ethic, and most important, our temperaments just clicked.

That Saturday on my own, I did have a few walk-in cus-tumers, mostly asking questions and picking up pamphlets for future reference. I was down to only five boarders, so I turned out each of them in the playroom for a spell, and dragged feather toys or threw catnip mice to exercise them.

Tough job, but someone's got to do it, right?

Determined not to intrude on Mark's weekend with the boys, I phoned my mother but got her voice mail. Not too long ago, Mom had a lot of time on her hands, but since she'd taken up with Harry she was on the go more often. I remem-bered that he had a lake house—maybe they'd decided to spend this gorgeous June day up there.

Now Cassie, don't pout!

I closed to the public at twelve and devoted the rest of my workday to housecleaning chores around the shop. To keep from feeling like Cinderella, slaving away while her stepsisters went to the ball, I booted up my laptop and played a mix of summer-themed music—everything from Jersey boys Springsteen and Bon Jovi to newer, upbeat numbers by Taylor Swift, Katy Perry and Justin Timberlake. Turning it up just loud enough not to disturb the boarder cats, I danced and sometimes sang my way through the sweeping and vacuuming.

Occasionally a passerby would glance through the front window in curiosity, then smile or shake their head: *Guess dealing with cats all day finally drove the poor girl around the bend!* For a while, the music took my mind off the more somber issues I'd been dealing with, such as Bernice's death.

That evening, when I expected even the post-funeral activities were over and Sarah would be home, I gave her a call to ask her how things went.

"It was . . . interesting," she said. "I met Chester's kids. Hard to believe two such sweet people raised such self-centered children."

Her criticism almost shocked me, because Sarah usually tried to see the best in people. "Wow, what did they say? Or do?"

"It's more what they didn't say or do. They sat in the same pew with Chester, of course, and near him at the gravesite. But they each stayed with their own families and didn't make much effort to console their father. He had a nurse with him, and I guess they felt that was enough, a paid helper to make sure he didn't fall apart. Chester needed the help, too—he was so wobbly on his feet, Robin said she thought he was sedated."

"That's awful." Stretched out on my sofa, I uncrossed my legs so Matisse, my calico, could settle on my lap. "Do you think he had some kind of argument or falling-out with his children?"

"No, but they're big shots now, I guess. Especially the son, Jimmy—calls himself James these days and has his own construction company. Sylvia is some kind of attorney. They both dressed well, drove up to the funeral home in nice cars, and came with spouses and kids. So I get the feeling old Mom and Dad had just slipped off their radar."

"I guess that explains why neither of them lent a hand when the Tillmans' house starting getting so run-down and cluttered."

"Robin said they finally saw it the day before the funeral and acted totally disgusted. Not sad or upset that their parents were living that way, just repulsed and embarrassed. At the repast, at least Sylvia thanked Robin and me for stepping in and trying to tidy up."

"Do they have any plans to help Chester, now that he's alone?"

"James wants to move him to assisted living as soon as possible. He wants to get the house cleaned out, fix anything that really needs it and then sell it off to the first buyer who'll offer a decent price."

Even though the place was in such bad condition, that still sounded callous to me. When we'd talked to the Tillmans, it was clear both had become very attached to their house because of the memories it held—particularly from the years of raising their family. It was ironic that their children had so little sentimental feeling for the place.

Stroking Matisse's multicolored fur, I remembered Chester telling Robin not to throw out some old video games because "Jimmy" might still want them. "They aren't interested in going through the contents first, in case there are things they might want to keep?"

"Robin brought that up, but James just shuddered at the idea. Said anything they've lived without this long, they obviously don't need." Sarah paused for a second on the line. "She and I have a plan, though."

That sounded encouraging. "Yeah?"

"It's going to be a while before they find a community

around here to take Chester. In the meantime, he's probably going to keep living in his house, with a caregiver to help with meals and cleaning. Robin and I will keep going through that junk and pull out a few things that are really meaningful to him—maybe tapes of his sports interviews, any scrapbooks he might have, his favorite music and photos. They say when someone has dementia, those things are important because they can spark the person's memory."

I'd known Sarah for a couple of years now, working with her five-and-a half days a week. We'd even helped each other through some frightening situations. But her sympathy for her elderly friend, and determination to help him, gave me an even deeper appreciation of her character.

"That's a wonderful idea," I told her. "Let me know if there's any way I can help."

"It would be great if FOCA could get at least some of those cats out of the house. If it's left to Chester's kids, they'll all go to the county shelter and he'll be heartbroken."

"I hear you—we should try to do that soon. Maybe I can get Becky and Chris to go up there with me tomorrow."

Sarah yawned on the line, then apologized. "Funerals take a lot out of me, especially now that I'm older. Maybe it's psychological."

"They are stressful," I agreed. "Especially when they're for someone you cared about."

"I forgot to ask, how did the Fosters' reception go?"

I answered with a dry laugh. "That also was 'interesting.' I won't burden you with that story tonight, though—you've had enough family drama for one weekend. I'll tell you at work on Monday."

"Clever way to make sure I show up bright and early! See you then."

Before turning in that night, I went down to the shop

again and ran a quick check on my boarders. We had only five at the moment, and they all seemed fine. But as I returned to the second floor and passed through my kitchen, my orange tabby Mango whined at me for more food. He had cleaned up any leftovers left by the other two cats, but still acted hungry. And in spite of his gluttony, he looked a bit thinner than usual.

Might be a question to ask Dr. Coccia, when he returns to town. For now, I am absolutely not going to worry about it.

I had enough troublesome questions, regarding humans, roiling around in my brain to keep me from getting a good night's sleep.

Chapter 10

Becky and Chris did coordinate with me to meet at Chester Tillman's house on Sunday afternoon. I let the two volunteers pull FOCA's good-size SUV into the driveway ahead of me and close to the garage. If all went smoothly today, they would be leaving with Autumn, Sugarman and Winky, lightening Chester's pet-care responsibilities and costs by more than half. I only hoped he wouldn't dig in his heels at the last minute and refuse to surrender the three cats.

When we rang the bell, Chester answered the door in clean, pressed clothes, and his hair looked freshly trimmed. Had the professional caretaker paid a visit already? He remembered me but raised an eyebrow at my two companions, the gamine young woman with short platinum hair and a boyishly handsome guy whose dark locks brushed his collar.

"Chester, this is Becky Newmeyer and Chris Eberhardt," I said. "They're from the animal shelter I told you about."

The widower's strong-boned, dignified face closed up a little. "Oh. You came to get some of the cats, huh?"

"To meet some of them, anyway," said Chris gently. "If that's okay with you."

Chester responded to this low-key approach by inviting us into the living room, shuffling ahead of us in his leather bedroom slippers. I had tried to prepare Becky and Chris for the appearance of the house, but their heads still swiveled a bit to take in the junk on all sides. I hoped neither of them suffered from claustrophobia. They probably would have been more astonished if I'd told them that, thanks to the efforts of Sarah and Robin, the hallway and living room looked a lot more organized today than when I'd first visited.

We all sat anywhere we could, and at first the three of us made chitchat with Chester. I asked him how he was doing and said that I'd heard his son and daughter had come to town for Bernice's funeral.

He sniffed. "First I've seen either of them in maybe seven years. Back then, my grandkids were little—now they're in high school. Who knows if I'll ever see any of 'em again?"

Though he had a right to be bitter, I tried to steer him onto a more positive topic. "I understand you've got someone coming by now to help you."

"She was here this morning. Nice enough lady—Megan, her name is." He turned his gaze out the living room window. "Haven't seen Bob, the guy who lives across the way, in weeks. Maybe now that Bernice is gone, he's afraid I'll be an old pest and start askin' him for favors."

Possibly to bring up a more pleasant subject, Chris pointed at a box on the floor near the sofa, from which a strangely shaped, light gray object protruded. "Hey, is that a model of the Millennium Falcon from *Star Wars*? Cool!"

The widower glanced in that direction absently. "It's one of Jimmy's models. He was always putting things like that together when he was a kid." Because Chris seemed so interested, Chester rose, fished the spaceship out of the carton and passed it to him.

"Gee, look at the detail." Becky ran her finger over the intricate surface. "Must have taken a long time to make, even from a kit."

Chris admired it, too. "I heard there was a model of this ship made by Lego that was, like, three feet long. It's such a collector's item these days, if you can even find one it's worth thousands of dollars. I think this size is more common. Though if you had one mint in the box, it probably would still be pretty valuable."

Chester returned to the sofa with a cynical sniff. "Only toy we ever bought our kids that never got used was a doll we got for Sylvia. Back when there were hardly any black dolls, Bernice found this really nice one with an old-fashioned dress and long curls. She was so excited to give it to Sylvia for her birthday, but that girl never played with it. I think because it was *too* old-fashioned."

"That's a shame," I said. "Do you still have it?"

"No idea. It sat on the shelf in Bernice's closet for years and years. I looked for it the other day after the funeral—thought my granddaughter might want it—but it wasn't there anymore. Lotta things I can't find these days."

The calico cat I'd seen on a previous visit crept out from under the sofa. She eyed the three of us warily, then wound around Chester's ankles. He lifted her onto his lap, his dark face finally creasing into a smile. "Therrre's my girl Candy! Say hi to the folks." He turned her toward us, though her golden-green eyes showed no enthusiasm for the strangers in her living room.

After asking permission, Becky leaned across to stroke the cat's head. Candy took that calmly enough, as long as she felt secure on her master's lap.

Suddenly Chester shot me a worried glance. "You're not takin' *her* from me, are you?"

"No," I reassured him. "Remember, we talked about possibly taking Bernice's three cats. You told me you wanted to keep Candy and Minnie."

He nodded, though his eyes remained sad. "Be a shame even to lose the others. When I see them around now, they remind me of Bernie. But . . . five *are* a lot of work."

"I'm sure they are," I said. "Two will still be plenty for you to take care of. You'll have three fewer dishes to wash and pans to scoop out, and you'll spend a lot less money on food and litter."

"I guess so." His gaze turned to Becky. "They'll be safe with you?"

"Cassie probably told you we're a no-kill shelter," she said. "We try very hard to find new homes for all of our animals, and usually we place them in foster homes until we locate permanent ones."

"We try to match up older cats with older adopters," Chris added. "Mostly, they just want a quiet pet that already has manners—knows how to use the pan, sleeps through the night, stays out from underfoot, that kind of stuff."

Since the ice had been broken, I thought we should let Becky and Chris move on to the day's business. "Are Bernice's pals still hanging out in her room most of the time?"

Chester nodded. "'Specially at night, they still sleep on her bed like they think she's coming back. The cops stripped the bed and took the sheets, but they still hang out on the bare mattress."

"Want to go have a look?" I asked the FOCA volunteers.

Becky and Chris headed down the hall, walking softly and toting two of the carriers. I kept the third one and told them I'd be along in a minute to help. First, I wanted to ask Chester some questions in private.

"You told Robin, too, that you found things missing from the house after the funeral. Anything else besides the doll?"

He clasped his hands on his lap and avoided my eyes. "So many people telling me I'm crazy, I'm starting to think I really am."

"Any of your own things? Your mementos?"

"Had a baseball on top of the bookcase over there." Chester glanced across the room. "Signed by Roger Maris. Put it under a little dome and everything."

I got up and crossed to the wooden bookcase. On the dusty top, which came to about my shoulder height, I saw a clean, circular spot about five inches in diameter. I seriously doubted that Sarah or Robin would have tossed out this treasured memento, and even if they had moved it, they probably also would have dusted the top of the bookcase. This evidence certainly gave Chester's story some credibility.

"Some of my records." His voice gained energy, now that I appeared to be taking him seriously. "My Blue Notes."

"Your what?"

"That's the record label. My dad left me a bunch of their old albums, all the jazz classics. Wayne Shorter, John Coltrane, Art Blakey." He crossed the room and pointed to a stained cardboard carton on the floor, loosely packed with old LPs. "They were in here. The morning after the funeral, I noticed the box was pulled out at an angle and wasn't as full. I went through it and realized some of my Blue Notes were gone."

"Just some, not all?" This new information started me thinking.

Chester must have heard my reaction as skepticism. "Yeah, the cops thought I was crazy, too. They almost believed me about the baseball. But who'd break into somebody's house just to steal an old doll, they asked me, and a few old records that nobody can even play anymore?" He returned to his sofa and sank down on it again, heavily. "Oh, and a few old Nintendo games."

Becky and Chris returned from Bernice's bedroom, their cat carriers filled. "We got the gray one and the white one with the red spots," Becky said.

"That's Winky and Sugarman," I told her, for Chester's benefit. I wanted him to feel that we knew their names.

"The tortoiseshell gave us a hard time, though," Chris told me. "She's still under the bed."

"Autumn. I'll get her."

I ventured alone into Bernice's room, set the third carrier on the bed and shut the door behind me. Before taking on Autumn, I pulled some grooming gloves from my pocket—who could say how resistant she'd be? The clutter complicated things, since I could hardly even see the tortoiseshell longhair under the bed because of the junk stored there, and couldn't pull the frame very far away from the wall without hitting some obstacle.

Eventually, though, Autumn retreated to a tight corner and got stuck long enough for me to grab her. I tried to cuddle and reassure her before slipping her into the carrier and securing the latches.

I was ready to leave Bernice's room when I noticed that her sliding closet door stood ajar and succumbed to curiosity. I opened it far enough to peer at the top shelf. Sarah or Robin must have been at work in there, because not much clutter remained; the few hats, purses and folded sweaters had been stacked neatly. If this was where Bernice had stored the doll she'd bought for her daughter decades ago, Chester spoke the truth—it was gone.

On my way past the kitchen, another thought occurred to

me, and I set Autumn down while I checked the back door. It looked closed, but I didn't even have to turn the knob to open it. Someone had used a strip of duct tape to keep the bolt from sliding shut.

That didn't make much sense to me. *I thought Chester propped this open so the outdoor cats could slip in and be fed. But it's a pretty heavy wooden door. If he closed it, even with the lock disabled, would a cat be strong enough to push it in?*

Maybe Chester is losing it, after all . . .

By the time I got back to the living room, all three trapped felines were mewing in protest, probably not having spent much time in carriers over the years. Chester was baby-talking to Winky through the mesh window of his enclosure, with a catch in his voice and a tear in his eye. The process would be easier on everyone, I thought, if we moved it along quickly. I mentioned this to the FOCA kids, and they agreed.

It occurred to me that, if these cats were the main "suspects" in Bernice's death, removing them from the house could constitute wrapping up the case. I just hoped they wouldn't have to remain incarcerated at the shelter for too long.

On the front stoop, Becky promised Chester that she'd keep him posted on how the cats were settling in and let him know if they found new homes. The feral ginger tom that I'd seen before trotted into the front yard, probably drawn by the cries of the other animals.

"What about him?" Chester asked. "Wanna take Buster, too?"

"Probably not a good idea," I told him. "That guy's too wild, so as long as he's not causing any problems he can stay. But don't let Candy or Minnie out, okay? Keep that kitchen door shut."

I would have asked him about the taped lock, but a loud

wail from Autumn spurred me along. I hurried to load her into the FOCA vehicle with her housemates, then got into my own car.

Chester waved to us as we pulled out of his driveway, but his posture slumped again as he stepped back inside his house. I hoped the two pets he'd hung on to would be enough to dispel the new sense of emptiness without Bernice.

That disabled lock also made me wonder, again, if someone had been able to slip into his house when he wasn't there or was sound asleep. But who would take a risk like that just to grab some old toys and memorabilia? The autographed baseball, maybe—that had been out in plain sight. But old LPs, Nintendo games, and a doll that even Sylvia didn't want?

Could all of those things possibly have something in common?

Though I'd promised Bonelli I wouldn't spread information about what had happened at the Fosters' reception, I cheated a bit on Monday when Sarah showed up for work. As my assistant, I thought she had a right to know what had taken place when I'd returned Leya to our client's home.

Sarah tied on her grooming apron while she listened, eyes behind her wire-rimmed glasses growing wide. When I finished, she shook her head. "I had a feeling you shouldn't spend any more time at that house than you absolutely needed to. Now watch Gillian try to accuse you or Nick of putting something in the food!"

"We can vouch for each other. Plus, the cook and Gillian's daughter would also know that we never came back into the kitchen while the dishes were being prepared."

"Unless one of them has something to hide," she pointed out, "and wants to implicate you."

Donning my own apron, I smiled. "You really have been

unraveling mysteries with me too long, Sarah. You're developing a criminal mind."

"It's not all your fault. Also comes from a couple of decades of teaching high school, with kids always trying to pull stuff behind my back."

"Well, if all else fails, I'm sure Bonelli can be my character witness. She called me last night, just to get my take on the incident. I tried to be as helpful as I could, but after this there's no reason for me to be involved. The cops may find out that someone from the historical society has a personal grudge against Adele, or else didn't want Gillian joining their exclusive little group. I had no motive, so I'm out."

"Lucky thing," said Sarah.

From one of the condos we retrieved Taffy, a Turkish Van cat whose owner would be picking her up that afternoon. Though she was a semi-longhair and mostly white, she needed only a touch-up to restore her natural elegance. It took two sets of hands, though, because she was not yet four and still a bundle of energy.

I started gently brushing the cat's rust-colored face, which matched her plumy tail. Sarah's phone buzzed in the pocket of her tunic, beneath the apron, but she ignored it and held on to Miss Taffy.

She returned the call only after we'd finished the task at hand. While I put the cat back into her condo, I heard Sarah tell someone, "Oh, dear . . . That's not good."

I busied myself straightening up the studio to give Sarah privacy, but as soon as she got off she reported back to me, anyway.

"That was Robin," she said. "New crisis with Chester."

"Uh-oh. Is he hurt? Sick?"

"No, but he called her and was going on about things

missing from his house. He's sure somebody got into the house while he was at the funeral."

"He told me all that yesterday," I said. "Of course, Chester doesn't have the more reliable memory, and he just buried his wife of forty-some years. I'm sure that's also affecting his mental state."

Sarah shrugged. "Robin says even though he may be vague about doing his laundry, or knowing what day of the week it is, he has a steel-trap mind when it comes to his collections. Can tell you who he interviewed on his radio show and when, and what songs are on every record album."

Possibly someone *was* sneaking into the house, I thought, especially with the lock disabled on that back door. "Did he call the cops?"

Sarah frowned. "Robin did, but she says they won't even come out again. Having been in the house once, I guess, they can't imagine anything of value could be missing. The one Robin spoke to joked that if Chester was lucky, some thief would come with a moving van and cart it *all* away."

I had the distinct impression, by now, that the Dalton cops weren't particularly sympathetic to the widower's plight or terribly conscientious about their jobs. I'd gotten spoiled, I guess, by the efficiency of the Chadwick police.

"I'll talk to Bonelli," I told Sarah. "I'll tell her that when I went up there with the FOCA kids, Chester sounded like he had a good grasp on what things were missing, and there's a real chance that someone's been stealing from him. Maybe she can talk to the Dalton guys."

"Would you? They've got a Chief Hill over there. I take it he's not the sharpest knife in the drawer, but he sounds stubborn . . . and kinda mean."

I laughed, with an edge. "He's probably never dealt with our gal. She'll kick his butt!"

Chapter 11

We were ready to close up that afternoon when Linda Freeman, Gillian's interior designer, walked in our shop door. I introduced her to Sarah and asked, "Are things settling down at the Fosters', I hope?"

Linda frowned, and I noticed faint circles under her dark eyes. Though dressed in a cute, trendy-casual outfit—a side-knotted tunic over leggings that played up her tall, slim figure—she gave off a troubled vibe. "Unfortunately, no. If anything, they're getting worse. That's why I wanted to talk to you."

I glanced at Sarah. "You can handle things if we go in back for a few minutes?"

When she nodded, I opened the wire-mesh door to the playroom and asked Linda, "Are you all right around cats?"

"Absolutely," she said with a grin.

In the play area, a gray Persian named Stormy, taking his hour of recreation, eyed us from a perch halfway up the wall. Though one of our most temperamental boarders, he always received five-star treatment because once he had helped to save my life.

I tossed a clean throw over a sturdy, carpeted perch and invited Linda to sit; I was long past worrying about cat hair on my own clothes. "So, what's up?"

"Basically, Gillian is still going nuts over what happened at the historical society reception. The police lab did find wheat flour in that pudding. I got the sense they might have dismissed it as just an accident—that someone added it without realizing one of the party guests had celiac disease—but Gillian insisted the cops find out who did it, anyway. So, they've been questioning the caterers, the cook, Donald and Whitney, and even the historical society members." Linda shook her head. "If Gillian had any prayer of winning those people over, and getting her home onto the register, of course that's blown to smithereens by now."

"And no one has owned up?" I asked.

"Not so far. Oh, they grilled your friend Nick Janos, too. Apparently Gillian overheard him making fun of the whole 'gluten-free' issue, and thought maybe he wanted to prove his point."

I'd forgotten he did that, but hurried to defend him. "Nick was with me the whole time. Once he finished repairing that kitchen cabinet, he never went back in there." Secretly, I was glad Linda had come by to feed me all of this new information. Bonelli probably wouldn't approve, but what she didn't know wouldn't hurt her.

"Well, there's some doubt about *when* the stuff was added to the porridge," the designer continued, shifting on her makeshift seat. "The caterers swore they used no wheat in the recipe, so the cops asked Herta if she 'stirred anything into' the pudding just before it was served. She also denied doing such a thing. But since they questioned so many of us who weren't involved with cooking or serving the food, they may think the wheat flour was added at the last minute."

I followed her train of thought. "Which would mean it was a deliberate attempt to make someone ill. But who? Adele?"

"I wondered, too," Linda said. "Her husband told me that maybe half of the historical society members who attended knew about Adele's condition ahead of time, and he couldn't think of any reason why any of them would want to harm her. But they probably didn't know Gillian had a wheat sensitivity, until she started talking about it at the reception."

Stormy had been making his way carefully down the stairsteps of wall shelves to approach us. He rubbed against Linda's legs and she reached her hand out to him.

"Watch out, he's a cranky one," I warned her. "Only pet his head, and if he stiffens up, back off!"

With a chuckle, Linda followed my advice and went for just a brief head stroke. But the big, pale-gray Persian sprawled at our feet, as if to eavesdrop on the gossip.

The diversion gave me time to think. If someone at the reception had a sudden brainstorm to doctor the pudding, they'd have had a very small window of opportunity. Plus, they still would have needed to get wheat flour from the kitchen—or somewhere else?—and to stir it in while no one was looking.

"The upshot," Linda went on, "is that Gillian thinks she was the target. Either someone on the historical society board wanted to make her look bad, or the caterer, the cook or someone else close to her pulled a nasty prank."

"If no one's confessing, I guess we'll never know," I concluded.

"Until we *do* know, she's on the warpath against everyone who came to the reception. Especially me." Linda lifted her gaze to the ceiling, as if praying for strength. "She thinks Donald and I are having an affair."

I could hardly have blamed Donald Foster if that were true, but still . . . "Why does she think that?"

"Just because he and I get along well, I guess, and because she knows I'm divorced. He and I have kidded around sometimes, about the décor or the renovations, but always while Gillian was nearby. Once he hung a chandelier for me, and that was probably the only time we were even alone in a room together. But there's absolutely nothing else going on! Why would I risk losing one of my most lucrative clients?"

I heard the subtext. Linda *was* attracted to Donald, and the feeling might be mutual, but neither wanted to incur his wife's wrath. On the other hand, Gillian saw her husband enjoying the company of a younger, prettier woman who also was easier to get along with. This might explain why she'd treated Linda so harshly the day the designer had been putting the final touches on the house.

"Of course," Linda continued, "anyone who's worked for her could have had a motivation. The way she talks to poor Herta, sometimes—! And she was micromanaging the catering staff that day, until I thought one of them would go at her with a carving knife."

I'd overheard some of that, too. "At least Nick had no motive whatsoever. She complimented his work and paid him on the spot. And he's not mean enough to make someone sick just for a prank."

"Yeah, I think he's safe enough. Donald even said he might ask Nick back to help him with the cellar restoration." Linda finally smiled again. "If it's any consolation, I don't think Gillian suspects you, either."

"I heard her being pretty hard on her daughter, too, a couple of times."

"Poor Whitney. She's smart enough to stay out of her mom's way whenever Gillian gets like this. Donald told me she's spending even more of her time out at Stirling Hill Farm—all afternoon, every day, lunchtime till supper."

I took a guess. "That's the stable where she boards her horse?"

"And complains to her, I think. Glory must be getting an earful this summer!" Linda straightened her posture with an air of relief. "I guess that's why I stopped by here, too—just to let off some steam. I'm sure there's nothing you can do about the situation."

"At least it sounds as if the Chadwick cops have been taking the food tampering seriously," I pointed out. "But if no one confesses and there's no proof . . . I guess Adele has recovered by now?"

"She'll have some aftereffects, but she's on her feet and back to work. She might like to sue the Fosters for negligence, but again, that won't wash if Gillian was the main target."

Could that be why Gillian was pushing the idea that she'd been the intended victim? I wondered. *To dodge a possible lawsuit?*

With a shrug, my visitor got to her feet. "I've taken enough of your time, Cassie, but thanks for listening."

I saw her back out to the front of the shop, where she and Sarah said their goodbyes. After Linda left, I rejoined my assistant at the sales counter and relayed the gist of my discussion with our visitor.

Sarah shook her head with a patient air. "Even when you try to stay away from the drama, Cassie, it keeps reaching out to find you, doesn't it?"

"No denying that I was a witness," I noted. "Though no one is even sure there was a crime, and even if someone did tamper with the food, the results weren't too serious. I'm mostly curious as to why someone would do such a strange thing, and whom they wanted to hurt—Adele or Gillian."

"And if it was Gillian, is that person satisfied now that

they've embarrassed her?" Sarah wondered aloud. "Or could they try something else even more drastic?"

I stared at my normally level-headed assistant. "For someone who keeps telling me not to get involved, you're doing your best to plant suspicions in my head!"

"Sorry." She laughed. "Guess all of this detective work *is* starting to get under my skin."

It was just about five o'clock, which was quitting time for Sarah, at least. She gathered her things, and I wished her a pleasant evening.

But my amateur-sleuth instincts did not turn off so easily. Left alone in the shop, I hit speed dial on my cell phone for Detective Angela Bonelli. She also worked long and irregular hours, so I caught her in her office and asked if I could drop by.

For a town that liked to play up its minor link to the American Revolution, Chadwick boasted a sleek, modern police station. This was hardly my first visit, though so far—knock wood—I'd never been brought in wearing cuffs. In fact, these days the clerk at the entry window waved me right through if I said Bonelli was expecting me. The bench where troublemakers usually sat was empty, but after all, it was a sleepy June Monday; it would fill up by Friday night.

Bonelli occupied a glass-walled office, as if she considered solitude less important than awareness of what was taking place around her. The private office and a little burgundy Keurig coffeemaker were her only apparent luxuries; she sat at an old L-shaped desk, its Formica top pretending to be granite, with a corded, black multiline phone in plain view. When I entered, she was on her personal cell, telling someone—probably her husband, Lou—that she should be home in half an hour. I'd never met Lou Bonelli, but knew he was a square-jawed, solid guy with a furry chest; her desk displayed a vacation photo of him at the beach with their two preteen boys.

When Bonelli put away the cell phone, I apologized for keeping her at work. "No problem, Cassie. Always a pleasure," she told me dryly. "Got something new on the Foster case?"

I hesitated to tell her about Linda's visit, but decided I should. "She's upset because Gillian thinks she and Donald are having an affair, and Linda swears they're not. Of course, it sounds as if Gillian's been pointing fingers at a lot of people."

"She has, and I was on the verge of suggesting she get some medication to calm her down. We've heard all of her theories, but . . . If the flour was added to the pudding at the last minute, there are only four sets of prints on the serving spoon. One set belongs to the maid, Herta, who served it. The others match up to Nick Janos, Adele and Gillian."

That would make sense, because I didn't see anyone else sample the strange-looking dish. "Nick ate some, but he certainly didn't tamper with it. He'd have had to bring along a packet of wheat flour in the pocket of his work pants!"

Bonelli dismissed that idea with a wave. "We grilled Herta pretty thoroughly, but she swore she wouldn't put her job at risk, and the Fosters have never had any problems with her before. Of course, there's a chance someone at the reception used a different spoon to stir in the wheat flour. Frankly, though, I think contaminating the dish after it was served would have been too difficult for any of the guests to pull off without being seen. It must have happened in the kitchen."

"The caterers?"

"Could be. Gillian harangued them about that dish in particular. She never told them anything about Adele's allergy, if she even knew about it. She only emphasized that she, herself, couldn't tolerate gluten. Some smart-aleck *might* have decided to get revenge by spoiling Gillian's big event for her. By the time she got sick, the pots and utensils used to make the porridge would have been washed, and their staff would be off the premises. Who could prove anything?"

"Kind of the perfect crime," I agreed.

"And not much of a crime, if Gillian suffered only a mild gastric upset. Of course, now that there have been more serious repercussions, no one on the caterer's staff is admitting to anything." With a restrained smile, the detective concluded, "I'm afraid this incident will have to go into our 'unsolved' file, which I like to keep as slim as possible."

I sensed Bonelli encouraging me to move me along so she could get home to her family.

"Actually, I wanted to discuss another case, though I know it's a little out of your territory." Trying to be succinct, I explained the Tillmans' living situation and about Bernice's unexplained death a week earlier. "For a while the Dalton cops believed Chester smothered his wife in her sleep, but they've never arrested him. I guess they found no proof."

The detective tilted her head at me in confusion. "And you have reason to think he's guilty?"

"Not at all. But I don't believe it was an accident, either. Chester said things have been disappearing from his house since the night his wife died. The local cops think he's going senile. But I was over there yesterday, and he sounded pretty lucid to me. The house is still a mess, but he remembers where certain items were kept and when they went missing."

"If Sarah and her church friend have been helping to clean the place out, maybe they threw away those things by mistake."

"I'm sure they would have known better, or at least asked him first." I explained that his children had visited only briefly, after Bernice's funeral, and showed no interest in any of the mementos; also, that Chester was out of the house most of the day of the funeral, and never locked his rear door. "It sounds as if someone may be handpicking certain objects, though I have no idea why."

"Valuable items?"

"Most don't sound like they would be. But he did claim to lose a baseball signed by Roger Maris. Would that be a big collectible?"

Bonelli arched one dark eyebrow, then swiveled to face her desktop computer. "Let's find out." The detective typed a phrase into her search engine and pulled up headers for several sites dealing in baseball-oriented memorabilia. She pursed her lips as if impressed by what she read.

"Well?" I asked.

"Did he say what year it was from, or a particular game?"

"No, but he might remember. Why?"

"Depending on those factors and its condition . . . could be worth more than twelve thousand dollars."

I sank back into my chair, feeling I'd made my point. "See?"

She swiveled to face me again. "Y'know, it's possible Chester killed his wife by accident, and has made up this story about some burglar to divert suspicion. Or that he feels so guilty, he'd rather believe it was done by an outside bogeyman."

I didn't like either of these explanations. "We can't rule anything out, of course. But I've talked with him a few times now, and Chester seems like an honest, standup guy. He misses his wife a lot, and I think if he'd been responsible for her death, he'd admit it and take his punishment."

Bonelli sighed and clasped her hands on the flat desk calendar in front of her. "Okay, what do you want me to do?"

"I know this is a lot to ask, but the Dalton PD doesn't

have a detective on staff. Would you consider taking a look at the case? At the very least, someone could have taken advantage of Bernice's illness, and Chester's poor eyesight and mental fog, to rob them of what possessions they had that might actually be worth something. And at worst, that person might have killed Bernice to cover up what they were doing."

I took it as a good sign that Bonelli didn't dismiss the idea immediately. "Dalton . . . that would be Chief Hill."

I said nothing, not wanting to repeat the negative gossip Sarah had heard about the police chief.

"Wouldn't be the first time *he* let something slip through the cracks," Bonelli muttered. "But he's not keen on surrendering his authority to an outsider, either."

"I'm sure you've handled tougher characters," I egged her on.

Her side-eye reminded me she would not be snowed by flattery. "Yes, but this time I might have to use a weapon I rarely pull out of my holster. Tact."

I grinned. "I'm sure you're an expert at that, too."

She locked eyes with me and seemed to weigh her words. "I have to warn you, Cassie—if I take over the Tillman case, I'll be looking at all of it. I'll want to see any evidence the Dalton cops may have against Chester. If I think it implicates him . . . he could go to jail."

Chapter 12

Mark had returned from Philly by Monday, but had his guitar lesson that night after work, so I suggested we have dinner Tuesday night at my place. Enthusiastic and skillful cook that I am, I picked up a Margherita pizza from one of our favorite local restaurants, Slice of Heaven. He showed up at seven, having stopped back at his condo to shower, change and retrieve a bottle of chardonnay.

I at least transferred the pizza to a large platter before slicing into it with the cutting wheel. Meanwhile, Mark opened the wine.

By the time I asked about his weekend, I already knew his team lost to the Mets. But Mark had half expected that outcome and wasn't the kind of sports fanatic who brooded about such things.

"I just wanted to get together with Eddie and Steve again," he said. "We had a good time, anyway. We walked around the campus, had beer and pizza at Smokey Joe's, like in the old days, and reminisced. We all said that it seems like more than ten years since we left—a lot has changed."

"Did they both go to veterinary school with you?" I asked.

"Steve did, but Eddie was in math and is a professor there now." He poured the wine into two glasses. "Speaking of my work, Becky and Chris came by the clinic today. Guess you all were up at Chester's place over the weekend?"

"We were, and I think he gave up those three cats pretty graciously." I lifted a pizza slice for each of us onto my aqua Fiestaware dishes. "How did they look to you?"

Taking his plate, Mark pulled out one of my chrome-and-vinyl kitchen chairs and sat down. "Winky, the youngest, is in the best shape. Sugarman has some dental decay and needs to lose a few teeth; we're keeping him overnight. Autumn has early kidney disease, but nothing that can't be managed with a prescription diet."

Though the news could have been far worse, I knew any ailment could hurt the chances of an animal headed for a shelter. "That could be rough for Autumn." I sat at the table across from Mark. "Less likely someone will want to adopt a pet that already has a chronic ailment and needs special, expensive food."

"Still, there are some good Samaritans out there," he observed. "My job was just to diagnose the cats, patch 'em up and send 'em along with Chris and Becky. Pro bono, of course."

"I'm sure they're grateful."

We toasted to that small success. For the next few minutes, conversation took a back seat as we both savored the gourmet-caliber pizza. The setting was less than romantic, because I still made do with the kitchen that had come with my renovated quarters—an older gas stove, shallow wooden cabinets I'd refreshed with white paint, and checkered linoleum that was missing a square or two. At least the ambience felt homey, though, and along with the good food and wine helped me relax after my busy day.

It also seemed to work for Mark. We shifted to the topic of his guitar lessons, and he said he felt he was making progress.

"Stan seems to think so, too," he added. "Quintessence is rehearsing some new material at his studio next week, and he invited me to come and sit in on a couple of numbers."

"Really? That's terrific." Surprised at first, I reminded myself that Mark *had* taken lessons in his college days, so he really was just reviving his skills. A smart and determined guy, he usually succeeded at anything he really put his mind to. And he'd done a decent job on the two songs he'd played for me so far. For each of those, he had the tune and the rhythm down fine, he just needed a little more creativity. Maybe Stan thought Mark would get inspiration from working with the group.

Although . . . not the wrong kind of inspiration, I hoped. "Does Tracy rehearse with them, too?"

He helped himself to a second mozzarella-covered slice. "Stan didn't say. I guess that depends on what they're working on." Then he narrowed his eyes at me. "Why? Don't tell me you're worried about her!"

That he'd guessed made it easier for me to admit it. "Well, she has got that whole forties pinup-girl thing going on. And when we saw them at the Firehouse, she was flirting with everybody in the band, except the balding guy with the glasses."

"Herb? I told you, he's her uncle."

"Exactly." I felt that only underscored my point.

Mark laughed and reached across the table to cover my hand with his. "First of all, I'm very happy with our relationship. And second, even if I weren't, Tracy wouldn't be my type at all."

My cheeks warmed. "I didn't really think so, but . . ."

"Tell you what. Stan said wives and sometimes friends often sit in on their rehearsals, to make it feel more like a real performance. When he's firmed up the date, why don't you come? I could use the moral support, and you could keep an eye on Tracy." His tone implied that there would be no need to keep an eye on him.

"I'd like to be there for your stage debut, actually. Yeah, please, let me know."

I had fed my cats before Mark and I ate, and they'd been hanging out in the nearby living room. Now I heard one of the metal pet dishes rattling in its stand, in the kitchen, and glanced behind me. Orange tabby Mango was licking the whole inside of the empty dish as if trying to gobble the stainless steel, too.

"Stop that," I told him mildly. "You already had a big dinner."

Mark wiped his lips with a paper napkin, while peering down at the frantic cat. "Does he do that often?"

"Lately he does. I've been feeding him the same amount as always, but he Hoovers it up and keeps whining for more. At the same time, I think he's losing weight." I added this information cautiously, both hoping for and fearing a veterinarian's opinion.

"Mind if I have a look?"

I picked up Mango, for the first time in a while, and immediately could tell he was a little lighter than he'd been a month ago. Mark swiveled in his chair so I could put the cat on his lap, and talked to Mango soothingly. Meanwhile, he ran a hand over my pet's marmalade-colored coat, felt his throat, palpated his upper hip area, and got the tabby to open his mouth so he could check his teeth. Although I also handled difficult animals for a living, even I wouldn't have tried that with Mango. Mark had the magic touch, though—no one could testify to that better than I.

He finished his mini-exam with a thoughtful frown. "I don't see signs of anything dire, and he doesn't seem to be in any pain. Still, you might want to bring him in for a workup. He's your oldest, isn't he?"

I nodded. "He was a rescue, so they didn't know his exact age, but by now he must be fifteen or sixteen."

"Mmm. At this point you have to watch out for kidney or thyroid problems. Diabetes is another possibility, though that's less likely if he's never been overweight. Has he been drinking a lot of water?"

"It's hard for me to tell," I admitted. "All three of them use the same water bowl."

"That could mean kidney problems, but he'd probably also be eating less. A voracious appetite combined with weight loss would more likely be diabetes or hyperthyroidism."

"I know." Like any other pet owner, I'd been in denial about the signs.

Once released, Mango galloped into the living room and sprang onto the back of the couch, as if to prove he was still spry as a kitten. Mark must have seen my morose expression, because he sent me a reassuring smile. "Like I said, whatever it might be, he doesn't seem badly off yet. His coat still looks healthy, which is another good sign. For any of those conditions, a change of diet or maybe a pill once a day could get it under control."

I said nothing, but got up to make coffee. I'd already had quite a few pets of various species in my lifetime and had lost several to diseases of old age. But the experience never got easier, and I didn't want to think about it happening to Mango. At least, not so soon.

I'd just put coffee on to drip, when my cell phone rang.

The sight of Nick Janos's name on the small screen got my attention. At eight p.m., when he wasn't even scheduled to do any jobs for me? My curiosity wouldn't let me ignore it.

"Hi, Cassie," Nick's rough-edged voice said. "I'm real sorry to call at this time of night. Maybe I shouldn't be bothering you with this, but I thought you might want to know. Because of the business with the woman who got sick at the reception."

"Why, Nick? What's wrong?"

"I'm calling from my truck. Just left the Fosters' place, and I'm parked a couple of blocks away." Before I could ask for an explanation, he added, "I've been helping Mr. Foster, Donald, work on the basement? Anyway, they had a *big* family row tonight. Gillian, him and even the daughter. Finally, I just walked out. I tell ya, if that's how the other half lives, I want no part of it." Nick paused, and over the phone I could hear his dark chuckle. "Uh-oh, a cop car just passed me, with flashing lights. Some neighbor musta called them. Guess I got outta there just in time!"

"You've got to be kidding." I tried to picture the respectable Fosters having a fight so disruptive that neighbors would call the police. "What was the problem?"

Nick took a deep breath, hinting it might be a long story. "Well, like I said, Don and I've been working on that basement. Boy, is it old—it needs *everything* brought up to code. He hired me mostly to repair the structural beams and the stonework, just to stabilize the walls. But even though Don says he knows electricity, he needs some help with that, too. I stopped him from making some pretty bad goofs."

Getting impatient, I prodded Nick. "So what started the fight?"

"At one point, Gillian came down and started talking

about what she'd like to do with the space, to make a wine cellar and a socializing area. Don said it sounded good, and maybe they could get that designer Linda back to draw up some sketches. Gillian hit the roof, saying she could design it herself. Got very sarcastic, then, and said Donald would use any excuse to bring Linda back. I guess she thinks there's something going on between the two of 'em."

I told him, briefly, about Linda's visit to me, and that she'd sworn the affair was all in Gillian's mind.

In the meantime, I saw Mark wander into the living room and settle on the couch, where my other two cats, Cole and Matisse, cozied up to him. All three must have decided I wouldn't be getting off the phone anytime soon.

Nick continued, "Don told her she was crazy—just in an offhanded way—but that only made her crazier. She said she knew Linda must have added the wheat flour to that pudding to make her sick and ruin her reception, maybe with his help. He tried to reason with her, but it didn't do any good. They were getting loud then, and the daughter came downstairs to see what was up. What's her name, Brittany?"

"Whitney," I told him.

"Well, she tried to stick up for her father, saying she knew he didn't do anything wrong. Finally, she said *she* put the flour in the pudding while she was helping out in the kitchen."

I reflected that I'd thought of Whitney as a possible suspect all along. "How did Gillian react to that?"

"She didn't believe her, and thought she was just covering up for Don and Linda. By that time, I'd packed up my tools and was halfway out the back door. You can't pay me enough to get mixed up in a family fight like that. Next time, Gillian might start throwing stuff and I might get in the way. That woman's got a screw loose."

I had to smile at the phrase, and told him, "The kind you can't fix, that's for sure! I'm really sorry my recommendation put you in the middle of things."

"Ah, wasn't your fault. You tried to do me a favor. But they got more problems than shoring up their basement— they've got to shore up their marriage. And I feel sorry for their kid being caught in the middle. I wonder if she really did mess with the pudding, or made that up just to get them to stop yelling at each other."

"Either way, it's not your problem. If I were you, I'd bill them for whatever work you did so far and tell them you're too busy to come back . . . ever again."

"You read my mind, Cassie!" Nick laughed. "Maybe before I head home I'll cruise back past the house, and see if the cops really did stop there. Anyway, you have a good rest of the night."

I wished him the same and finally got off the phone. Shaking my head, I joined Mark on the sofa and told him about the messy soap opera at the Foster house. To my surprise, he seemed annoyed with Nick.

"He shouldn't have called you so late and bothered you about that," Mark said. "I heard you tell him it's not his problem, but it's not yours, either."

Mark knew me too well by now. He probably guessed that I was already fighting the urge to call Bonelli—to ask if the Chadwick PD had gotten everything under control, and if she knew that Whitney had confessed to doctoring the food. Grudgingly, I admitted, "I guess you're right."

He slid closer and put an arm around me. "I speak from experience, hon. Day in and day out, I get animal patients that have been neglected or abused. Sometimes I suspect a woman or a kid in the family has been abused, too. Once in a while I have mentioned my suspicions to the Humane Society, or to the cops, if the situation looked really serious. But other times I just have to do what I can as a veterinarian—repair the damage, give them some advice and let it go. If I agonized over every single case, it would drive me crazy, and then I couldn't do my job at all."

"I can see that, and I'm sure you're right," I told him. "I guess it wasn't fair of Linda to come by the shop and unload her problems on me, either."

"No, it wasn't. Whether or not she's messing around with Donald Foster, at this point her best move would be to follow Nick's lead. Send Gillian a bill and never set foot in that house again."

I agreed with Mark's assessment and slumped back comfortably against his shoulder. That definitely would be the right solution for both Nick and Linda. But what about poor Whitney? She had to go on living in that stressful home. With her mother hurling wild accusations at her father, whom the girl clearly got along with much better.

I remembered my last glimpse of her, when Adele was being rolled out the front door on a stretcher. Whitney standing at the end of the hall, near the kitchen doorway, her eyes enormous and her hands over her mouth in shock.

Because a woman she hardly knew might die, from a prank Whitney had meant to play only on Gillian? To ruin the reception, embarrass her in front of the historical society board and take her down a peg?

Could she hate her mother that much?

Chapter 13

The next day, it was back to work early for both me and Mark. But while his clinic never lacked for patients, business remained pretty slow at Cassie's Comfy Cats. Sarah and I took turns staffing the sales counter and keeping our charges amused during their turns in the playroom. I again told myself that, since the cats' owners were technically paying for this, it wasn't so bad to make part of my living playing with other peoples' pets.

Just before noon, Dawn called me on my cell phone to complain about her own lack of customers. "I'm bored, and I need some business advice. Any chance you can get away for a quick lunch?"

"Well, I don't know," I said. "I'm trying to get this Siamese to move his butt, only so far nothing I've tossed through the air or pulled on a string has tempted him. I'd hate to be a quitter."

"Maybe he's more into zen meditation. Allow him to be himself."

I laughed. "I like the way you think."

By the time I told Sarah that I would be ducking out for

an hour or so, I'd thought of another good use for that time. "I also plan to do some more sleuthing on Chester's behalf, okay?"

"You're the boss," she reminded me with a smile. "But sure, anything more you could do for him will be appreciated."

Downtown Chadwick is very walkable, so Dawn and I met at Chad's, our retro diner. She made an entrance in her "new" vintage skirt, the black one with the art nouveau daylilies, which flowed almost to her ankles. She'd combined it with a simple T-shirt the same coral shade as the flowers, and with her long, wavy auburn hair it all looked spectacular. By Chadwick standards—and most people's—Dawn would have been overdressed for a weekday lunch at the diner. But since she had opened her store three years ago, she'd become familiar to the town's population, at least by sight. I'm sure they knew by now that Dawn marched to a different drummer, and some may even have envied the way she carried off such outfits. I certainly did, and felt dull that day by comparison, in my pastel-striped camp shirt and khaki shorts.

At Chad's, they made no hard distinctions between breakfast and lunch, so even though it was past noon we both ordered omelets. My experiences that week had provided me with lots of gossip to share, but I tried to be judicious.

First, I told Dawn about Nick's call to me the night before and the Fosters' boisterous argument. I omitted Whitney's confession that she had tainted the pease porridge with wheat flour. That tidbit might have legal repercussions, so I hesitated to spread it around.

Dawn did empathize with Whitney as the innocent victim of the turmoil. "Boy, I remember when my folks were breaking up, I hated so much to hear them argue. I'd lock myself in my room, put on headphones and listen to music to drown them out. By the time they divorced, I actually was relieved. Living with just my mom was so much calmer—you know how well she and I get along."

I tried to relate this to Whitney's situation and came up with a grimmer scenario. "Unfortunately, if the Fosters split and Donald is accused of infidelity, custody will probably go her mother, and that's the last thing Whitney would want. She's still under eighteen, so she might not have much say in the matter."

"Oh, I don't know. All kinds of things can influence that, I think. Your mom could probably tell you."

That was true; as a paralegal with a respected Morristown firm, Barbara McGlone had lots of information of that kind at her fingertips. "I could ask her, except then she'd warn me not to get involved, just like Mark did."

Dawn flashed a wide keyboard of pearly teeth. "Gee, do they even *know* you by now?"

"Doesn't seem that way, does it?"

Once our omelets had arrived—mine Greek with spinach and feta cheese, hers Spanish with assorted peppers—we moved on to Chester Tillman's dilemma. I told Dawn that for the present he seemed to be doing okay at home, with a caregiver visiting, but in the long run his absentee children planned to move him into an assisted living facility.

"Y'know, there's a pretty decent one not far from Dalton, called Mountainview," Dawn told me. "I gave a talk there once on natural foods and supplements to help treat various old-age problems. The staff was very nice to deal with, and the complex is really cheerful and homey. They have a whole memory care wing for dementia patients, marked in ways that make it easier for them to get around on their own. Of course, I don't know how much it costs to live there."

"Chester's kids have money," I recalled. "Just depends on

whether they'd be willing to pay for him to have the best care. From what I've seen and heard about them so far, I wouldn't be optimistic."

Finished with our lunches, we ordered coffee—it was excellent at Chad's—and Dawn filled me in on her news, such as it was. "Business has been slow this spring, so I'm brainstorming on how to improve that. Start filling orders by mail? Do more advertising or promotion? I'm stumped."

"Maybe there are some new target groups you could reach out to," I suggested.

She cupped her chin in her hand and squinted, as if thinking hard. "Is it too late for me to hold a summer solstice promotion? Those pagans and Wiccans do buy a lot of herbs."

I laughed. "You'd know more about that than I would!"

As we paid our tab at the front counter, Dawn hinted that she should drop by the antiques shop so Philip could see her in the skirt.

I startled her, I think, with my quick response to that suggestion. "Yes, let's! I have some questions I want to ask him."

Philip Russell always decorated his front show window with some eye-catching arrangement of pieces, dating anywhere from the distant past to the 1980s, but following a certain theme. The concept for June appeared to be "Summer Fun." In the large window with its deep inside sill, he had brought together an antique fishing pole, an old picnic basket, and a wicker rocker, all probably from the early 1900s. On top of a "beatnik"-themed beach towel from the 1950s rested a child's pail with matching shovel and a boxy portable record player, both probably from the sixties.

While Dawn and I paused on the sidewalk to admire the setup, these collectibles reminded me why I'd wanted to pay Philip a visit.

Inside, we found him carefully wrapping up some pieces

of Depression glass for a young couple, so we browsed until he was free. He instantly recognized the skirt he'd sold to Dawn and complimented her on how well she'd matched it to her top.

"I got some more long skirts in last week, if you want to check them out." He pointed toward the rear alcove, where he kept the vintage clothing.

"Might as well have a look, right?" With a happy shrug, she headed in that direction.

I considered this lucky, because I could talk to Philip alone. Quietly, I explained to him about Chester Tillman's dilemma, and the types of things he'd been missing. "You carry a lot of video games. Are any of the old Nintendos really valuable? Would they be worth stealing?"

The antiques dealer wore a guarded expression, though I hoped he could tell I wasn't accusing him. "Some are more collectible than others. Ironically, if the story and characters are well-known, the game's probably not worth very much. Certain games are rare—maybe they were sold mostly in Europe, they were limited editions or for some reason they never really caught on. But because of those elements, collectors really value them today."

When I pressed for specifics, Philip said the cartridge for a rare game might be worth several hundred dollars in itself, but in the box it could sell for a couple thousand.

As a cautionary note, he added, "There has to be something special about a piece for it to command a high price."

Since I couldn't tell him which games in particular Chester had lost—and I wondered if even Chester could remember—that didn't help much. "How about jazz albums? He said he had a few from the Blue Note label that seemed to be gone from their carton, as if they'd been handpicked."

Philip pursed his lips in thought. "I'm not an expert on those—if someone brings one in, even I have to look it up online. But yes, in the very early days Blue Note recorded some of the jazz greats, the real innovators. Even the cover art for the albums was very avant-garde and creative. Again, if Tillman could remember exactly which ones went missing, you could check online auction sites for the current prices."

Meanwhile, Dawn had wandered back from the clothing alcove. She carried no major garments, but a long necklace of colorful beads. She still scanned the knickknacks in the front room of the shop, giving me time to ask Philip one more question.

"And Chester said his wife had a doll that they bought for their daughter when she was small. I guess this would have been in the late eighties or early nineties." I repeated the widower's description of the doll's appearance and costume. "He said his daughter never even played with it, but his wife kept it in her closet, still in the box. Wouldn't that increase its value?"

The dealer looked thoughtful again. "Probably. Did he know the brand?"

"I don't think he could remember, but he did say it was very good quality and cost them a bit."

Philip pulled out an iPad, a strange sight among all of the timeworn merchandise around him, and did some tapping and scrolling. "I'll bet it was an American Girl. They started doing high-quality ethnic dolls right around that time." Pretty soon he pulled up a photo of one in an elaborate Victorian dress.

"That looks like what Chester described, all right," I said.

"American Girl has produced quite a few African-American dolls in historic costumes over the years. They came with booklets telling the stories of the characters. They're only eighteen inches tall, but if your guy bought one of the first, and it was never really used . . . Yeah, that could be worth hundreds today."

Chester's suspicions began to sound more and more credible. Someone certainly could have been raiding his "junk" with an eye to any collectibles worth fencing to an antiques shop or on the Internet.

"Thanks so much," I told Philip. "I may pass this information on to the Dalton police. They think Chester's just a dotty old man."

As Dawn and I left Towne Antiques, I explained why I'd been quizzing the proprietor so intently.

"Poor Chester," she sympathized. "The police do need to take his reports seriously. Just because his house is cluttered, and he's careless about leaving his door unlocked, that shouldn't mean someone could just walk in there and get away with robbery."

Or, I thought, *maybe even with murder.*

I got back to my duties at the shop after that. But later on, during a post-grooming coffee break, I phoned Bonelli.

She also was in her office and had a few minutes free to talk. She told me she'd had a conversation with Chief Eddie Hill of the Dalton PD. When she'd offered to "assist" his department by taking a second look at the Bernice Tillman case, Hill had assured her that it would be a waste of time.

"On the other hand," Bonelli said, "the fact that he cares so little about her death could actually work in my favor. His last words to me were, 'If you think there's something more to the case that we missed, Detective, then be my guest. Knock yourself out!'"

"Not very respectful," I observed.

"No, but technically he gave me permission to investigate.

So I hope to get over to Chester's this afternoon, have a look around and ask him a few questions."

"That's great, thank you!" With Bonelli on the case, we might start getting some real answers. "I also found out some stuff today, at the antiques shop, that might help."

I explained about the latest items Chester claimed were missing from his home, and what Philip Russell had told me about their possible value.

"Interesting," she said. "It seems like two people we can definitely rule out are his children. They'd have no reason to sneak stuff out of the house, since they stood to inherit everything."

"You're right. Chester said he was actually keeping some of the video games for his son, all these years, and the doll for his daughter. If they'd shown the slightest interest, he'd probably have insisted they take those things home with them."

"You don't think that might have happened, and Chester just forgot?" Bonelli wondered.

"Sarah said both James and Sylvia just stopped by the house for a few minutes and turned up their noses at the mess. As far as she could see, they left empty-handed."

"Maybe they would have felt differently if they knew how much their old toys might be worth. We have their contact information, so I can give each of them a call. Anyhow, I'll do some more digging."

"Thanks so much." Sensing the detective was about to hang up, I squeezed in one more question. "Was there some kind of to-do at the Fosters' house last night?" I explained what Nick had said, about seeing a police cruiser headed toward the place just after he'd left.

"We did send a unit to a domestic disturbance around eight thirty p.m.," she confirmed. "Not so unusual, except most of the time those calls come from the seedier part of town."

"Nick said Gillian was blaming her husband for pulling that prank at their reception last week."

"According to the officers, she was making a lot of accusations, but didn't have any proof. Our guys just tried to calm everyone down, and said by the time they left things seemed okay. But if I were your friend Nick, I'd steer clear of that household. He can't need the work that badly."

I chuckled. "He's already decided that on his own. Well, the Fosters have put up with each other for what, seventeen years so far? Long enough, at least, to have a daughter that age. They should be able to work out their issues eventually."

"Unless the wife is really going off the rails this time," Bonelli said soberly. "Now, Cassie, much as I've enjoyed our gossip session . . ."

"Yes, I'm sure you have other cases to get back to. But thanks for the updates."

I also returned to my work. The owner of Pepper, a silver Ocicat, would be returning for him that afternoon. While he was being boarded, Pepper's beautiful spotted coat did not really need grooming, but his master had requested that we trim his nails and add soft caps to them. The young man had tried to do this himself, without success, so it was up to me and Sarah.

Normally I could trim a cat's claws myself, but after handling Pepper a few times during his stay, I could see it would be a two-person job. He was a friendly cat until you touched his paws—then he declared war. He hissed, growled, twisted himself every which way, and threatened to bite, though so far he'd never followed through on that.

I misted the grooming studio with an herbal spray that supposedly calmed fractious cats, and managed to get Pepper into a padded grooming harness that also had a soothing effect.

Sarah and I both wore rubber gloves. While she held his body, I took on the riskier job of gently squeezing each paw to expose the nails, and clipping each as short as possible without exposing the "quick," or the vein that ran down into the nail.

Though Pepper grumbled under his breath, this worked okay for his front feet. When Sarah carefully laid him on his side and I dealt with his hind feet, though, his fighting spirit revived. Luckily, an Ocicat isn't a large breed—a blend of Siamese and Abyssinian genes—so the two of us could hold him in place. Still, I never liked to subdue a cat by force, because it stressed them so much.

I got the hind feet clipped, and I had purchased a set of the nail tips, but started to have second thoughts about adding them. Maybe when the owner came, I'd suggest just a bimonthly clipping instead, and advise him on teaching Pepper to use scratching posts as a better way to spare the furniture.

Sarah and I had to concentrate so intently during the session, we didn't have a chance to chat as we normally do while grooming a cat. After we put Pepper in his condo and took a much-needed coffee break, though, I told her the latest news about both the Foster and Tillman cases.

"Sounds like our friend Gillian doesn't believe her husband is innocent until proven guilty," Sarah concluded with a twinkle in her eye.

"I wanted to ask if Whitney told the cops she doctored the porridge," I said. "But Bonelli didn't mention it, and I didn't want to be the one to bring it up. Even if the daughter lied to take the heat off her father, it could still open a can of worms. The Dugans could sue them for Adele's hospital costs, pain and suffering, and who knows what." With a paralegal for a mother, I'd heard about such cases.

"Well, you got that information from Nick, so it's only

hearsay. At least nobody died as a result. Might as well step back now, and let the Fighting Fosters work out their own problems."

Sarah took more of a personal interest in Chester Tillman's case and was also encouraged to hear that Bonelli would be looking into it.

"Y'know, yesterday after church, Robin reminded me about something," she said. "A couple of the Dalton cops got in trouble, a few years back, for pulling some funny stuff on the job. They stopped a driver who was slightly drunk, made him step out and do the sobriety test. I guess he wasn't that impaired, so the cops sent him off with a warning. But the next day, the guy went back to the police station claiming that he'd had an iPod on the passenger seat that went missing."

I set my empty mug back on the small table next to the coffeemaker, to be rinsed later in the studio sink. "During the traffic stop?"

Sarah nodded. "He swore that while the one cop was testing him, the other guy must have swiped the iPod. Of course both of them denied it, saying he was so drunk he'd probably lost it somewhere, and he should just be glad they didn't arrest him. The driver complained to their captain, too, but he backed his guys up."

"That's Hill. Even Bonelli doesn't think much of him." This story opened up a whole new field of possibilities. Would the Dalton cops have known that Chester left his house open at night? But even if one of them was capable of stealing from a homeowner, would he sink so low as to smother an elderly woman to death?

Possibly. If she woke up, saw his face, and he thought she might recognize and report him.

We were winding up our break when an electronic chime told us someone had come in the shop's door. Sarah offered to go up front, while I checked to see if Pepper had settled down by now.

The Ocicat seemed to have recovered from his ordeal, but my assistant returned from the sales area wearing a slight frown. "So much for my advice that you should stay out of the Fosters' business."

"Why, what's wrong?"

"Donald Foster is out there with Leya. He wants to board her again . . . and they both seem kind of upset."

Chapter 14

Compared to the times I'd seen him before, at his house, Donald Foster looked as if he'd aged ten years. His hair and his complexion both seemed a shade grayer. Even so, he put on a good-natured smile when I stepped into the front sales area of my shop.

Leya's hard-sided beige carrier already rested on the counter, agitated meows coming from inside. I remembered that when I'd picked the cat up at her home, and even when I'd returned her, she'd stayed calm and quiet.

"Bet you didn't think you'd see us again so soon!" Donald tried to joke.

"I certainly don't mind," I told him, "but is everything okay?"

"Yeah, sure. I just think we should leave Leya with you until we've finished work on our cellar. The noise seems to be bothering her, and she'd be better off in a quieter environment."

Sarah had slipped away into the adjoining playroom, and through the screen I saw her waving a wand toy at another of our boarders.

I opened the carrier to have a look at Leya. Usually I check a cat over physically only on its first visit, but because the Himalayan had been so vocal since her arrival, I wanted to be sure she didn't have any new problems. Sure enough, I found a bald patch on her tail and another on a hind leg.

When Donald noticed me examining these, he shifted from one foot to the other. "Yeah, those skin problems are new. I don't know if something got into the air, with all the construction, that she's allergic to . . ."

When I let go of the fluffy cat, she immediately twisted around to lick to her tail. I pointed this out to Donald. "Or she could be overgrooming those areas. That's a common reaction to stress."

He nodded. "I guess that would make sense. Like I said, it's been noisy, with people traipsing in and out of the house and up and down the cellar stairs. Leya doesn't go outside, so we've had to shut her up in the guest room more than usual, but I'm sure she can still hear all the activity."

Well did I recall that creepy guest room. *If I was shut up in there all day, I'd probably start pulling my hair out, too.*

"I'm sure it's been stressful for everyone," I said, trying to keep my tone casual. "Nick Janos was helping you with that project, wasn't he?"

Donald sank onto one of the tall stools on the customers' side of the counter, letting down his guard. With another tight smile, he told me, "I think he's given up on us."

"He did say you and Gillian were having some disagreements, and it was making him uncomfortable."

Donald ran a hand over his short, combed-back hair. "She always does this. She takes on these very challenging projects and then expects everything to go perfectly. Years ago, when we started, I had no problem with it. I like planning the renovations and even doing some of the work myself. But if there's a delay, or something doesn't turn out exactly as expected, I can roll with that. Somehow, Gillian just can't."

I stroked Leya's vanilla coat. Unlike most of my boarders, she seemed calmer and happier now, *away* from her home. "I'm sure you can't predict or control everything in a whole house renovation."

Donald let out a brief snort. "Or in life!" Before I could think of a response to that, he slid off the stool, straightened, and pulled a checkbook from his back pocket. "Anyhow, I'm sure we'll get things under control in another week or two. But since I don't know how long it will be, Cassie, how about I give you twice the usual deposit?"

I wasn't going to turn down that offer, especially since having Leya back on the premises might once again involve me in the Fosters' problems. Accepting the check, I asked him, "How's Whitney getting along?"

Her father laughed. "She's at the stable so much, we could have rented out her room for the summer. But I suppose she wants to make the most of her time off from school."

He tried to put a positive spin on the fact that Whitney took every opportunity to escape from her mother's orbit. He probably knew, though, that I wasn't fooled.

On his way out, Donald thanked me again for accommodating Leya. "If you see Nick, tell him I'm going to miss working with him. He was a big help!"

"I will," I promised.

"Sounds like things are kind of spinning out of control with the Fosters," said Mark when I gave him this update Wednesday evening. We had grabbed a quick dinner at his condo, and now were in his cobalt-blue RAV4, headed across town to Quintessence's rehearsal. His college guitar, in its case, rested on the back seat.

"That's the impression I got, too," I said. "Donald seems like a pretty low-key guy, so I felt that, if anything, he was soft-pedaling the situation. But, of course, I'd already heard from both Nick and Bonelli that all three members of the family got into a screaming match on Tuesday."

Mark kept his eyes on the road. "Well, at least their cat's out of the house, and you're being well paid to take care of her."

"That's Sarah's attitude, too," I told him. "But something about Donald's explanation bothers me. He said Leya was upset by the renovations going on in the cellar. Really? More than when the main level was being worked on, over the past year or so?" I shook my head. "If you ask me, the cat's freaking out because the humans are fighting all the time. And if Whitney's hardly ever home . . . I got the feeling she's the one who's really bonded with Leya."

In the sunset glow that suffused the car, Mark shot a sideways glance at me. "Cassie, you're doing it again."

"Doing what?"

"Getting involved in your client's personal problems. Your job is to board the Fosters' cat, not to fix their marriage."

"But you suggested, yourself, that sometimes issues with the animals are tied into issues with their owners."

"I also told you that unless it's very serious—like, criminal—I try not to interfere. If I got a reputation for poking my nose into my customers' business, or telling them how to live their lives, pretty soon I wouldn't have any clinic."

He was right about that, of course. Still, I wondered if there had been something more behind Donald Foster's visit to my shop the previous day.

Mark went on, "Y'know, sometimes at the clinic we have animals dumped on us! The owners bring in a pet that's hurt or sick, we tell them the cost, they agree to it and leave the animal . . . but they never come back. We've even had people give us fake addresses and phone numbers, as if they planned to skip out all along."

I frowned in sympathy. I knew in a case like that, the vet could only try to place the animal with a no-kill shelter; send it to the town shelter, where it would promptly be gassed; or, if it were old or sick, they could humanely euthanize it at their own expense.

Still, sad as it was, I couldn't see how Mark's example related to my problem. "I highly doubt the Fosters intend to do that. For one thing, Donald prepaid me for a month's board. I know they can afford the bills, and I sure know where to find them if I need to collect more."

He fell quiet for a moment. "I don't mean to give you a hard time, Cassie. I just don't want people to take advantage of you, because you care so much."

"I don't think Donald was trying to do that, exactly. But I did sense maybe he was trying to reach out to me, through Leya," I admitted. "So someone else, outside the family, would know what was going on."

"Apparently, the Chadwick cops already know what's been going on. At this point, he should be reaching out to a marriage counselor. Or maybe a lawyer."

Again, Mark was right. Maybe Gillian refused to see a counselor, though. And to consult with a lawyer might look like first step toward divorce. Awful as life with Gillian sounded, Donald didn't seem to want that.

Who's got the money in their marriage? I wondered. *Maybe it's mostly hers. Maybe that's why she's gone on the offensive, accusing him of adultery . . .*

There could be more behind their clashes than meets the eye.

A few minutes later, we arrived at our destination—Stan Burrell's guitar shop in a neighboring town. It stood at the center of a whole block of turn-of-the-century brick storefronts. Gleaming guitars of various designs and colors filled the front display windows, which were guarded at this hour by pull-down metal gates. Mark drove around back, where several vehicles already occupied the lot. I accompanied him to the building's rear door. He pressed an intercom button, announced himself, and got buzzed in.

"Convenient that Stan has a rehearsal space over his own store," I commented.

"Pretty cool, huh? And as you can see, after dark this block is dead, so even if he had the world's loudest rock band, they wouldn't bother anybody."

We climbed one flight of stairs, covered by tweed industrial carpet that was worn down the center, and reached a corridor lined with fake-wood paneling. Mark, accustomed to the layout from his weekly lessons, automatically headed for the one door that stood open.

About a dozen people already occupied the room. A platform against one wall held the band's drum kit, electronic keyboard, big double bass, and Stan's electric guitar, which rested on a sky-blue chair. More of the metal folding chairs, in assorted bright shades, had been set up in two rows to accommodate the small audience.

I asked Mark about the multihued but adult-size seating.

"During the day and some evenings, Stan rents this space out for other uses," he said. "Support groups of different kinds, I think."

"That's interesting. Maybe the colors are supposed to help cheer them up?"

On the platform stage, Stan and a teenaged boy fiddled

with an amplifier. Herb, the bland, balding keyboard player, and Nash, the pumped-looking black drummer, stood talking and joking with people in the front row. As Mark had suggested, they seemed to know the audience members well.

He and I took seats in the second row and he set his guitar case on the floor, which was covered in the same commercial carpet as the stairs. I guessed that, combined with the paneled walls and acoustic ceiling tiles, it helped mute the volume during the band's practice sessions . . . and maybe any outbursts during the support groups?

Mark leaned forward in his seat, forearms resting on his lean, denim-covered thighs, and hands tightly clasped. Picking up on his tension, I asked, "What exactly are you supposed to do tonight?"

"I'm not too sure, myself. Stan's had me working on two numbers in particular, though. I guess the group will go through their normal rehearsal, and then he'll have me join in toward the end."

"Ever played in front of an audience before?"

He chuckled grimly. "Not since college, and then it was just a group of friends, not strangers. Damn, I didn't expect to be this nervous."

I covered his clasped hands with one of mine in support. I would have suggested that he picture the audience naked, but since it included a few women who might be wives and girl-friends of the band members, that seemed unwise.

Even more unwise when I noticed that Tracy, the sizzling singer, occupied a front-row seat.

I recognized her first by her shoulder-length blond locks, although tonight she had skipped the crimped, 1940s waves. She was chatting vivaciously with a more sedate-looking woman who had a roundish face, short auburn hair and glasses. At one point I overheard Tracy ask her, "So when do we meet this mysterious new student of Stan's? He's told us just enough to make me really curious."

The older woman smiled and shrugged. "You probably know as much as I do. He talks sometimes about how well a student is doing, or isn't, but he usually doesn't bring them to the house."

Kenny, the bass player whose moussed-up hair made him look even taller, entered from a hallway with a Coke can in his hand. He spotted Mark, waved and ambled on over. The two of them shot the breeze for a few minutes about Mark performing for the first time in front of a real audience. Kenny tried to put his fears to rest.

"Everybody here's like family," he said. "Nobody's looking to judge you. From what Stan's told us, you're already pretty good. This is just to give you a feel for working with an ensemble." He confirmed that Mark would just be sitting in on a couple of numbers at the end of their set. "Otherwise, you guys will be part of our audience. You'll be here awhile, so if you need a break, there are vending machines out there." He gestured with his soda can toward the hallway.

"Thanks, man." Mark shook Kenny's hand.

When the bass player stepped away, I noticed that Tracy had twisted around in her seat in front of us. Clearly she'd been eavesdropping on the conversation and now she fixed a wide-eyed stare upon Mark. When he faced forward again, happening to catch her gaze, she smiled and winked.

I felt myself flush. Who did she think she was? With me sitting right beside him? *This girl has a real problem!*

Mark must have felt me freeze up, because he subtly took my hand. "Now, don't go all crazy. She's probably one of those ladies who just likes to flirt. You remember how, when we saw them at the Firehouse, she kidded around with the guys in the audience."

That reminder helped to ease my worries, as did the fact that a minute later Quintessence took the stage for their rehearsal. At the mic, Stan explained that they were trying out some new material, and later on would be bringing in one of his students, Mark Coccia. Mark nodded modestly while I and the rest of the small audience applauded. Even though the male band members were too cool to join in, Tracy made a show of clapping for him, too.

Just watch your step, honey, I warned her silently.

Stan then announced the group was going to do "Exactly Like You," written by Jimmy McHugh and Dorothy Fields in 1930, and "One-Note Samba," written by Antônio Carlos Jobim around 1960. "This will be our first venture into bossa nova," he said of the second song, "and since Tracy doesn't speak Portuguese, she'll be singing the English lyrics by Jon Hendricks."

While the members of Quintessence prepared to start, I whispered to Mark, "Stan really knows his musical history, doesn't he?"

Mark nodded. "You know, you might want to ask *him* about the value of Chester's jazz albums."

"Just what I was thinking." It surprised me that Mark would encourage my sleuthing.

Quintessence didn't sound as if they needed much rehearsal, interpreting both numbers with style. But both were love songs, and though I might have been getting paranoid, I felt Tracy kept focusing in our direction—Mark's—while she breathed that she prayed each night for someone "exactly like you." At least the second number was more of a novelty song, fast-paced and quirky, but she still seemed to aim lyrics such as "all the love I feel for you" in the direction of Mark. *My* Mark.

Stan announced that after a short break Mark would be joining the group onstage. "He's a hard-working veterinarian with a busy clinic in Chadwick, so I'm glad no rottweiler-related emergencies interfered with his coming here tonight."

A few audience members chuckled and Mark managed a weak smile, but he still looked tense to me.

"Can I get you anything from the vending machines?" I asked. "A soda?"

"Maybe just a bottle of water, if they have it. Thanks."

I found the hallway alcove well equipped with both drinks and snacks. Had Stan installed the machines just for his rehearsals, or did the support groups who met in the space make use of them, too? Could be a problem for Overeaters Anonymous!

It took me only a minute to purchase water for Mark and a Diet Coke for myself, but even that might have been too long to leave him alone. By the time I returned, he'd taken his guitar out of its case and Tracy had stopped by to admire it.

"It's an older model," Mark was telling her. "I'm sure they make fancier ones now. But hey, it gets the job done."

"I'm sure it does," Tracy purred.

At that point he spotted me approaching, and dodged awkwardly around her. "Anyway, I'd better grab my water and get on up to the stage."

Her eyes followed him as he took the chilled bottle from me, with a sheepish shake of his head.

"Don't let her rattle you," I whispered, and kissed him on the cheek. "Good luck!"

At least with Mark on a chair toward the rear left of the stage, Tracy couldn't focus on him anymore. When Quintessence launched into "Summertime," guitarist Stan took the lead at first, then Mark picked up the tune for a bit. He'd definitely made progress since the evening he'd played for me at his condo. He still emphasized the core melody over any wild improvisation, but when he did get creative he showed a style of his own, clearly distinct from his mentor's.

The small audience applauded, and the group ended with "Sunny," one of the numbers Mark had played for me before. Again, he built on that foundation while adding more of his personal touches. He might never be as brilliant a jazz guitarist as he was a veterinarian, but for a hobbyist he sounded pretty darn good.

When the band finished, Stan invited the audience to give Mark a special hand. They did, and I saw a blush creep up his cheeks. I knew he must have felt great to have conquered his fears and acquitted himself so well. Almost predictably, Tracy went to congratulate him, too, and her touch on his arm lingered longer than was necessary. He laughed it off and tried politely to extricate himself and leave the stage. Meanwhile, he even seemed to be easing the guitar in between the two of them!

A strange, visceral sensation shot through my nerve endings. I needed to put a stop to this, but how? In the past I'd been mildly jealous of some other women who'd chased after Mark, but when he'd said he had no interest, I'd believed him. He'd always followed through by ignoring them, which ended the problem. I had a sense, though, that Tracy was not used to taking no for an answer. Mark still might never give in to her, but in the meantime she could make him very uncomfortable. And she had no right to do that!

He left his guitar near the stage and disappeared in the direction of the men's room, which gave me an opening. Did I dare to take it? As Tracy stepped down from the platform, our gazes locked and I rose to the challenge.

I walked straight up to her and put out my hand. "Hi, we haven't met. I'm Cassie McGlone. Mark and I saw you once before, at the Firehouse in Chadwick."

She accepted the handshake. "Oh, were you there, too?"

I'd been prepared to play nice and compliment her on her singing, but this slightly snarky comment made me drop all pretense. "Yes, he and I were there together. We *are* together."

"You're lucky," she simpered. "He seems like a very nice guy. Not many of those around these days."

And even if there are, you don't attract them, do you? I thought.

Tonight she'd dressed more casually and discreetly than at the Firehouse, but still wore tight jeans and a snug red T-shirt with a suggestive zipper running down from the neckline. My choice of a floral peasant top, to dress up my own jeans for the evening, felt almost puritanical by comparison.

"So, you're married?" she asked. "Or living together?"

"I'm his girlfriend."

"Oh. Well." Her tone implied that could change.

My heart hammered in my chest at this challenge, but I held my smile. "Listen, honey, almost every day at work I get hissed at, spat at, scratched and bitten, so don't get into a cat-fight with me. You think you're tough? How many times have you been held at gunpoint?" That startled the smirk from her face. "I'm up to three so far, and all of those jerks are behind bars now. If you think I'm lying, ask Detective Angela Bonelli of the Chadwick PD."

The pink of Tracy's cheeks faded. Whether she was guilty of some secret felony or whether she just thought I was insane, she backed away and raised her hands in self-defense. "Hey, whatever you say, sister! The nice-guy vet is all yours."

Mark had returned to the rehearsal room by then. With

no idea of what had taken place between me and Tracy, he advised me to talk to Stan before the guitarist headed home.

I decided not to mention to Stan that Chester's albums had mysteriously vanished, and said only that he'd been wondering about their value.

"Depends on different things," Stan told me. "The old ones by top artists, in good condition, usually go for five to seven hundred. But even a little scratched up, I've heard of a rare one going for three or four thousand."

"He mentioned Art Blakey, John Coltrane and Wayne Shorter," I said.

The guitarist nodded. "All top names. Again, some of their records are more in demand than others, but the prices still should be up there. Sounds like your friend's got a good collection. If he's interested in selling any, he should go through one of those sites online. They're easy to use, and he could do well."

I thanked Stan, though this was not such great news for Chester.

"That's too bad," Mark commented, as we walked out to his car. "Sounds more like Chester has *lost* part of a very good collection."

"If somebody's been ripping him off for thousands of dollars, I'm going to get to the bottom of it. I swear I will!"

As we took our seats in the RAV4, he sent me a startled look. "You're in a feisty mood tonight, aren't you? Did you also have some kind of go-round with Tracy, earlier? When I came back in the room she was, like, slinking away from you."

I smiled sweetly. "I told her you were my man, and not to mess with me because I'd already put a few perps behind bars."

After a second of disbelief, Mark laughed out loud. "No kidding? Wow, I'm just glad it didn't come to blows!"

"Did I go too far? I don't want to get you in trouble with Stan, or embarrass you with the other guys."

"Don't worry about it." Pulling out of the rear lot, he grinned. "I kind of like being a jazz musician with a gangsta girlfriend."

Chapter 15

Work remained fairly quiet the next day, so in between helping Sarah care for the boarders, which now included Leya, I used my laptop to search the web for information about vintage jazz LPs. I found eBay auctions and ads posted by individuals that seemed to bear out what Stan had told me—depending on the reputation of the performer and the rarity and condition of the recording, certain albums could command at least four figures.

There also were ads by specialty stores and private vendors who sold vintage records, including jazz, and posts by collectors looking for certain rare LPs. In other words, a lot of money seemed to be changing hands in this hobby.

The eBay vendors generally identified themselves only by e-mail addresses, at least until you won the auction and got to the point of making a transaction. They had to be approved, though, to do business on the site, and were rated by customers for how quickly they filled an order and the quality of the merchandise. Was there any way to tell if a seller had come by something illegally?

More likely, if you were a thief, you'd bring your stolen treasures to one of the specialty shops. Or offer it to a rabid individual collector who'd be even less likely to ask any questions.

Sarah noticed me scrolling and tapping away, and asked what I was up to. I told her what I'd found out from Stan the evening before. "If we knew the name of even one particular album that Chester lost, we could see if anybody is reselling it."

"If he'd even remember," Sarah pointed out. "But I'll tell Robin to ask him. She still looks in on him two or three times a week."

I closed the laptop for the time being. "How is he getting along with his new caregiver?"

"I guess it's a little rocky. Robin says the woman doesn't have much patience with him. She's at least persuaded him to close the back door at night, and she put a big hook-and-eye lock on the inside. But now Chester says he's got a plan to catch the thief."

"Oh, no."

"There's a recipe for disaster, right? If anybody has been breaking in, confronting him would be the worst thing Chester could do. He could end up like Bernice."

Sarah bent to pour clean litter into a boarder's pan, but I stared at her back. "Sounds as if you're also coming around to the idea of a burglar."

"I don't know what to think." She slid the pan back into the cat's condo and straightened up, dusting her gloved hands on her apron. "Have you heard anything more about it from Bonelli?"

"Not lately. Last e-mail I had from her, she'd hit a stone wall with the Dalton cops. She was planning to talk to Chester and some of his neighbors."

"Well, she's persistent. I'm sure if she suspects anything hinky, she'll keep digging until she gets some answers." Sarah crumpled the empty, economy-size cat litter bag and stuffed it into the trash can just outside the condo corridor. "By the way, we're almost out of this stuff, and of the pan liners, too." "Okay, thanks. I'll make a run out after lunch to restock."

I had recently discovered an animal-supply warehouse along one of the back roads. Though it might have opened originally to meet the needs of people with farms and breeding operations, it also offered pet supplies in large quantities at deep discounts. The only downside was that those thirty-pound sacks were a challenge to lift into my hatchback, but I'd gotten pretty fit over my past two years on the job, and at this rate I'd never need a gym membership.

I'd restocked on the cat supplies and was cruising back to my shop when I happened to notice a graceful wooden shingle on a post up ahead: STIRLING HILL FARM. Why did that name sound familiar?

Right. Linda Freeman had said that was where Whitney stabled her horse.

I slowed the car, my conscience warning me all the while. *You have no business talking to her, especially with neither of her parents around. They'd probably be furious. Depending on what you discuss with her, Bonelli might also be furious!*

But without her parents around, I thought, Whitney might be more willing to tell me the truth about what was going on in her home.

It's none of your business.

But if Whitney did stir wheat flour into the porridge, and wasn't just protecting her father, wouldn't that put an end to Gillian's fantasies that Donald was trying to kill her?

Or would she then accuse her daughter of attempted murder instead?

Surely not, if it was only meant as a prank.

I didn't even convince myself of that one. Still, I'd come to almost a full stop at the foot of the drive that I assumed led to the farm. In spite of my misgivings, I made the turn.

On this lovely June day, the property couldn't have been prettier. Across the middle distance stretched a long barn of picturesquely weathered brown wood. A center cupola sprouted from the well-kept roof, and crisp white trim accented the windows. Beyond this I could glimpse several green paddocks, where equines of various breeds, colors and sizes roamed and grazed.

But what interested me most was the action in the foreground, which featured three fenced riding rings. A female instructor stood in the center of one, shouting corrections and encouragement to the four children who trotted around her on safe, sleepy-looking mounts. The middle ring was empty at the moment. In the farthest one, a helmeted rider with a blond ponytail was sending a long-legged red horse over a series of practice jumps.

Could I possibly have gotten that lucky? But both Linda Freeman and Donald Foster *had* said that Whitney spent practically all of her time here lately. And why would the girl waste a fine, sunny day like this any other way?

Still keeping a low profile, I parked in the common lot and nonchalantly strolled past the ring with the children's class. I had no idea whether a stranger on the grounds would be suspect, but their teacher paid me no attention. I passed the empty ring and quietly approached the one where the blonde was practicing. Before I even got very close, I could confirm this was Whitney.

The way she rode, she needed a ring to herself. Whether the horse was a handful or Whitney was goading her on, Glory charged around the circuit of jumps at top speed, with the occasional snort or flip of her tail. When she veered out

toward the fence, she raised enough dust for me to retreat a
few steps. Not a bad idea, anyhow, since I wasn't sure her
rider would welcome my presence. Once they knocked a rail
down, but most of the time they sailed over clear. From a distance, I guessed the jumps were all around three feet high,
pretty challenging. The effort and excitement on this warm
day had raised a sheen on the chestnut's curved neck and mus-
cled shoulders.

On that pass close to the fence, Whitney finally must have
recognized me, because soon after she slowed her talented
mount to a walk. She loosened the reins and Glory stretched
her neck to take advantage of the freedom.

I raised my voice to carry halfway across the ring. "She's
quite a horse."

Whitney patted the mare's neck, as if to acknowledge this,
and walked her in my direction. "Hi, Cassie." So far, she
hadn't smiled. "What brings you out here?"

"Just curiosity. I was driving back from the feed store, saw
the sign, and I remembered that someone said you kept Glory
out here. I must have driven by a dozen times and never knew
it was such a big place."

"It is, I guess, compared to the last one we were at, up
north. The guy who ran that stable was a jerk. At least here,
when I tell them what to feed Glory and how much to turn
her out, they actually do it, and don't treat me like some
dumb kid." She swung lightly out of the small jumping saddle,
and wiped her brow beneath the visor of her black helmet.
"You wanna come in here and talk? I have to walk her before
I bring her in."

"Of course." I ducked between the wooden rails.

"You're not afraid of horses, are you? I know you handle
cats a lot, but—"

"I'm not as used to horses, but I actually studied to be a vet tech, years ago, and took courses in animal behavior. So we dealt with a little of everything." Up close, I could admire Whitney's tall mare, whose eyes remained bright and eager, scanning the horizon. "She doesn't even seem very tired after that workout."

As Whitney let out the horse's girth a few holes, she laughed. "Omigod, Glory needs to work like this practically every day. Otherwise she starts kicking her stall and driving all the other horses crazy. She used to give me a hard time and go around too fast. But since I've ridden her so much this summer she's started listening better, and we're getting to be good buds."

"It sure looked that way." I patted the horse's damp shoulder. "Speaking of bonding with animals, I guess you know that your dad brought Leya back to my place to board? He said he couldn't be sure for how long."

Whitney walked on, leading the horse; her gaze dropped to the toes of her tall boots, which scuffed up dust with every step. "Yeah, it's been kind of crazy at our house lately. I guess he thinks she'll be better off at your place."

I mentioned the bare spots I'd noticed on the cat, and my theory that she could be grooming herself too hard due to stress. "If it's having that effect on her, I can only imagine what it's doing to you."

The teen shrugged. "I've lived through our renovations before."

"Is that really all it is, this time?" When she responded with a pained look, I pressed further. "You know that handyman Nick and I are friends. He told me what it was like there last Saturday night."

"Yeah, he bolted. Poor guy, I couldn't blame him."

"He said you told your mother you added the wheat flour to the pudding. Was that true?" Whitney looked spooked, so

I reassured her, "He hasn't told the cops, and I won't, either. I'm just wondering if you'd really do something like that, and why."

Walking on, the young woman shrugged. "I don't know. I just did it on impulse. Mom was so wound up about that reception, as if impressing those historical society snobs was the most important thing in the world. It made me see that this whole project, that she and dad spent more than a year on, was really just for that goal—getting the place on the historic register. That it was supposed to be *our* home for us to live in didn't even matter, as long as it was this perfect period piece."

"I can see why that would be hard to accept," I sympathized.

"You have no idea how crazy she made Dad and me and everybody who came to work on the house. Anyway, that day when she was fussing at the caterers, and bitching about that stupid cabinet door being off-kilter, I just got so angry. I heard her tell the cook a couple of times to follow that recipe *exactly* because it had to be gluten-free, and suddenly I thought, *that's it*. I took a mixing cup to the pantry, sprinkled a little wheat flour in it, and when the cook wasn't looking I stirred it into the porridge."

Although there was nobody else nearby, Whitney dropped her voice to a hush and recalled how the trick had backfired. "I felt so awful when Mrs. Dugan reacted to it instead. And when they had to take her to the hospital, I was terrified that she might not recover!"

I nodded. "I guess since you didn't know Adele had celiac disease, you had no idea anyone might get really sick, except your mother."

She stopped the horse and faced me. "But that's the thing. Mom goes on and on about having to avoid gluten, but she's never gotten *really* sick from it. Sometimes she gets stomach cramps, but she's never had to go to the hospital like Adele. I thought she'd be embarrassed, maybe would have to run to the john a few extra times. And as for anybody else . . . Cassie, you saw what that stuff looked like. I didn't think a single other person at the party would even try it."

I gave her a grudging smile. "It would have been a fairly harmless trick, then, if not for Adele."

"The crazy thing is, I confessed Tuesday night! I told Mom I did it, but she wouldn't believe me. She's got this idea that Dad and Linda Freeman are conspiring to kill her so they can be together. It's not true, but she'd probably rather think that than believe I just wanted to give her a hard time. Isn't that twisted?"

I couldn't come up with a tactful reply, but Whitney didn't wait for one. Pulling off her helmet, she opened the gate of the riding ring, led Glory out, and didn't seem to mind when I followed. Through a wide door we entered the cool, clean barn, which smelled sweetly of hay and horses and very little else. When asked, I held Glory's reins just under her chin while her owner stripped off the saddle and its similarly curved pad. Then she changed the horse's bridle for a halter and cross-tied her in the aisle. Glory would not be in anybody's way there, because although several horses occupied nearby stalls, the closest human was a stablehand working at some distance from us.

With this amount of privacy, I stepped away for a second to phone Sarah and tell her I'd made a side trip but would be back soon.

By now Whitney had begun grooming the horse, scrubbing with the currycomb in small circles. I dared to ask her, "Has your mom always been jealous over your dad, or is this unusual?"

"Sometimes she's joked about it, but this is the first time she's acted seriously worried. And it's weird, because Mom hired Linda herself, based on good things she'd heard about her work. They got along okay at the beginning; even though Mom is so picky, Linda usually rolled with it. But after a while she started giving both Linda and Robert such a hard time, I don't know why they didn't quit." The teen paused for a second, biting her lip. "Tuesday night, Mom was absolutely out of control, screaming at Dad about this supposed affair. Finally, I got in between them, which I guess was a stupid thing to do. I told Mom she was imagining things, obsessing over nothing, and she should get help. Meaning a shrink, which I'm sure she knew."

Out of the mouths of babes, I thought, even though Whitney was no longer a child. "What did she say to that?"

"She slapped my face." The girl reddened, but also tried to laugh it off. "Guess I should've expected it, but she hasn't done anything like that since I was a little kid."

I could imagine what a shock the blow must have been to a young woman of seventeen, almost an adult.

"It's not like what I said was so outrageous," Whitney went on. "Mom *was* seeing a therapist for a while, where we lived before. I don't know why she got so mad—unless she believed me about the pudding, after all." The girl paused in her grooming and faced me. "Cassie, do you think I should tell the cops I messed with the food at the reception? I'm worried that if I do, Adele could sue my parents. They'd probably blame each other, and it might turn into an even bigger mess than it is already."

Whitney could be right about that. "Maybe your folks could tell Detective Bonelli it was an accident. The caterer needed more flour and you grabbed the wrong kind. Then, when Adele got sick, you realized it could have been your fault, but you were too scared to say anything."

The teen thought this over. "That could work, if I could count on Mom's support. Maybe she'd go along just to avoid gossip, but . . . it feels like we're at war lately. I had Glory entered in a show next month, and now Mom's forbidden me to go. Some days she even threatens to sell Glory." Whitney switched to a large brush and started polishing her horse's coat with brisk strokes, until it glowed like copper. "She's gotten crankier than ever, too. She used to fuss over Leya and baby-talk to her, but now if she gets underfoot Mom yells and stomps to scare her away."

That did sound like a major change, I thought. "Gee, and she seemed so concerned about the cat when she first brought her to my shop."

Though Whitney was facing half away from me, I saw a tear side down her cheek. "I was upset when Dad took Leya to your place, and I really miss her . . . but maybe he was right. The way things are at home these days, she's probably safer with you."

Chapter 16

When I arrived back at my shop, I parked in the rear and hauled the bags of litter into a storage closet. I washed my hands in the first-floor powder room and made my way to the front sales area, where I found Bonelli shooting the breeze with Sarah. That made me glad I hadn't told my assistant exactly where my "side trip" was taking me, even though she probably would have known better than to share the information with the detective.

Bonelli sat on one of the stools in our sales area and held an open bottle of water, no doubt provided by Sarah. A small plate of chocolate-chip cookies also rested on the counter between them.

"Cassie, you sound out of breath," the detective commented, never one to miss the smallest detail.

I explained about the thirty-pound bags and quickly changed the subject. "You've got a new look, I see."

Bonelli had trimmed a few inches off her usually chin-length dark bob, and instead of gray roots it sported a few subtle reddish highlights. On the job, she always wore some version of a uniform, but today it took a summery turn—a lightweight navy jacket with rolled-up sleeves over a pale blue polo shirt and pressed khakis.

"Thanks. Lou gave me a gift certificate to a salon at the mall, for Mother's Day, and I just got around to using it. Pretty sad when your husband has to give you that big of a hint, eh?"

Sarah laughed. "Well, a busy lady like you sometimes needs reminding."

The detective ran a hand through her straight hair, a brisk, tomboyish gesture. "I have to admit, it is a lot easier to take care of this way. And Lou seems to like it okay."

I got some water for myself out of our small refrigerator, slid onto my customary stool behind the counter and snagged a cookie of my own. "I don't suppose you dropped by just to discuss your makeover, though."

Sarah turned to me. "She says she was up at Chester's yesterday and found out a few more things."

"I stopped by there around five thirty so I could interview his neighbors as they were getting home from work," Bonelli said. "One young couple claimed they haven't lived there very long and seldom even saw the people in the ranch house, much less spoke to them. The fellow who lives right in back of them, Bob Smiley, was more receptive. He said he'd visited the Tillmans and talked with them sometimes over the years."

My assistant nodded. "He visited once when I was there. Seemed very nice. He's interested in sports, and drew Chester out about his experiences writing for the papers and covering games on the radio. Bob seemed impressed by the celebrities Chester had met and interviewed over the years. It was a kind thing to do, I thought, and seemed to keep Chester's wits sharper. I don't think Bob has come around much, though, since Bernice died."

"I asked Smiley about that. He said he was between jobs for a while, but now he's back to work and hasn't had the time. He acted sorry to hear about Bernice's death and told me he'd try to look in on Chester again soon."

I picked up on the detective's turn of phrase, since she never used words carelessly. "You say he 'acted' sorry?"

"When I'm doing interviews at a scene, I never take anything people say at face value. He sounded sincere enough."

"What's his new job?" I asked.

"He was vague about that, said it was part-time, in retail. But he's also picking up extra bucks by helping out a local contractor, Superior Home Renovations. They're working on the house a block or so away from Chester's."

"Oh, yes," said Sarah. "That's turning into a big project. They're putting on a second story and adding to the back. When Robin and I are at Chester's house, we can hear them sawing and hammering half the day."

Bonelli turned thoughtful. "You'd think that would annoy Bob, too. Maybe the guy hired him partly so he wouldn't complain about the noise."

"Chester told Sarah and Robin that he's hatching a plan to catch his burglar," I remembered. "Did he mention that to you?"

"No." The detective's smile slipped sideways. "Maybe he was smart enough not to. If there is a thief, that would be a seriously stupid thing to try to do."

"Yes, I'm worried," Sarah said. "His caretaker only comes three times a week, and she doesn't stay overnight, so he's still alone then."

"I can ask the Dalton PD to have a car cruise by his place at night," Bonelli said, "though I doubt they'll want to make the effort."

I locked eyes with Sarah. "Did you ask Angela about the Dalton cop who was accused of theft a while ago?"

She passed along Robin's story, about the officer who might have stolen a man's iPod during a traffic stop. "I don't know if there's any truth to it," Sarah added.

"I don't, either." Bonelli made a quick jot in her small, vinyl-covered notebook. "But I'll see what I can find out. For what it's worth, I'm also going to research Superior Home Renovations and maybe give them a call."

Since she seemed to be ferreting out everyone's secrets, anyway, I thought it wise to tell her that Donald Foster had brought Leya in to be boarded, because of all the "disruption" in their household.

"She's turned out in the playroom now," Sarah told Bonelli. "Want to meet her?"

The detective, more of a dog lover, paused briefly. "Why not? Always a chance she might turn out to be evidence!"

Sarah stayed out front while Bonelli joined me in the play-room. Leya already had made it to the top of a tall, carpeted cat tree, and her bushy tail hung gracefully off the platform to one side. She looked much more relaxed and confident than when she'd been cowering under the bed in the Fosters' guest room.

The spectacle even impressed our detective, though she still approached the longhaired diva gingerly before stroking her head. "She *is* beautiful. What kind did you say she was, again?"

"Himalayan. Sounds exotic, but it's really just a type of Persian with Siamese coloring—a light-toned body with dark points."

Bonelli looked amused. "Really, Cassie, how in the world do you keep track of all these breeds and the variations?"

I'd never even questioned that before. "To tell the truth, when I started grooming professionally, there were some types even I didn't know much about and had to read up on. But I guess I remember easily because I find them all interesting." I joined her in petting Leya. "At least she seems to have mellowed out since Donald brought her here."

"Considerate of him, to get her out of the line of fire." Bonelli crossed to one of the carpeted cubes and sat down. "Last I heard, Gillian still thinks Donald messed with the food at the reception, or maybe even put Whitney up to it."

"That's ridiculous." From what Whitney had told me, her father had nothing to do with the prank.

"Gillian did tell me one other disturbing story," the detective continued. "She said the brakes on her Acura have been making noise for a while. Donald told her it was probably the pads and he could replace them himself . . . I guess he's done it before. Thinking he'd fixed the problem, Gillian took the car out a couple of days ago and the brakes failed—she lost control just a few feet from their house and almost went into a ditch. That was one of the things they were fighting about Tuesday."

"Maybe Donald never got around to working on the car."

"That's what he claims. Gillian had it towed to a dealer, and they said the pads were fine but the rotors were shot, which is more serious. I guess they showed unusual wear, so now she thinks Donald sabotaged them. He knows she's the only one who drives the Acura."

That did sound a bit fishy, but I remained skeptical. "So, Donald doesn't know as much about cars as he thinks. He misdiagnosed the problem and never actually checked it out. That doesn't mean he's a killer."

With her customary wry expression, Bonelli stood to leave.

"No, it doesn't. But if anything did happen to his wife, a jury could have said he had means and opportunity. They'd only have to decide if he had sufficient motive."

My mother, Barbara McGlone, lives about forty-five minutes away from me in Morristown—which, compared to Chadwick, is almost urban. Up until last winter, she and I talked several times a week and had dinner together as often as once a month. But at the end of last year, Mom had started dating again for the first time since my father's death, three years ago.

Not that she'd launched into a wild social life—that never would have been her style—but she took up with someone I didn't much care for, at least in the beginning. I'd met him, in fact, before Mom had. Harry Bock, a divorced local architect, had boarded his cat at my shop and then threatened to sue me after she'd developed a nasty rash. Mom, a paralegal with the Morristown firm of McCabe, Preston & Rueda, had interceded on my behalf. For her and Harry, the rest was romantic history.

At least now I didn't have to picture her spending every night in front of her TV alone. She also called me less often just to make sure I was okay (a good thing, considering how much trouble I tended to get myself into), or to hint around that Mark and I should tie the knot before I was too old to give her grandchildren (also a good thing, since he and I agreed we both liked our relationship as it was, for the time being). I'd gotten in the habit of calling Mom at least once a week, on Sunday night, no matter what.

But she'd been on her way out to a movie with Harry this past Sunday, so our conversion had been brief.

My talks with Whitney Foster and Angela Bonelli raised

some questions that Mom probably could answer. It was Thursday night now, and I didn't think she'd mind another call to share her legal expertise. Sitting amidst the cats on my living room sofa, I punched her number.

Mom had caller ID and answered the phone with a cheerful "Hi, Cassie!" I had to admit her spirits seemed better since she had been dating Harry, and she didn't pull that clichéd lonely-mother act as often, implying that she never heard from me. We chatted for a few minutes about what was new with each of us, and she enthused about Sunday's movie, a weighty historical drama. I was sure it would get many Oscar nominations, though it wouldn't have been my kind of thing.

As soon as I could, without being too obvious, I got around to the ulterior motive for my call. I gave Mom the general outline of the Fosters' situation, not mentioning any of them by name.

"The wife in this marriage seems hell-bent on accusing her husband of adultery, though he and the supposed other woman both deny it," I told her. "Could that work in the wife's favor if she has more money than he does? The guy seems to have a good job, but if she either earns more or inherited a pile, could she end up paying him alimony?"

I heard Mom sigh. "That depends on so many things— how long they've been married, whether either of them gave up career possibilities to support the other or to relocate, who did more of the child care . . . But off the top of my head, I'd say no. If he's been working full-time and makes a good living, I don't think any judge would require her to support him."

That made sense to me. "If she could prove he cheated, though—and she didn't have any big inheritance of her own—could *she* demand alimony?"

"That might be more likely, but she also has a career,

right? And from what you said, her daughter is almost of legal age. He might be required to help with support of the daughter—college tuition, and all that—but not of his ex-wife." Mom paused. "Again, Cassie, when lawyers get involved, anything can happen, but all I can tell you is what would be most likely."

And of course, I thought, there could be hidden aspects to the Fosters' marriage, about which I knew nothing, that could come out during divorce proceedings. Matisse jumped on my lap for a cuddle, drawn by the fact that I was talking to *someone* and jealous that it wasn't her. Massaging her dense, tricolored fur helped to counteract my dark thoughts—somewhat.

My mother was still musing on the Fosters' situation, her logical brain clicking away. "If Gillian has most of the money, the only way her husband would be almost sure to get it would be if she died."

That grabbed my attention. "What?"

"Well, unless they were divorced, or she cut him out of her will. Otherwise, a spouse automatically inherits everything."

"Yes," I realized, "of course."

Long after I'd gotten off the phone, this simple and obvious fact preoccupied my thinking. Still stroking Matisse, I thought about Gillian's near accident, which she blamed on her husband either neglecting to repair the brakes on her Acura or deliberately sabotaging them.

Whether or not he was involved with Linda the designer, did Donald Foster have a financial motive to murder his wife? That seemed absurd, until I considered how long he had persevered in their marriage, despite Gillian's difficult temperament. If it was for her money, he might be starting to think the aggravation wasn't worth it . . . but if they divorced, he might be worse off. And which of them would get custody of Whitney, who obviously preferred her father?

So much better if Gillian was completely out of the way . . .

I thought of a twist on the old joke. *Just because you're paranoid doesn't mean someone isn't out to kill you.*

Chapter 17

On Friday morning, I finally got around to bringing Mango to the Chadwick Veterinary Clinic to get his blood work done. It wasn't that I didn't care about his health, or even that my mind was preoccupied with other issues. I always dreaded bringing Mango to the vet under any circumstances. Just getting him into his carrier was a struggle—even for someone with my skill and experience—and things generally went downhill from there.

At my apartment, Mark had been able to hold the orange tabby and poke and prod him with very little drama. But whatever the reason—maybe the first faint whiff of antiseptic—by the time we took a seat in the waiting room, Mango began softly growling in his carrier. Another vet, where I used to live, told me her staff had posted warnings such as *Danger— will bite!* all over Mango's chart. They could vaccinate him on the fly, but for a more thorough exam and blood work, he had to be at least mildly sedated.

The routine always depressed me slightly, because it seemed so harrowing for the poor cat. It also embarrassed me, as if I were somehow responsible for his being so difficult to handle. But I'd gotten Mango as a five-year-old rescue and had little idea of what he'd gone through in his early years. Luckily, our vet these days was Mark, who knew that I didn't terrorize or abuse my cats at home.

A tech ushered us, with a smile, into one of the examining rooms. Most of the staff at the clinic knew by now that Mark and I were a couple.

I set Mango's square gray carrier on the stainless steel table and, while we were alone, tried to talk some sense to him. "C'mon pal. Jeez, it's just Mark. You like him fine when he comes to the apartment!"

But the tabby remained haunted by some trauma from his past, I guess, and my reassurances fell on deaf, pointed ears.

Dr. Coccia himself stepped through the door a few minutes later. When he heard the rumbling protests coming from the carrier, he smiled at me. "I see that Mango is as delighted to be here as ever."

"Unfortunately. I didn't want to let him out, because I figured you might need to take him in back and sedate him."

Mark ruefully studied my pet, who spat at him through the mesh window in response. "If it were something simple like a shot, we could probably just hold him down with a big towel. But when we're drawing blood, too much could go wrong. Besides, I'd always rather keep an animal as calm as possible. I wouldn't want to risk a heart attack or a stroke."

Though I knew the danger was real, I couldn't resist a macabre joke. "For him or for you?"

"Ha-ha. Mango's the older guy in this scenario, if you adjust for cat years." Mark picked up the carrier. "We won't totally knock him out—a light gas should do it, and he'll shake that off pretty fast. We'll keep him here for a few hours to recover, though."

I knew that was my cue to leave. On the way out, I asked, "By the way, how did things go with the three cats from the Tillman house?"

"Okay, I think. We released them to Chris Eberhardt, to go to the FOCA shelter, and sent along medications for two of them. I haven't heard anything since."

Mark said I'd get a call when Mango was ready to come home, and I thanked him. Though sedating a cat made a simple blood draw more expensive, I suspected he'd give me a break on the bill, even if he didn't admit to it.

After our relationship became serious, Mark had implied that he'd be glad to treat my cats for free. But I insisted on paying the same rate as everyone else, as long as I could afford it. I knew that Mark and his partner, Maggie, did a lot of pro bono work, and I'd rather see the really needy cases benefit from their generosity.

The day outside had turned overcast and muggy. I hadn't come prepared for rain, so I walked briskly back to my shop, fitting in some much-needed exercise.

Sarah was already on the job, of course. She asked after Mango's health, and I gave her an update.

"Poor little guy, I hope he'll be okay," she said. "Even though he almost scared me away from this job, when I first tried out for you!"

"He was scaring off all my prospective assistants," I confessed to her with a laugh. I remembered how my orange menace had flattened his ears and hissed at Sarah when we'd started to work on him. She had flinched a bit, but stood her ground. "That was the acid test—whether they had the nerve to work with Mango. One girl burst into tears, and a couple people gave up immediately."

"But I hung in there," she recalled proudly.

"That's right. And you have ever since!"

When Sarah and I took our lunch break, I retreated to the playroom to phone Dawn, whom I hadn't talked to in a few days. She actually had tried a Summer Solstice Sale, promoting it among her known Wiccan and neo-hippie customers, and saw a slight boost in her business. She said she was still mulling the possibility of taking mail orders.

"Even though I already have a website, it's designed just to lure people into the store," she reminded me. "Every once in a while I will send merchandise to someone, as a favor, but I've always been reluctant to get into taking orders as a major part of my business. I'd probably have to get an assistant just to handle that, which would eat into my profits, anyway. What do you think?"

I saw her dilemma. "I think you're right to consider all the angles before you make any new moves. Since the summer promotion worked well, why not try that for every new season, every holiday, and see how it goes?"

Dawn murmured agreement. "I could make up a mailing list, ask Keith to design flyers for me, and send them out to my regulars. That would cost a little, but not nearly as much as shipping goods all over the country."

Keith, her lanky, brown-bearded significant other, was a sought-after graphic artist. He lived and worked in a loft across town, in a former commercial building.

"Sounds like a good plan," I told Dawn.

When she asked what was new with me, I brought her up to date on the situations with Chester and the Fosters, and told her Bonelli was looking into both cases. I kept to myself, though, any sensitive information, such as the possibility of a dirty cop on the Dalton force, and Gillian's claims that her husband and/or her interior designer were out to kill her.

When asked about Mark's rehearsal with Quintessence, though, I did describe Tracy's brazen attempt to put the moves on him and how I'd handled it.

Dawn howled with laughter over the phone. "Catwoman unsheathed her claws, eh? I won't say I didn't know you had it in you, because I've seen you face down even tougher characters. But I'll bet you surprised the hell out of Tracy!"

"Well, I meant to scare her off, and I hope it worked. It's not that I don't trust Mark, but he shouldn't have to put up with stuff like that. If he gets a chance to perform with the group sometime, for real, he might think twice if he'll have to watch out for the niece of the keyboard guy. I mean, a woman has no right to sexually harass a man, either!"

"Absolutely not," said Dawn, though I heard a smile in her voice. "If he's not interested."

"Of course he's not interested!"

"I know, I'm just yanking your chain." I heard the bell over her shop door ring, and she lowered her voice. "I'd better go, now—I may actually have a customer. We'll talk again soon."

Back up front, Sarah had just hung up from a phone call of her own. "Robin says Chester's all excited," she told me. "He thinks he has proof that somebody got into his house last night. He claims he set a trap for the guy, and it worked."

"Does she have any idea what he's talking about?" I asked.

"He wouldn't tell her, said she needed to see for herself. She promised to come to his place around three thirty, but she's worried about what she'll find."

I could see Sarah also was troubled. "Maybe she should ask the cops to swing by, too, just in case."

My assistant frowned. "The Dalton police have been brushing off Chester's complaints from the beginning and already have him labeled as a troublemaker. I guess Robin wants to make sure there's really something to his story before she calls them again. I could try to persuade her, though . . ."

I agreed that might be a good idea. "Sarah, if you want to take off early and go help her out, it's okay with me. We haven't got any more grooming jobs today, just one more cat to turn out and the evening feeding. I can handle all that myself."

She looked apologetic. "Are you sure? It's just that Robin said Chester sounded very worked up, and I know folks with dementia can sometimes be hard to handle. She's younger and stronger than me, and she does have nursing experience. Still, two of us might do better than just one."

"Go!" I told her. "I have to pick up Mango after work and bring him home, but after that maybe I'll pop over to see how you guys are making out."

My feisty feline friend already had shaken off most of the sedation when I picked him up at the Chadwick Veterinary Clinic, and of course his only "procedure" had been routine blood work. It would take another day or two for the results. So I didn't feel there was any risk in leaving him in my apartment while I drove to Chester's place. I confined Mango to my bedroom, though, because if his buddies caught a whiff of that medicinal smell on his fur, they might squabble with him. It's a common problem, though nobody's ever figured out if cats actually don't recognize a feline friend until that odor has worn off.

Around five thirty, I found a lineup of cars in front of Chester's homely little ranch house—Sarah's Camry sedan, Robin's dark gray Ford Fusion, and a white police cruiser bearing the Dalton town seal. I guessed someone had managed to convince the cops that Chester's "evidence" was worth a look, after all.

The front door stood ajar, but I knocked on the jamb, anyway, and Sarah let me in. "The police actually came?" I whispered to her.

"One, anyhow." She accompanied me to the kitchen, where a rangy man stood talking to Chester and Robin. The cop wore navy pants, a lighter blue shirt and a peaked cap with the same official seal as his patrol car.

Not wanting to interrupt, I circled around until I could view the "crime scene" for myself. The floor just inside the back door looked as if someone had spilled a full two-pound bag of white rice. Some grains were pushed back an angle, as if the door had been opened inward.

Meanwhile Robin noticed my presence and introduced me to Officer Marty Brewer. The tall, thin policeman shook my hand with a smile that spanned the width of his narrow face. He gave off a boyish vibe, though a few creases around his eyes suggested he might be nearing forty.

"Is Chester right?" I asked him straight out. "Did someone get into his house last night?"

Brewer cocked his head and squinted in skepticism. "More like his imagination is running away with him, as usual."

The older man stepped forward and spoke for himself. "Cassie will believe me!" He stabbed his arthritic finger toward an area deeper into the kitchen. "Look there—footprints! I left the door unlocked last night. He sneaked in, didn't see the rice and walked on it. Then maybe he realized I'd set a trap, got scared and snuck back out again!"

I *could* detect some long, oval outlines where the white grains had been crushed or scuffed aside. Though they could have been made by shoes, they weren't enough to prove a stranger had entered the house, and certainly not enough to identify that person. It would have taken mud, or at least soft dirt, to capture a real impression of a sole.

"Did you *hear* someone come in?" I asked Chester.

He frowned. "Naw, I tried my damndest to stay awake, but I couldn't. I thought I would still hear if someone crunched on the rice. But my ears aren't that great anymore, either, and I guess I was too deep asleep. I could kick myself!"

Robin laughed, with a nervous edge. "If somebody came in here last night, thank God you *didn't* wake up. You'd probably have picked a fight with him and gotten yourself killed!"

"Maybe you're right," Chester conceded. "'Specially if it was the same guy who smothered Bernie."

Brewer scanned the ceiling for heavenly help. "Not that again! Chester, no one smothered your wife except those damn cats of hers. Glad you at least got rid of some of them."

I reflected on the scene for a minute, then asked the cop, "Can you get somebody to check for fingerprints on the back doorknob?"

He gave his head a half shake. "We checked after the wife died. No prints then except hers and his."

Of course, this was an entirely new situation, but Brewer didn't seem to consider it worth another visit by the fingerprint guy.

Chester still fumed about having slept through the supposed nighttime intrusion. "This mighta been the same guy who killed Bernice. Boy, I wish I'd stayed awake. I coulda used one of her old cast-iron skillets and brained him!"

Brewer planted his hands on his hips and regarded the homeowner as if he were a small child. "Chester, how do you know you didn't wake up sometime during the night? And went to check the door, and made those footprints yourself?"

The older man looked rattled for a second, then scoffed. "I'd know, I'd remember. I'm not crazy!"

Robin put a hand on Chester's arm to soothe his wounded ego. "Instead of spilling rice all over your kitchen, why don't you get some good locks and an actual alarm? I'll gladly buy them for you."

Though he seemed to consider this, he protested, "But then I'll never know."

"Know what?" Sarah asked gently.

"Who killed Bernice. And who's been stealing our stuff . . . is *still* stealing it."

Brewer's shoulders rose and fell in a deep sigh. "Mr. Tillman, nobody's taking your stuff. Nobody wants any of this old junk! You should just have it hauled away. Dan's even offered to do that for you." The cop jerked his head backward. "You could just chuck it all in one of his Dumpsters."

"Who's that?" I asked.

"Dan Pressley. He owns the company that's working on that house down the road."

I wondered how the house flipper would know so much about Chester's hoarding habits. But it was a small town, and I guessed cops and neighbors would talk about such things. Especially since there had been a death in the home.

Brewer had started out of the kitchen toward the front hall, when Sarah asked him, "So, it's okay if I sweep up all of this rice?"

"Someone better," he told her with a hard laugh. "That's slippery footing. Wouldn't want Chester to break his neck on his own 'trap.'" As Robin and I followed him to the door, Brewer dropped his voice a little. "Poor old guy. It's not really safe for him to be alone here at night. Hasn't he got kids, somebody he could move in with?"

Robin explained that Chester's grown children lived at a

distance, and they had talked about moving him to an assisted living home. "The nicest one around here is Mountainview," she said, "and it even has a dementia wing. But I think it's a little pricey. I don't know whether that's an issue for them."

Brewer scratched his scalp under the uniform cap. "Y'know, Dan probably would buy this place from him at a fair price. Might make it easier for Chester to afford the move."

"I'll mention that to his son," Robin said. "James heads up a construction company, himself."

The cop nodded with some enthusiasm. "That house they're working on started out just like this one, a run-down ranch from the nineteen seventies. Gonna be terrific, though, when they're done. Ought to bring up the property values in the whole neighborhood."

"Dalton sure could use more of that," Robin admitted.

As Brewer paused by the front door, sounds of vigorous sweeping from the kitchen reached our ears. He frowned and told Robin, "If you do get a good lock for that door, you might want to skip the alarm. Between Chester and his cats, it'll probably be going off at all hours, and we haven't got enough manpower to deal with that."

After Brewer drove away, Robin and I rejoined Sarah in the kitchen. I didn't see Chester and asked where he'd gone.

"Into his bedroom." Sarah dumped the last dustpan full of rice into the trash. "To sulk, I guess."

Robin told her what Brewer had suggested, about selling his house to help pay for the upscale assisted living facility.

"That might be a good plan," Sarah agreed. "And as long as Chester has help, there's really no reason why he can't go on living here until Mountainview has an opening. The biggest problem is this obsession of his, about someone breaking in."

"Of course," I reminded her, "if someone really is breaking in, that's an even bigger problem."

I knocked on the closed door of his room, and Chester mumbled that I could come in. He sat on the foot of his bed, and did seem to be brooding over the fact that the cop had not taken his "evidence" seriously.

This visit, I had remembered to bring a small notepad with me, and pulled it from my purse. "Chester, can you tell me everything you noticed missing around the time your wife . . . died, and since then? Be as specific as you can."

I interviewed him this way for about twenty minutes, which he told me was far more than the police ever had done. Chester's recall impressed me—obviously, he'd given the missing items a lot of thought—and again I reflected that he wasn't as addled as some people believed.

He also seemed to appreciate my effort to catalog his losses. "You really think you might be able to get some of my stuff back? Or at least to find out who took it?"

"I can't promise anything, but it's possible. With computers today, there are all kinds of ways to search."

Sarah knew I'd brought Mango to the clinic, and after I'd finished with Chester, she asked how my tabby was doing.

"He seemed pretty good, no aftereffects from being knocked out," I told her. "But he's stuck by himself in my room, so I still don't want to leave him alone too long."

"Go home, then," she told me. "Robin and I are going to hang around a little longer and make Chester some supper."

I said my goodbyes and headed out to my car. It was about six twenty, but the day was still warm and the sun still high in the sky. The slam of a vehicle door drew my attention toward Bob Smiley's house. I saw him exit his old red truck, a few tools visible in the flatbed, probably after a long day of working for the neighborhood contractor. His posture weary, Bob trudged up the flagstone path to his front door.

Maybe because I was watching him from the back, his closely shaved nape and army-green T-shirt struck a familiar note with me, especially combined with his rather discouraged-looking gait. I realized he very well might have been the man Dawn and I had run into—literally—when he was leaving the antiques store a few weeks ago.

The one Philip said had tried to sell him some '80s video games.

Chapter 18

Saturday morning, after Sarah and I had done the initial cleanup of the condos and feeding of the boarders, I retreated to the grooming studio with my laptop. For about twenty minutes, I searched online auction sites for objects that might have been pilfered from Chester Tillman's house. I found a bewildering amount of memorabilia for sale online, but nothing correlated closely with any of the items on the list I'd handwritten at Chester's place, and typed out for legibility the night before. I didn't want to spend too much time on the quest during work hours, leaving Sarah to staff the counter by herself.

Just as I was giving up on this project, I got a call on my cell from Becky. A visitor to FOCA the previous week had expressed some interest in adopting Autumn, and even sounded perfectly willing to deal with her health issues.

"She's coming back for a second visit Monday," Becky told me, "and I'd like Autumn to look her absolute best. Could you possibly stop by tomorrow and work your magic on that heavy coat of hers? I'll help you, naturally!"

The next day, of course, was Sunday, when both my shop

and FOCA would usually be closed. Also, I had made plans with Mark for the afternoon, but grooming one cat wouldn't take that long. I agreed to meet Becky at the shelter around ten a.m.

While on the phone, I'd heard someone come in the shop's front door, and as I pocketed my phone, raised voices reached me from the sales area. I left the studio and headed out to the playroom, where I met up with Sarah.

"What's up?" I asked her.

"Gillian Foster is here, and she wants Leya."

That was a surprise. I accompanied my assistant back to the sales counter, where Gillian wheeled upon me.

If I'd been startled by the recent changes in her husband's appearance, I was even more alarmed by Gillian's. She looked thinner, the rather aristocratic bone structure of her face now verging on haggard. Her usually sharp, hawklike hazel eyes had taken on a wilder cast. She wore makeup but, horror of horrors, she'd actually put her coral lipstick on crooked.

She seemed to struggle to control herself and spoke in a frosty tone. "I understand that my husband brought our cat here earlier this week without my knowledge. I've come to take her back. Your assistant"—she shot a glance at Sarah—"would not release her without your say-so, which I guess I can understand. But please tell her to bring Leya out here immediately."

The way Gillian was acting, I could easily believe the things Whitney had told me, about her treating the cat roughly these days. It wouldn't be the first case I'd heard of where someone upset with another member of the family, or with a romantic partner, took out their anger on a pet.

She tried to interpret my hesitation. "I'll pay you for the days she's been boarding here, of course."

I needed to stall, and this gave me the perfect opening.

"That won't be necessary. Your husband prepaid, enough for Leya to stay here for at least another month."

That seemed to startle Gillian. "Well, no matter. He shouldn't have brought her here in the first place, and I want her back, now."

Sarah glanced at me nervously, and I knew we both were dreading the outcome if we complied.

"I'm afraid I can't do that," I said. "Donald brought the cat here and paid in advance for her upkeep. That makes *him* my client. Legally, it wouldn't be right for me to hand her over to anyone else."

Under normal circumstances, I wouldn't hesitate to give a pet to someone's spouse, as long as I knew it was okay with the person who'd brought me the animal. But in this case, I didn't know. What if Donald deliberately had left Leya in my care because he was afraid his wife would abuse her?

This time, I was going to stand on ceremony.

As I could have predicted, Gillian's face went scarlet. "That's ridiculous. I bought the cat originally, so she's more mine than his! And if he paid you by credit card, it's got both our names on it."

"He paid with a personal check. It has just his name, and his signature."

She looked about to explode, and I felt glad that Sarah and I stood behind the sales counter, though it was only a little more than waist-high. I do have an alarm button under the counter to press, though, in case of a stickup or other emergency. I hoped I wouldn't need it.

Gillian let go a stream of curses such as I never would have expected to pass her lips, at least not when we'd first met. Of course, I knew a lot more about her these days. "You're just a snotty, ignorant kid with a crappy little business! You think you can hold on to a valuable animal that belongs to me, when I'm standing here in person demanding that she be returned? And as far as honoring my husband's wishes . . . let me tell you something about Donald. He's trying to kill me! That business with the porridge was just a test, I suppose. But this week he got serious, tampering with my car."

She must have read my silence—correctly—as skepticism, because she added, "I told your friend the police detective all about it. If you don't believe me, ask her."

I kept my voice level. "Detective Bonelli says there's no proof connecting him to either of those incidents."

"I'm not leaving here without that cat!"

Gillian started for the gap between the sales counter and the wall, trying to dash through the playroom door to the back of the shop. Just as swiftly, Sarah stepped sideways to block her. My assistant is only about five-four, her bulk more motherly than brawny. But decades of teaching in inner-city schools has made her pretty fearless, I guess.

Arms crossed over her chest, she braced herself like a stone statue, and her dark glare challenged Gillian—*Just try it, lady!*

The suburban social climber backed off so quickly that I hid a smile. Not willing to take us on in physical combat, Gillian threatened another means of attack.

"I'll sue you!" she shouted at me. "For keeping my cat and my money under false pretenses."

Technically, it's Donald's money, I thought, but wasn't about to point that out again. This time, I kept my mouth shut and only shrugged.

Gillian paced out the front door and slammed it so hard I feared the glass would break. Luckily, it stayed intact, along with my resolve.

I congratulated Sarah on calling the woman's bluff.

"She doesn't scare me," my assistant said, "but you see why I called you out here. What on earth is her problem?"

"Whatever it is, I'm really glad her husband stashed Leya here and paid us in the way that he did. I'd hate to hand any animal over to someone with that kind of temper!"

Gillian's visit left us both rattled, so after some thought I decided to report it to Bonelli. When I called her office phone I got a recording, then left a message. Just in case Gillian did try to sue, or cause us some other kind of trouble, it might help to have my side of the story on record with the Chadwick PD.

We closed the shop at noon, as per our usual Saturday schedule. That gave me a chance to take my list of missing items over to Towne Antiques.

Philip Russell flattened the sheet of paper on the glass top of his sales counter. A tall floor fan whirring a few feet from us dispelled some of the musty smell that pervaded the antiques shop on warm days like this one. Still, I enjoyed a sense of traveling back through time, while surrounded by beautiful ceramics, amateur oil paintings, UFO-shaped chandeliers and colorful, 1960s Pop Art furniture.

"Yes, I do recognize some of these Nintendo games," he told me. "I may even still have a few of them in stock."

"Did you get them from Bob Smiley?" I asked.

"Nooo, I don't think so. Bob tried to sell me a few earlier this month, but they weren't especially rare. He seemed disappointed at the prices I offered him, and he took them all with him when he left."

So I had part of my answer—Smiley *had* been peddling some electronic games. "Does he bring things to your shop often?"

"Now and then. He's sold me some toys that were worth a bit more—vintage Star Wars and Star Trek stuff."

"Any of it on this list?"

Philip narrowed his eyes and went over the items again. "Maybe this model kit. I sold that earlier this spring. Can't remember whether it came from Bob, but it's the kind of thing he tended to bring me."

Early spring . . . months before Bernice's death.

Supposedly he had been visiting Chester often, at that time, and chatting about the older man's experiences as a sports writer and announcer. Had Bob been smuggling things out of the Tillmans' house even then?

"Smiley never offered you any of these LPs, autographed pictures or baseball cards?" I pointed to one particular item. "This is the doll Chester lost, the one you said was probably an American Girl design. Did Bob bring that in?"

The antiques dealer shook his head sadly. "If I ever had anything like that I would have told you, back when you first described it to me."

I still held out a slim hope that I could recover some of the pieces that meant the most to Chester. "How about a baseball signed by Roger Maris? Chester said it was under a protective dome."

Philip smiled. "I'd sure remember seeing that! I'd be keeping it under a dome, too, and under lock and key. But no, sorry."

Discouraged, I took the list back, folded it and stuck it in my purse again.

"Don't give up, though," he told me. "Search online and see if those things show up for sale anywhere else. Look on eBay, Etsy, and any specialty sites you can find. If Bob took them, or someone else did, he could be trying for the best possible price by putting them out on the web. Even if you do find something, though, I don't know how easy it will be to trace the seller. Maybe someone would have to pose as a collector to flush him out."

That sounded like a job for the actual cops, although probably not the blasé Dalton force. "Thanks for your time, anyway. Even what you told me could be helpful."

At least I knew now that Smiley *had* been trying to sell old toys and games, and could easily have picked them up at Chester's home.

Later that afternoon, Bonelli called me.

"In it up to your neck again, aren't you, McGlone." It wasn't a question.

"Don't tell me Gillian Foster went crying to you? I just expected her to sue me, not try to have me arrested." I explained that Donald had brought me the family cat and strongly implied Leya might be safer with me, at the moment, than in their home. "To give her back to Gillian would have been to go against the wishes of a paying customer."

"You may be within your rights," Bonelli conceded, "but putting yourself in the middle of their marital spat might not be the wisest move, either."

"There's only one person who can make me return Leya, and that's Donald. Technically he hired me, and brought her here for a reason. If he's found another way to keep her safe, or honestly feels there's no more danger, I'm perfectly willing to give the cat back to him."

"That sounds fair. I'll have a word with him about it." The detective paused, switching tracks. "You've gotten yourself on the radar of Chief Hill, too, and he's not pleased."

"The Dalton guy? How come? I've never even met him."

"Maybe not, but he said you were up at the Tillman house yesterday encouraging Chester to make wild accusations—his words, not mine—and insisting someone dust the back doorknob for fingerprints."

I also gave her an accurate account of that incident. "Sure,

Chester's stunt with the rice on the floor was dumb, but it does look as if someone came in his house. Officer Brewer wasn't taking it seriously at all."

"Well, Hill was already ticked off because I had a chat with the guy from Superior Home Renovations, the one who's flipping houses in that neighborhood. The chief insisted Dan Pressley is doing a service to the town, and we shouldn't go making trouble for him."

I smiled to myself. "Hill's going to regret his invitation to let you investigate the case."

"Yeah, I'm like a vampire," Bonelli agreed in a rare moment of whimsy. "Once you let me in, it's hard to get rid of me. I was only asking Pressley if he or his workers had seen anyone strange hanging around Tillman's house, but I didn't really expect that they would have, since they only work during the daytime."

"You said you also talked to Bob Smiley, right? He lives in back of Chester, past that little patch of woods?" I told her about the collectibles Bob had tried to sell to the antiques shop.

"Interesting," the detective said. "Sounds like he might be worth another visit."

"Try around five thirty or six. That's when I saw him getting out of his truck yesterday."

"Will do." I heard a pause on the line. "The Dalton cop who came out to check on Chester's story . . . did you say his name was Brewer?"

"That's right, why?"

"Same guy who beat the rap, a couple of years back, for stealing the iPod during that traffic stop."

Chapter 19

FOCA already maintained a designated room where the volunteers did light grooming of their rescues, so on Sunday Becky and I used that space to tidy up Autumn. I commented that the tortoiseshell's coat actually seemed to have grown healthier and bushier over her two weeks at the shelter.

"We've got her on a low-protein diet for her kidneys," Becky told me, "so she's not as dehydrated. The downside is, she's more prone to matting now."

I noticed that, too. The tortoiseshell tolerated my initial brushing well enough, but objected when I tried to work out the more stubborn knots in her long coat. I misted the air around the table with my herbal calming spray, and Becky used several gentle but firm holds that I had taught her to keep the cat from squirming free.

"It's great that you found a potential adopter so soon," I said.

"Yeah, she saw Autumn on our website and read the sad story—that her elderly owner had died and she needed a home to live out her last years comfortably. This woman is older, herself, and one of those big-hearted folks who's actually looking for a cat with special needs."

"Sounds like a match made in heaven."

The mention of special diets pulled my thoughts back to Mango's ailment. His blood work had revealed, as Mark expected, that my aging tabby suffered from hyperthyroidism. Unfortunately, controlling that took more than just a change of food. I'd begun giving him tablets embedded in pill pockets, but already he was getting wise to that, eating the pockets and spitting out the pills. The evening before, I'd tried giving him the pill by hand; I succeeded after several attempts, but came close to getting bitten. I worried that my luck might not hold up over the long haul.

"Winky should be easy to place, too, since he's very cute and lively," Becky went on. "Sugarman could be more of a challenge—he's more ordinary-looking and on the shy side."

"He'd also be well suited, though, to a mature person who just wants a quiet companion," I said.

"Actually, Chris and I have an idea along that line. Once or twice, we've visited nursing homes, or geriatric wards in hospitals, and brought along kittens. The seniors always brighten up and want to pet them. Of course, kittens are easy, because they're always friendly, and can't bite or scratch hard enough to do anyone much harm. But we've been wondering if we should bring some older cats, too."

"Sugarman might be a good candidate for that," I suggested. "I've also heard of nursing homes that keep a couple of cats on the premises, and they wander around visiting the residents. You might be able to place a couple that way."

And FOCA might need to make some room in their shelter, I thought, if Chester moved to assisted living and needed to send them his last two cats. The whole situation was very sad, and once again made me angry that his grown children weren't doing more to help.

Finally, we'd completed Autumn's transformation from grungy to glamorous, and returned her to her stainless steel cage. Although FOCA tried to provide their animals with all the necessary comforts, Autumn was used to a house to roam around and a loving owner. I wished both her and Becky success in their meeting with the prospective adopter the next day.

I'd walked to the shelter, because it was only about five blocks from my shop and the weather was clear. Eleven a.m.—just enough time to clean up a bit before Mark came by. He'd proposed a picnic in Riverside Park, and I wasn't about to turn that down!

As I've mentioned already, cooking is not my strong suit, but I at least made the sandwiches for our park excursion— deli-sliced chicken, organic and free range, with mayo on whole wheat bread. Mark probably put more effort and finesse into the salad of dark greens and tomato chunks that he brought along. Both in shorts, we spread out a blanket under a shade tree, not far from the river bank, to eat our picnic. Plenty of other people had already done the same.

Mark also brought along his guitar, figuring he'd use the leisure time to practice some new pieces he'd been working on with Stan. After lunch, he surprised me with a lively version of "Stray Cat Strut," which I'd playfully challenged him to learn. Mark didn't really know the words, though, so while he concentrated on his fingerwork I sang along.

The singer was supposed to be a tomcat, but I had fun with the lyrics, anyway.

I slink down the alleyway looking for a fight . . .

A family of four, passing by, actually stopped to listen to

us. When we finished, they grinned and applauded our efforts. We probably should have handed out our business cards; they might have been amused by our professions.

After they moved on, Mark confided, "I pretty much taught myself that one."

"Really? It sounded great. You're getting better all the time."

"Thanks. You weren't bad, either. I never heard you sing before! You could give Tracy a run for her money."

"Hold that thought," I purred.

He laughed self-consciously. "Speaking of which, Stan thinks I might be able to sit in with Quintessence for a real gig later on this summer."

"That would be terrific."

Mark might have heard a note of caution in my voice, because he added, "I mentioned my problems with Tracy to him. I made light of it, at first, just to see how he'd react. He got the message, though. I guess it isn't the first time she's made some guy in the band uncomfortable."

"Oh, yeah?" I wondered again what the woman's issue was. She was attractive enough not to need to chase after everything in pants.

"Herb, her uncle, told Stan that she just went through a bad breakup, so I guess she's rebounding pretty hard. Anyway, Stan said I shouldn't worry, he'd deal with it. I just hope he's subtle—I don't need Tracy as an enemy, either!"

"No, you don't. I have a feeling she can fight dirty." *And I'm sure she's already not too crazy about me.*

A tinnier version of the Stray Cats hit drifted from the pocket of my shorts, and I checked my cell phone. I didn't recognize the number, but it was local, so I answered.

Donald Foster's voice sounded weary and apologetic. "Cassie, I know Gillian went to your shop yesterday and raised a stink about the cat, and I'm sorry. I guess it wasn't fair of me to put you in this position. Can you bring Leya back to us?"

His defeated tone concerned me. "Are you sure she'll be okay at your house?" It would be awkward to also ask if he and Whitney would be okay, though I wanted to.

"Yes, she'll be fine. I think that will be the best solution, to keep the peace. Things have settled down a bit—we've put the basement work on hold for a while."

Okay, he was sticking with his story that the cat was disturbed by the noise. "I don't want to cause any problems with Gillian, of course. But if the construction starts up again, feel free to park Leya here with me anytime."

"For sure. And keep the check I gave you. With all this drama, you've certainly earned it."

I'd been dodging concerned looks from Mark, and I didn't want to interrupt our time together on a customer's whim. "Did you want me to bring her back today? I'm not at the shop right now."

"No, no, it's your day off, and I'm sure you made other plans. But can you swing by tomorrow morning, say, around ten? I won't be here, but Whitney and Herta should, and Gillian definitely will be."

Great, I might have to face Gillian by myself. Oh, well, why should she give me a hard time? She'll be getting what she wanted.

"Okay, I'll do that," I said.

Donald hesitated before adding, "Gillian gets wrought up sometimes, but she's had kind of a tough life. She grew up an only child, and I guess her parents were the same as she is now, maybe worse. Both very high achievers, and pressured her to be the same. To get top grades, take on all kinds of extracurriculars, get a high-paying job. It was almost literally, 'Unless you're perfect, we won't love you.'"

I said nothing, but thought of the inspirational slogans on

Gillian's website, and even the samplers in her guest room—as if she had to have the perfect home, too.

"I saw through all that," Donald went on, "and told her she didn't have to try so hard all of the time. When we were first married, she did seem to relax a little more. Maybe getting older has revived those anxieties for her. She was taking some medication for a while that I think helped her, and so did this hobby of renovating houses. But our latest restoration project seems to be making things worse instead of better."

It was my first hint that Gillian's obsessiveness might be more than just a personality defect, but a real mental illness. "That must be very hard on you and your daughter."

Donald sighed. "Yes, she does tend to nag Whitney sometimes. Usually about her weight, though the poor girl certainly isn't fat! But by now Whitney's mounted some heavy defenses of her own against Gillian." He chuckled dryly. "She probably can take care of herself!"

It was quite a confession on Donald's part, and I hardly knew how to respond. "I just hope things settle down for all of you soon. I'll bring the cat back tomorrow, then. If you're sure it'll be all right."

"Yeah, Cassie, everything's going to be okay," he assured me. "I'll make certain of that."

His vow lingered in my mind as I tucked the phone back into my pocket. I met Mark's curious eyes and sighed deeply. "You won't believe this!"

Chapter 20

"*As you requested, Ms. Foster, I'm returning Leya to you. You'll notice that the balding area on her tail has started to grow back, so it seems that she was over grooming herself from stress. After you spoke to Detective Bonelli, I also asked her advice; she agreed that, since your husband paid Leya's board, I was within my rights to wait until I had his okay to bring her back home. Donald has assured me that the most disruptive renovations in your house are over now. If that situation changes, though, I'll be happy to accommodate Leya again.*"

I guess I am my mother's daughter, because when necessary I can craft a prim, rather legalistic speech, and I rehearsed this one on my way to the Foster house. If I had to hand the cat back to Gillian, I wanted to put her on notice that even the local PD knew I had misgivings about doing so, and if anything bad happened, we'd all hold her responsible. In reality, our local cops don't deal directly with animal cruelty cases, but I also have clout with the county SPCA.

When I pulled into the driveway of the historic Ramsford-Cooper house, now better known as the Fosters' fortress, I tried to determine who was home by the other vehicles parked there.

No sign of Donald's silver BMW, so he must be at work. Whitney's bike was absent, too. I saw only a glossy cream-colored Acura that, because of the fracas over the faulty brakes, I knew must be Gillian's.

Odd . . . Donald had said that at least Herta would also be around. Maybe she commuted to their house by bus, or even lived near enough to walk? At any rate, the quiet, conscientious maid probably wouldn't be much of a buffer—she seemed unlikely to take my side against her strong-willed employer.

Oh, well, at least I had my speech. *"As you requested, Ms. Foster, I'm returning Leya to you . . ."*

Toting Leya in her carrier, I climbed the three steps to the front porch and rang the pewter doorbell, a colonial pineapple design. I heard it chime inside, but no one answered; rang it a second time with the same result. A twist of the knob confirmed the door was locked.

Great. Does Gillian want her cat, or doesn't she? I hope Donald told her I was coming at ten!

I wondered if she could be in another part of the house, or even the yard, where she couldn't hear the bell. Leaving the cat on the porch, I stole around the back to have a look. The garden was still weedy, and a shed probably intended for a lawnmower and other large tools needed shoring up and repainting.

I smelled the smoke before I saw it—seeping out around the low, bulkhead doors that probably led to the cellar. I grabbed a big ring attached to one door and yanked, but it didn't budge. There was a keyhole next to the ring—did the Fosters keep the outer doors locked?

No more time to waste. Retreating a few yards, I dialed 911. I gave the address and added, "It's the Ramsford-Cooper house. I think there's a fire in the basement."

While I waited for the trucks, I brought Leya back to my car. Then I rang the front doorbell again, even banged with my fists, and yelled for Gillian. I checked the rear, kitchen door and found that also locked.

By now I feared that, if Gillian was home, she might have more urgent things to deal with. If she still was capable of dealing with anything. Could she, or somebody else, be trapped in the cellar?

I stewed over this question for a minute, then decided to take action. The back shed was open, and inside I found an old, rusted shovel. I used the blade to whack the lockset on the bulkhead doors a couple of times. Finally, the old wood around the ring began to splinter, and with a good yank I was able to open one side.

The thick, noxious cloud that billowed out made me stagger back, and I realized I couldn't safely venture down the steps. I already heard sirens approaching, so I jogged back out front to meet the firefighters. As soon as their hook and ladder pulled up, they glimpsed for themselves the dark haze spreading across the back yard, and began to unreel the massive hose.

"Two people were supposed to be home," I told the captain, "and Gillian Foster's car is here. But the doors are locked and no one answers the bell."

Once the pros were on the job, I gave Sarah a quick call and told her what was happening.

"This business with the Fosters gets crazier by the day, doesn't it?" she marveled over the line.

"I know. Makes me wonder what more could happen."

I found out about fifteen minutes later, after the firefighters who had been hosing down the cellar finally put out the blaze.

The captain called me into the back yard. "You broke through these doors with the shovel?"

"Yes, but when I saw how thick the smoke was I didn't even try to go down. I was worried that, if someone was trapped in there, every minute might count."

He looked grim. "You were right about that, but I don't think even you could have gotten to the lady in time."

An icy sensation trickled down my back. "Lady?"

His radio came to life then, and he relayed to his chief, "Found a deceased Caucasian female inside, forty to fifty years old. Possibly the homeowner."

"They were able to ID Gillian with no problem," I told Mark on Tuesday evening. "Apparently she crawled some distance away from the fire, but she still died from smoke inhalation."

He and I were having dinner at Slice of Heaven, the town's best pizza parlor. It was a date we had made before my Monday had gone so terribly wrong. Mark insisted we go through with our plans, because he thought I needed a break from all the death and disaster. I had to agree with him.

We had ordered a mushroom-fontina pizza that came topped with a fried egg, parsley and thyme (what, no rosemary?). While we waited for it, I noticed that the popularity of the cool, modern restaurant, with its industrial pendant lights, concrete floor and tomato-red tables, worked in our favor. It was crowded for a weeknight, and all the other couples and groups chattered happily among themselves. This ambient noise let me and Mark talk about serious matters without having to worry about eavesdroppers.

Tonight, however, I could have done without the symbolism of the large, central brick oven, bright flames leaping within its arched doorway.

"Could they figure out how the fire started?" Mark asked me.

"Not right away. An investigator came out, and because of

the death they brought Bonelli in on the case, too. Last theory I heard was some problem with the cellar wiring. Of course, Donald and Nick had been working together on that."

Mark took a thoughtful swallow of his Chablis before reminding me, "And Gillian accused Donald of trying to kill her."

I hadn't forgotten about that. Admittedly, it didn't look good that her end came just a week after she accused him of neglecting—or maybe worsening—the faulty brakes on her car.

"Bonelli contacted Donald right away, of course," I told Mark. "He'd been at work, at his ad agency, since nine a.m. She said he sounded genuinely upset, but she's told me before that she doesn't take people's reactions at face value."

"Do you think he could have rigged beforehand something to catch fire, then locked Gillian in the cellar and headed off to work, so he'd have an alibi?" Mark shook his head. "That would take a pretty cold character."

"It would, and I really don't think Donald Foster is capable of that. I only know him superficially, of course, but his daughter thinks the world of him. And if he was faking concern for their cat's welfare, when he brought her to my shop, he deserves an Oscar for his acting."

"He might've liked Leya better than Gillian." A wry smile curved Mark's lips. "Meanwhile, you've still got the cat?"

I sipped my own wine before replying. "Until the dust settles. Her board's paid through the rest of the month. The cellar of the Foster house is being treated as a crime scene, and the fire not only damaged much of that area, but some of the structure underneath the first floor, too. It's got to be stabilized."

"I guess no one else was around yesterday? Not the daughter or the maid?"

"No, even though Donald thought they would be. Whitney was at the stable riding her horse, which is typical for her, and she has witnesses. But Herta said Gillian gave her the day off. According to Bonelli, it was short notice and unexpected. Herta said Gillian called her early that morning, unusually cheerful, and told her there wasn't much to do and she might as well enjoy the nice weather. Now that sounds out of character!"

"Hmm." Mark pondered this. "If *Donald* had given her the day off, it would be suspicious. But I wonder why Gillian would."

I stabbed a finger at him. "You see? You ask me why I keep getting sucked into these cases, but it's hard to resist, isn't it?"

"I have nothing against the theoretical sleuthing," he said. "I just wish you'd stay out of the line of fire. That's what the actual cops are paid for."

"Can't argue with you there." At least, not unless I wanted to ruin a nice evening.

When our pizza arrived, we polished it off quickly so we could make the seven thirty movie at the Paragon. Chadwick's 1939 downtown theater had been lovingly restored, a few years back, by a local history buff. By day, its brown brick exterior with limestone, art deco trim lent some character to the otherwise mundane block of storefronts. In the evening, the vertical sign announcing its name in gold-and-green neon added a touch of Old Hollywood glamour.

To stay in business, the owner had to screen at least some first-run films, but Mark and I went there primarily for the oldies. Whether a movie dated from the 1930s or the 1980s, it was still new if it was new to us. We'd both even taken "memberships" in the Paragon to help support it.

Now that summer officially had arrived, the theater favored flicks appropriate to the season. As soon as *Jaws* had gone up on the marquee, Mark and I had bought our tickets.

We settled into the welcome air-conditioning, shared a

box of Good & Plenty candies, and thoroughly enjoyed the 1975 thriller. Of course, we'd each seen brief clips from it over the years, but never watched it start to finish. When an occasional shock made me jump in my seat, Mark would chuckle and slip a protective arm around me. Near the end, though, when the giant shark lurched onto the small boat and almost nailed Roy Scheider, it was Mark who flinched. With a smile, I patted his hand and whispered, "There, there . . . It's only a movie!"

Later, on our way out, we ran into one of the regular ushers—a skinny blond guy named Dave, who was a communications major at the County College of Morris and a serious film buff. He usually shared some trivia about the night's movie, and for *Jaws* he told us the book actually was inspired by a great white shark that killed four people at the Jersey shore in 1916; author Peter Benchley has a cameo as a TV reporter on the beach; the mechanical shark was so much trouble to use that it appears very seldom; and Scheider's famous line, "You're gonna need a bigger boat," was actually improvised during shooting.

"Well, that shark might have been fake, but it scared the heck out of us," Mark told him happily. "And we both work with animals for a living."

"Guess you won't be taking any veterinary jobs at the Camden aquarium?" I needled him.

"Hard pass on that."

Dave grinned. "Scary movies always bring people in, though. We're already brainstorming on our lineup for Halloween. The boss likes to keep things pretty PG-13, so there won't be anything too violent or gory—mostly old classics. But I'm trying to talk him into a werewolf marathon."

I laughed and elbowed Mark. "That's more in your wheelhouse, right?"

He nodded confidently. "You bet. I patched up one of those just last week."

It was nearly ten, and both Mark and I had to be at work early the next morning, so we got into his RAV4 for him to drop me back to my shop. On the way my phone summoned me yet again. If the screen had shown Dawn's name or my mother's, I would have postponed answering it, since they'd probably just be calling to chat. But the last time Nick Janos called me, it was to report that big blowup at the Foster house.

Gillian was gone, though. What could be wrong now?

Chapter 21

I explained to Mark and apologized, but he waved for me to take the call.

"I keep interrupting you, Cassie, during your time off," Nick acknowledged.

"That's okay," I told him. "I guess you heard what happened to Gillian Foster."

"Heard about it! I was down at the police station yesterday, being grilled about it. I guess 'cause I've been working in the cellar with her husband."

"Oh, no! The cops can't think you had anything to do with the fire."

"Well, Madam Detective did ask me how I got along with Gillian, and about the argument the Fosters had a week ago. She might have been fishing around as to whether I crossed some wires to get back at them for some reason, or if maybe Donald asked me to do something to scare his wife."

As usual, Bonelli was leaving no stone unturned. "I'm sure you didn't do either of those things."

"I didn't, and I finally managed to convince her. But after

that, she picked my brain for more technical details. Asked me to expand on some stuff from the fire investigator's report."

Mark had begun eyeing me in concern, so I reassured him that Nick wasn't under arrest.

"Good to know!" he half joked, because my handyman had suffered through one wrong accusation in the past. Mark turned his attention back to the road and let me continue my conversation.

Nick continued. "I guess you never got into the cellar yesterday, did you?"

"No, and once the firemen started to investigate they shooed me off the property," I said. "Bonelli did tell me later, though, that Gillian didn't actually burn to death."

"Sounds like she almost made it up the stairs to the inside door, before the smoke got to her. But they found a wire-cutting tool and a pair of work gloves near the wall that caught fire. Whoever was messing with the wiring, I guess it's hard to tell what they were up to, because that wall is pretty charred."

I knew enough about the electrical system in a typical house to ask him, "If something was wired wrong, that might have given her a nasty shock, but wouldn't it take more to cause a serious fire?"

"Hey, Cassie, you're good. That's pretty much what the detective asked me, too. Whoever did this, maybe they didn't figure on the gaslight piping."

"The cellar has gaslights?"

"Used to at some time, probably in the late eighteen hundreds. The fixtures are long gone, but Don and I found the pipes behind the walls. That's one reason he stopped work on the project—we needed to figure out the safest way to deal with that stuff."

"But if the lights weren't being used anymore, wouldn't the gas to the pipes be shut off?" I asked.

"Technically, yeah, but some usually stays in those narrow pipes and leaks into the air behind the walls. It's not really dangerous to breathe, and it can be so subtle that you don't even smell it, but you can't take a chance of igniting it. Plus, their cellar has old knob-and-tube wiring, which is brittle. So, if you mess with that stuff and set off a spark . . . *whoosh!*"

"Someone must have done just that," I guessed. "Someone who didn't know about the gas in the walls."

"Or else, somebody who did." Nick's voice went low, serious. "I like Don, so I didn't want to say anything to, y'know, implicate him. But I could see he was getting pretty fed up with Gillian's nonsense—abuse, really. The night I walked out, when she was accusing him of having an affair, she told him, 'You'll leave me for that tramp over my dead body!' Whether he was playing around or not, maybe he decided a little accident in the cellar would solve all his problems."

Wednesday morning at work, I spent some time in our playroom with one of our boarders, Latte. Her owner traveled a lot, and while Sarah and I were always happy to host the lovely Abyssinian, she did crave plenty of exercise. Trailing around a feather toy on a wand for her to chase, I technically put in some work time while I gave Bonelli a call. I wanted to get her latest take on the Foster family tragedy.

"The fire investigator drew pretty much the same conclusion as Janos," the detective told me. "He also thought the piping behind the walls looked like the source of the fire. One of those old, cloth-covered wires was sticking out at an angle, and he said the end appeared frayed. The gloves and wire cut-ter could have either been left there earlier, by Donald or by someone else tampering with the scene that morning. There's no real way to tell. Those things were partially burned, so I don't know how much good they'll be for fingerprints."

I remembered something. "Y'know, when the Fosters hosted the reception, they took all of their guests on a quick tour of the house. So, all of those board members knew the basic layout of the cellar and heard about the old wiring."

"But Donald probably didn't mention the gas pipes, right? Supposedly he and Nick didn't find out about them until they opened up the walls. Linda Freeman might have known about them, because Donald talked to her about redesigning the cellar. I doubt she ever got a chance to really study them, though, because Gillian didn't want her back in the house."

Donald could have allowed her to sneak back in, I thought. And Linda might have had good reason to want Gillian dead. Heck, even Linda's assistant, Robert, might have been willing to do the deed, because Gillian had treated him so rudely.

Somewhat reluctantly, I mentioned all of this to the detective.

"Linda said both she and Robert were working in their office all Monday morning and can alibi each other," Bonelli told me.

While luring the Abyssinian up the wall shelves with the feather toy, I explored this idea further. "Professional interior designers have to know the basics about electrical wiring and plumbing, don't they, so they can rework the spaces in a house? Still, it's hard to imagine that Linda would deliberately come by on a day when Gillian was home, somehow hatch a plot to set the basement on fire, and trap her there."

"Yeah, and this doesn't exactly look like an impulse crime—it would have been pretty risky. If the killer went into the basement with Gillian, always a chance he or she would get caught by the fire, too."

"I had to break through the outside cellar doors with a shovel," I remembered. "So they must have been locked from the inside, right?"

I heard a beat of silence, as if Bonelli checked something. "Yes, that's noted in the investigator's report. The interior door leading up to the hallway was closed, but didn't even have a lock. Which may be why Gillian tried to escape that way."

Finally tired, Latte stretched out elegantly on one of the wall shelves. I let her rest and settled myself on the low, carpet-covered cube. "I guess the whole thing could just have been a complete accident," I said into the phone. "She smelled smoke coming from the cellar, went to check, and somehow got trapped down there."

"Possible," Bonelli admitted. "What concerns me is Gillian giving her maid the day off for no apparent reason, when she'd never done anything like that before."

"It does suggest she was trying to get Herta out of the way," I agreed.

After we'd hung up, I continued to follow this train of thought. Had Gillian been expecting a secret visitor? Someone who had no business coming to the house at that time of day . . . or at all?

Someone who'd killed her?

But both the front and kitchen doors were locked from the inside.

Sarah appeared in the doorway between the playroom and the front sales area. Quietly, she told me, "Whitney Foster's here. She says she wants to visit Leya."

Hoo, boy. I wondered when dealing with that dysfunctional family had officially become part of my job description.

Have a heart. The girl did just lose her mother.

I sighed. "Okay, sure. I'll put this cat away and bring Leya out here."

When I returned with the Himalayan in my arms, Whitney sat waiting on the top platform of a carpeted perch. She'd shrouded herself in a baggy sweatshirt and faded jeans—maybe the teenager's version of mourning garb. She also had pulled her long, straight hair over one shoulder and twisted the whole hank nervously. The same as she'd been doing the night she watched the EMTs load Adele into the ambulance.

She bounced up when she saw Leya, though, and met me halfway to fuss over her.

"Poor sweetie, have you been okay here? Did you miss us? We miss you!"

I handed over her pet so they could have a better reunion. Meanwhile, I couldn't help wondering if Whitney was channeling her feelings of loss into the cat . . . or whether she'd missed Leya at least as much as her mother, if not more so.

After a minute she finally acknowledged me again. "Cassie, thanks so much for noticing the smoke and calling the fire department. If they hadn't gotten there so quickly . . . there might have been nothing left."

I nodded, though this comment also stirred my curiosity. Did she mean nothing left of their house, or of Gillian?

"Sorry I wasn't able to do more," I said. "How are you holding up? This must have been a terrible shock for you and your father."

"Neither of us can understand how it happened. Mom had no reason to go into the cellar by herself on Monday. A couple of weeks ago, she drew up plans about how she wanted it to look, with storage in one half and a wine cellar in the other, but since then she's left all the work to Dad and Nick. Even when they talked about the nuts-and-bolts stuff in front of her, she just acted bored."

"Is it possible someone else dropped by and she was show-ing them around down there?" I suggested.

Whitney looked up at me and cocked her head. "I don't know who that would be. When I left for the stable, Mom didn't mention anything like that to me. I thought Herta would be coming, as usual, but Detective Bonelli says Mom gave her the day off."

"You already spoke to Bonelli?"

"Yeah, she asked me a lot of questions, because of the por-ridge incident. As if that means I'd try to kill my mother!"

Not so far-fetched, I reasoned. On the one hand, Whit-ney's prank probably wouldn't have done Gillian any serious harm. On the other, it had landed Adele Dugan in the hos-pital.

"The cops are giving Dad an even harder time," the girl went on. "They think maybe he rigged up something in the basement and told her to go down there, but that's ridiculous! Not only would my father never kill anyone, but would he risk burning down our house, too?"

"Is there a chance he did something wrong down there and accidently created the conditions that started the fire? The inspector found work gloves that looked like a man's size right near the spot where the blaze started. Could they have been your dad's?"

She shrugged. "I suppose they must have been, either his or Nick's. Honestly, I was afraid something like this might happen, but not to my mother. I worried that Dad would get electrocuted fooling with that old wiring. He probably didn't know as much about it as he thought, because once I heard Nick warn him about it. The wires weren't color-coded right, or something, and Nick told Dad to always check whether or not a wire was live before touching it."

I asked Whitney if her mother was aware of the gas pipes

behind the walls, and she looked surprised. "I'm not sure. This is the first I heard about them. That's what started the fire, the gas?"

Hoping Bonelli wouldn't think I was sharing confidential details with a suspect, I nodded.

"Wow. Dad did tell us he needed to stop the work for a while and get a plumber in to deal with some pipes, but I figured they were regular water pipes. I think Mom did, too. Just yesterday she was nagging him about it, asking why he couldn't work around the plumbing and get the electrical stuff done. It made her antsy not to have the house completely finished. You know how she was—needed to know everything was done *perfectly*."

"I do."

Whitney started wringing her hair again. She gazed sideways, toward the wall of cat shelves, but I could tell her vision really was turned inward. "Mom almost baited Dad to just deal with the wiring himself, without Nick. Like, didn't he know just as much about that kind of thing?"

I could almost hear Gillian's sarcastic tone in my head, and it set some gears rolling in a new direction.

"Well, speaking of Dad, I'd better get home or he'll worry." Whitney ruffled Leya's fur once more and planted a kiss on her head, then handed her back to me. "Thanks for hanging on to her a little longer. Once we've had the house checked and repaired, Dad will come to get her."

I followed the girl as she headed for the playroom door. "Whitney, right before the fire, did your mother say or do anything else that seemed strange? I mean, like giving Herta the day off?"

"I can't think of anything." She paused, and for the first time her voice thickened with sadness. "But she did do some-

thing weird on the day of the fire. I didn't know about it before, just found out about it yesterday. Mom died wearing my
shoes."

"What?"

"We wore the same size, and once in a while we bor-
rowed shoes from each other. Mostly she'd talk me into wearing her heels, when I was dressing up, even though I like flats
better. But after the fire, I was missing some running shoes,
and when I asked Bonelli, sure enough, Mom had them on."

"Did your mother go running?"

Whitney gave a dry laugh. "Never! She didn't like to
sweat that much; Pilates was more her thing. And she absolutely hated those particular sneakers on me, because they
were so thick-soled and clunky—she called them my Franken-
stein shoes. But for some reason, without even asking me, she
wore them on Monday."

By the time Whitney left, it was about four thirty. Sarah
and I had no other appointments that day, so we began
straightening up the place in a leisurely way, sweeping floors
and scooping out litter pans. We made chitchat about various
things, including the Fosters, but I kept my newest, half-
formed suspicions about Gillian's death to myself. I'd save
them for someone who'd be in a better position to follow up.

Near five, Sarah got a call on her cell. I stepped away to
avoid eavesdropping, but could tell from my assistant's low,
serious tone that the news worried her.

"That was Robin," she told me minutes later.

"Chester again?" I guessed.

"He said he heard noises last night in his back yard—a cat
yowling and music playing. Saxophone music. He said it
sounded like something from the Coltrane album that went
missing from his house."

I paused, in the middle of filling a boarder's dish with dry food, to stare at Sarah. Her expression told me she also found this story absurd.

"I know, it's crazy," my assistant agreed. "Even Robin thinks his mind really could be going this time. But she's worried that, because Chester set that 'trap' in his kitchen, somebody might have decided to try luring him out of the house instead. The other day, his caretaker told Robin she found an empty beer bottle in the outdoor garbage can, and since she's been coming there she's never known Chester to have beer in the house. Robin thought of grabbing it for possible evidence, but the trash already had been picked up."

"The bottle could have been dumped by someone just passing by, through the woods back there," I said. "But yeah, it also might mean somebody shady has been hanging around his house."

"Exactly. Robin has told him to lock his doors, and not to go outside by himself at night under any circumstances, but she's afraid he won't listen to her."

I shook my head. "I'd tell her to call the Dalton cops, but we all know how much good that will do."

"Anyway, she's going to stay over there tonight with him and sleep in Bernice's old room, just to see if there's anything to Chester's story. If she does hear noises, at least she can stop him from leaving the house. Cassie, do you think she also could call the Chadwick cops? Since Bonelli's on the case now, would they respond?"

"Worth a try," I said. "But I really don't like the idea of Robin putting herself at risk like that."

"I don't, either, but she's hardheaded. Robin thinks because she's a nurse and in good shape—and has handled some rough situations working in the schools—she can take care of herself. But she doesn't know who or what she'd be up against. None of us do!"

I glanced at my wall clock and wondered if Bonelli would still be in her office. Seemingly not, because I got her answering machine.

I gave her a brief heads-up about what Chester reportedly heard the evening before, and Robin Stoppard's plan to stay over and check it out. I doubted the detective would investigate unless there was some real evidence of wrongdoing, but it didn't hurt to alert her.

As long as I was leaving a message, I also mentioned Whitney's visit to my shop and our conversation. "She said her mother died wearing a pair of running shoes that belonged to Whitney, even though Gillian didn't run and always complained that the shoes were ugly. I was just wondering . . . did they happen to have thick, rubber soles?"

Chapter 22

By around eight thirty that evening I lay exhausted on my sofa. Matisse sprawled across my lap, and Cole sat in a meditative Sphinx pose nearby.

Mango observed the rest of us from a wall shelf across the room. He had begun avoiding me since I'd started giving him his daily thyroid pills. I'd fooled him with the first two by hiding them inside the chewy cat treats, but he'd soon gotten wise to that trick. The next few times, I'd had to prop him on my lap, facing away from me; I'd gotten his mouth open, shoved the pill as far in as I could, held his jaws closed, and massaged his throat until he swallowed. The element of surprise had worked in my favor.

But Mango never had been known for his mellow temperament, and over the last few days he'd been ready to do battle. I resorted to the time-honored vet tech method of wrapping him completely in a bath towel, except for his head, before I poked the tablet into his mouth. Even so, one pill that I could have sworn he'd swallowed later turned up between the sofa cushions.

He was his own worst enemy, I told myself. The pills did

seem to be helping his condition and would be the easiest way to manage it. But if he refused to take them, the next step would be surgery to remove the thyroid tumor. I dreaded that, because anesthesia was always risky for cats past a certain age.

Earlier, I'd put in a call to Dawn but got voice mail. I told her it was nothing urgent and to call back when she got the chance. Too tired to focus on a book, I began watching a lackluster episode of a forensic-mystery series. Fatigue soon got the better of me, though, and my eyes closed.

I'd probably dozed for a good ten minutes—the TV episode was winding up—when my cell phone rang. Not Dawn, though. Sarah.

"Sorry to disturb you, Cassie, but I'm worried. I've tried calling Chester on his house phone and Robin on her cell, several times. Neither of them answers."

I woke sufficiently to understand why this was a bad thing. "She's staying over at his house tonight?"

"That was her plan. Do you think I dare call the Dalton cops?"

My mind clearing, I advised Sarah, "No, call the Chadwick PD and drop my name. Tell them it's about the Chester Tillman case, that he's supposed to have a caretaker with him, but no one's answering at the house. Let me know what they say."

While giving her time to do this, I pulled myself together. I had showered after work and now wore my Kelly-green CAT WRANGLER T-shirt with floral pajama pants; I exchanged the pants for jeans and pulled on sneakers. A glance out the window told me the night had turned rainy and foggy, though, and I hoped we wouldn't have to go out.

Sarah called me right back. "The desk sergeant said most of their officers have gone out to a multicar accident on the highway. He'll try to pull somebody off to look in on Chester, but it could be awhile."

"Okay, we can't wait that long." *Rain and fog be damned.* "Want to go up to his house?"

She chuckled darkly. "I was afraid to ask you."

"Since you're nearer to his place, I'll pick you up."

I locked my apartment door and trotted downstairs, by the glow of a ceiling safety light. Passing my sales counter, I paused to grab the can of pepper spray I kept underneath. (Store stickups weren't a common problem in Chadwick, but I'd had issues with a few specific bad guys in the past.)

When Sarah got into my car, about fifteen minutes later, she brought along a good-size flashlight, which I imagined could be helpful, too. Both of us had worn dark pants and hooded jackets, like burglars. The rain had eased a little, but the fog remained. I had to be careful driving out to Dalton, because the roads grew more rural with fewer lights.

Meanwhile, Sarah and I plotted our strategy: Park a little distance from the ranch house, survey the property, and see if anything looked immediately suspicious before we went inside.

I left my car in a patch of woods, and we approached the house on foot, our jacket hoods raised against the drizzle. Through the garage window, I could make out Robin's sleek gray sedan inside. Had she pulled it in to keep it dry, or so her presence wouldn't be too obvious?

The living room's high front window showed only one dim light, probably from a table lamp. Maybe Robin had decided to stay up and read while keeping watch? But why hadn't she answered her phone?

You're making too much of this, Cassie. She and Chester are probably both asleep, in their respective rooms. Could be she just forgot to charge her phone.

But what about Chester's landline?

When we reached the front of the house, I heard voices. One shout that sounded like Robin, then a man yelling at her. A healthy baritone, not Chester's elderly rasp.

"Stay low so they can't see you," I told Sarah. We eased through the overgrown bushes at the front of the house, and I stood on tiptoe to peer inside. The living room window bowed outward, in the style of many 1950s and 1960s houses, and my nose just came to the sill. The vertical blinds had suffered even more damage over the past couple of weeks, and the gaps allowed me a decent view of the room beyond.

Robin sat in an old wing chair, bound to it by several coils of a thick rope. The stiff way her hands lay in her lap suggested her wrists also were tied. While I watched, her captor, a medium-tall man, tore some duct tape off a roll and plastered that over her mouth.

He stepped back to approve his work, and tucked what looked like a small pistol into the pocket of his sweatpants. He wore a gray hoodie, but the top was pushed down far enough for me to recognize Bob Smiley.

Beside me I heard Sarah gasp, and knew she'd also glimpsed the scenario.

I ducked below the window and texted a 911 message to the Chadwick cops, knowing it still might take them a while to come.

"What can we do?" Sarah whispered.

"Let's go around the back."

We crept up the steps to the rear porch, while I tried to devise a game plan. Smiley's gun complicated things. It explained how he'd persuaded Robin to sit in the chair while he tied her up. But if he'd meant to kill her, wouldn't she be dead already?

"Where's Chester?" asked Sarah.

Another good question. Smiley could have felled him with one good punch. We'd just have to worry about that later.

We found the back door unlocked, made it to the kitchen and crouched behind the counter. From there, the clutter helped conceal us, but we had a decent view of the living room.

Smiley backed away from the immobilized Robin, rubbed a hand over his thinning hair and tapped out a number on his phone. He started talking to someone, too rapidly and quietly for me to hear very much. Just two phrases reached me: ". . . more than I signed up for . . ." and "You better get over here!"

My mind was on other things, anyhow. While he faced away from me, I scanned the cluttered kitchen counter. Spotted something useful—a chrome-sided, 1980s toaster oven.

I held up my hand, signaling Sarah to stay where she was. Bob seemed caught up in his agitated conversation, but still kept an eye on Robin. I slipped from my hiding place and quietly picked up the greasy old appliance. Stole up behind him . . .

And, as hard as I could, swung it at the back of his head.

Robin darted a glance at me, which might have tipped off Bob, and he half turned. My blow landed not quite square, glancing off the side of his head and his shoulder. In spite of that, he let out one groan and dropped—like a trash bag full of old eight-track cassettes.

Sarah, armed with a kitchen knife, dashed across the living room to Robin. In a few seconds she had freed her friend's hands, and the two of them untied the thicker rope that bound her to the chair.

Once Robin had pulled the tape from her mouth, she started to tell us what had happened. "After Chester went to bed, I sat up for a while in Bernice's room, reading. I'd tried to lock the back door, but that hook-and-eye lock is pretty flimsy. Before too long, I heard someone padding around out here. I told Chester to stay in his room until I gave him the okay, and sneaked out to see who it was . . . but Bob got the drop on me." She glanced at the fallen man. "At least you got the drop on him!"

"Who knows how long he'll stay out, though," I said.

"Oh, could be awhile. You hit him in a good spot, behind the ear. That's an instant KO. Just as well you didn't get him right at the base of his skull, because that could've killed him."

Sarah nodded. "And we still need him to tell us just what's been going on here!"

I laughed at this cold-blooded statement from my usually gentle, humane assistant.

"Well, are you gonna let him just lay there? Tie him up before he comes to!"

This suggestion, coming from the kitchen, startled all three of us. Focused on Bob, we hadn't noticed Chester sneaking down the hallway, wearing a bathrobe over pajamas.

"Are you okay?" I asked him.

"Course I am. I woulda come out and helped, but you and Sarah had stuff under control. I figured I'd just get in the way." He edged nearer to view the unconscious man and called him a few names. "Some friend and neighbor! Visiting with me, askin' me all kinds of questions about my career, famous people I'd met and my sports souvenirs. Is he the one who's been sneakin' in here to steal my stuff?"

"I'm afraid it looks that way." Robin grabbed some of the leftover rope and started to bind Smiley's wrists and ankles, which must have been especially satisfying for her.

She and I went through Bob's pockets, and in one I found a microcassette recorder. When I pushed Play, it produced a few seconds of the cat sounds, followed by some saxophone music. Chester listened with a satisfied smile, and I handed him the device. "Just in case anybody else tries to tell you that you've been imagining things."

From the fallen man's sweatpants, Robin withdrew the semiautomatic pistol. "Beretta, .22 caliber."

"You're lucky he didn't shoot you, instead of just tying you up!" Sarah told her.

"Yes, it's strange," she said. "I think he was really shocked to find me here. He kept warning me to cooperate so he wouldn't have to hurt me."

"Maybe he was just hoping to steal some more stuff while Chester was asleep," I guessed. "He didn't have a plan, though, for dealing with you."

A car door slammed outside. We all flinched. Robin peered out through the front window blinds and visibly relaxed. "Better late than never!"

I checked for myself. A police cruiser, but not from Chadwick. White, with the Dalton shield. And if the cops suspected a break-in, or any other dangerous situation, wouldn't they send two guys?

Only one tall, lean figure got out of the vehicle and approached the house. Officer Marty Brewer.

"Chester," I said, "can you go back in your room for a while and pretend to be asleep? We don't want you to be accused of anything we did!"

He looked about to protest, but Sarah backed me up with a nod and a finger to her lips. Silently, the older man retreated down the hall once more.

When the doorbell rang, Robin answered it. I heard Brewer, on the stoop, ask her, "You reported an intruder?"

"Yes, I did." She let him into the living room and stepped to one side. His long face registered shock as he took in me,

Sarah and the balding man who lay trussed and unconscious on the floor.

"What the hell?" said Brewer.

"He broke in here, pulled a gun and tied *me* up," Robin explained. "Fortunately, my friends arrived and were able to disarm and subdue him."

"But how— What did you do to him?"

"Does that really matter?" I countered, not trusting Brewer as far as I could hurl him. "He's alive, though he probably should get medical help. But most likely, he's the one who's been sneaking into this house and making off with the collectibles. This proves Chester wasn't imagining things, after all."

"Okay, okay." The young cop seemed to be reassuring himself, rather than us. "How about you ladies tell me exactly what happened here, step by step?"

"Shouldn't you call an ambulance for him, first?" Sarah asked, as if she shared my misgivings about Brewer. "Cassie gave him a pretty hard whack on the head, and he's already been out for at least ten minutes."

Brewer seemed reluctant to make the call, though. Instead, he just crouched next to Smiley and took his pulse. That finally brought the other man around, though Bob acted disoriented.

"Where . . . How did I . . ." He tried to roll to one side and howled in pain. "*Jeeeez*, my shoulder!"

"Take it easy there, pal," Brewer told him. "These ladies have made some pretty serious accusations against you."

Smiley's baffled expression confirmed what I'd thought. He knew Marty Brewer; they were in it together. But Brewer had to go on acting like a cop.

"Ladies, this man obviously is in a lot of pain," he said. "I think we can untie his feet, at least, don't you?" Without waiting for an answer, but keeping an eye on us at whole time, Brewer tugged those knots loose. "What did you catch him stealing?"

"He didn't get that far tonight, I guess," Robin admitted. "As soon as he got inside the house, he saw me."

While Smiley rubbed the circulation back into his ankles, Brewer faced us with a patronizing air. "I think this is probably just a big misunderstanding. Most likely, Bob here just dropped by to check on Chester. But because of all the crazy stories the old man's been telling about burglars and break-ins, one of you got excited and clobbered him."

"It was no *misunderstanding*." Robin's sarcasm told me she was finally catching on. "He brought these ropes with him and tied me to that wing chair. My friends can testify to that."

While Smiley still sat with his hands bound, the cop appeared to frisk him. He looked unnerved to find Bob's pockets empty.

Robin must have hung on to the Beretta.

"Just your word against his, isn't it?" Brewer told her. "Still, I'll go with yours, for now." He hauled the injured man to his feet, while Smiley moaned in misery.

"I screwed up, Marty. I didn't know she'd be here. I thought he'd be alone . . ."

"Shut up," Brewer growled.

"You were late! That's why I had to tie her up."

The cop pulled his service revolver and trained it on us. "You shoulda just shot her, you loser. Saved us all this trouble."

"You said you'd deal with the old man, so I figured you'd handle her, too. I might be a thief, but I'm not a killer."

"Oh, you aren't, huh? What about the old lady?"

"That was an accident! She woke up, and I couldn't let her see my face. I just tried to cover her eyes . . ."

Smiley's lids fluttered and he sank to his knees again, jerking Brewer off-balance. I saw Sarah edge nearer to the cop and wondered what on earth she was up to. Maybe she figured if the three of us spread out, he'd have a hard time knowing where to aim?

Ready to do my part, I slipped my hand into the pocket of my soggy fleece jacket.

"Grow a spine, will ya?" Brewer snarled at Smiley. "You made this mess, and now I'm going to have to clean it up."

In the corner of my eye, I saw Robin take a couple of steps forward, too, flanking the two men on the opposite side from Sarah. Brewer caught her stealthy movement and shouted, "That's far enough!"

From the kitchen behind him rose an unearthly series of high-decibel caterwauls, like a whole feral colony in heat. Startled, Brewer threw a glance over his left shoulder.

I lunged forward to blast him with the pepper spray. While he flailed in agony, Sarah grabbed his gun arm and dropped to the floor, pulling the tall man down with her. His weapon discharged into the dingy shag carpet, then bounced from his hand.

I rushed to grab it, and Robin finally produced the Beretta.

Sarah backed away from Brewer, who still crouched on the floor, coughing and wheezing. I remained awestruck by the way my rather petite, sixtyish assistant had disarmed the young cop. "Where did you learn *that* move?"

"When I was still teaching middle school, we had active-shooter drills," she told me, a little short of breath herself. "Lucky I never had to use it . . . before now."

Chester shuffled out from behind the kitchen counter. "Anybody shot?"

"Nope," I reassured him, my gun trained on Smiley. "Just one blinded cop and one disabled burglar."

"Burglar, my ass!" Chester, his face a scowling mask of vengeance, loomed over Smiley. "It was you that killed Bernice! Wish t' God somebody'd put a bullet in you!"

"I'm sorry," Bob wailed from his seat on the floor. "I didn't mean to."

"An' even after that, you kept coming back to rob me? You—!"

Sarah clutched Chester's arm gently but firmly. "Take it easy. Bob will pay for what he did. Brewer, too."

The tall cop staggered to his feel, still wiping his eyes, while Robin pinned him with the Beretta. "You th-think anybody will believe your story?" he screamed at us between coughs. "I've got twelve years on the f-force, and Chief Hill is my father-in-law. You're the ones who'll pay, for interfering with an ar-rrest and as-saulting a police officer! Who's going to take the testimony of three hysterical broads and a c-crazy old man over mine?"

The rotating lights of another cruiser appeared through the living room window. My heart sank, and Brewer smirked, when a male voice outside bellowed, "Police!"

Sarah opened the front door. In walked officers Mel Jacoby and Chris Waller of the Chadwick PD . . . with Detective Angela Bonelli.

Chapter 23

The Chadwick cops took Brewer and Smiley into custody. They interviewed Chester at his house, then called his caretaker and arranged for her to watch over him for the rest of the night. Robin, Sarah and I went to the police station for debriefing.

Bonelli told Officer Waller to interview my friends and dealt with me herself. The day's events had left me drained, but I took courage from the sound of the detective's Keurig coffeemaker burbling on top of her file cabinet. As soon as it stopped, she poured us two mugs of Green Mountain Nantucket Blend. It was yummy, and comforting, and I didn't expect to sleep that night, anyway.

I explained that Sarah and I had our suspicions about Brewer for a while, but no concrete reason to accuse him of anything.

"He and Smiley are cousins, by the way, which is how they ended up in this mess together," Bonelli told me, settling behind her Spartan desk with her aromatic brew. "Marty's not talking, but Bob spilled his guts. His reward was a trip to the

ER, to see whether or not you gave him a concussion. What
the heck did you hit him with, again?"

"A toaster oven. Not even a very big one."

With an amused shake of her head, the detective consulted
some notes. "He admits he was 'between jobs' for several
months, and while visiting with Chester he started to wonder
what those sports collectibles might be worth. He researched
different sites online, and found out that even some of the old
toys and vinyl records sold for many hundreds of dollars to
collectors. Because the Tillmans' place was so messy, and
Chester's eyesight was poor, Bob started to slip things into his
pockets during his visits."

"Including, I'll bet, that baseball signed by Roger Maris,"
I said.

"Probably. Of course, then he set his sights on some of the
larger stuff, which he couldn't smuggle out so easily. He told
me that once, while Bernice was right in the next room, he
filled a whole trash bag with cassettes of video games, then offered to take it out to the garbage pick-up for her. Of course,
he just brought it to his house."

Slime! I thought.

"He noticed that the Tillmans always left their back door
ajar, for the cats, so he began slipping in at night. He concentrated on things in the front rooms, so he'd be less likely to
wake anybody. But I guess Bernice had mentioned the unusual doll that she still kept on her closet shelf because her
daughter never liked it. Smiley looked that up, and found out
it could be worth several hundred dollars. He knew Bernice
took medication to help her sleep, and that she snored. He
gambled that he could sneak into her room and get the doll
without her ever knowing. But the three cats fussed and woke
her up."

I remembered Bob's admission earlier that evening. "He knew she would recognize him, so he pressed the pillow over her face. He told Brewer that he was just trying to cover her eyes, but I'm sure he was desperate to keep her quiet. Maybe he thought she'd just pass out, though, not smother to death."

"After that, Bob said, his guilty conscience made him stop visiting Chester," Bonelli continued. "He might have stopped stealing from him, too. But by that time, he'd bragged to Marty about how much he'd made selling these collectibles. Chester had complained to the cops that someone was breaking into his house, so Brewer knew his cousin had to be the burglar. He threatened to expose Smiley unless he kept pulling the mini-robberies and cut him in on the profits."

I sipped my coffee, as most of the puzzle pieces started to fall into place. "Since they were getting away with all this, though, why pull that prank of trying to lure Chester out of the house at night? They had to be intending some harm to him."

Bonelli held up one finger. "That's where the renovator, Dan Pressley, comes in. After Bob went to work for him, they got chatting about the Tillman house and how run-down it was. Apparently, Pressley had approached the old couple, offering to buy it. But especially once Bernice was gone, the decision lay with Chester and he wouldn't budge. Bob told Pressley that he was friendly with Chester and maybe could talk him into selling. Pressley said that would be great, and if Bob could help there might be a nice bonus in his next paycheck."

"But by then, Bob wasn't visiting Chester anymore, right?" I reminded her. "Couldn't look him in the eye, I guess."

"Hence, the scheme to either frighten him into selling, or injure him so he had to move elsewhere. After all, if Chester went outside at night to check out the weird sounds, he might fall down the back steps or hurt himself in the woods. Brewer was glad to help with that scheme, too, because he thought Pressley was upgrading the community with his renovations."

I marveled at the complicated plot, which sounded pretty straightforward when you broke it down. "Seems like Smiley has given you everything you need to wrap up the case."

"He and Brewer might have gotten away with it, though, if not for you, Robin and Sarah. Those are a couple of tough ladies! I've always had the greatest respect for nurses and schoolteachers, but I didn't realize they also had commando skills."

I laughed ruefully. "Schools aren't the safe havens they used to be, I guess. Robin told me she's never fired a gun, but kids sometimes try to bring the small-caliber ones to school, so she knows one from another. It was Sarah who really astonished me!"

Bonelli agreed. "She said in her last year of teaching, mass shootings already were becoming a concern. The teachers and students were taught how to hide, but the adults also learned how to disarm a shooter in a real emergency—grab his gun arm, point it at the floor and fall, taking him with you. Since Sarah's no spring chicken, I'm just glad she came out of it okay, barring a few bruises."

The detective added that she still had to sort out the case with Chief Hill, but if he gave her any trouble, she was prepared to go over his head to the county Internal Affairs Bureau. If Brewer continued to claim innocence, she warned, we all might be required to testify in court somewhere down the line. For now, though, the plot against Chester seemed to have been successfully foiled.

As I rose to leave, Bonelli added, "By the way, I guess I never answered your question about the shoes Gillian Foster was wearing when she died. Yes, they did have thick, rubber soles."

I lingered by her desk. Even though it was so late and I was so beat, I started to sit down again.

She waved me along. "Another time. Let's just say that I can see where you're going with that idea, Cassie, and you could be onto something. I'll do some more checking and let you know what I find."

Though the next day was Thursday, I gave Sarah some well-deserved time off. We had no important groomings scheduled, and no pick-ups or drop-offs, so I also intended to do as little work as possible—at least cat-related.

When I checked the latest issue of the *Chadwick Courier* online, I found a belated story about Gillian Foster's demise. It stated that "the proprietor of a pet boarding facility, who came by to return the family cat, noticed the smoke and called the fire department." The reporter probably got his information from the police, and I appreciated their efforts to keep my name out of the story, though some folks probably would suspect my involvement, anyway.

The only person in my circle whom I hadn't yet told about the incident was Dawn, and after seeing the news item, she e-mailed me. "We're due for a dinner together," she wrote. "Let me know when you're free, and we can catch up."

The story also triggered a call from my mother, who fretted about the fact that this was the second time I had stumbled over a client's dead body. I pointed out that, since I was unable to go down into the Fosters' cellar, I had not actually stumbled over, or even seen, the deceased Gillian.

"Do they think there's any foul play involved?" Mom asked.

"I guess they're not sure yet," I told her.

"Because the other day, after you'd been asking all of those questions about wills, and when a spouse could or couldn't inherit," she said, "I remembered one very nasty divorce I heard about. Not handled by our firm, fortunately!"

"Oh?"

"A wife suspected her husband was fooling around, but couldn't prove it. She also wanted his money, and thought she deserved it, so she tried to kill him. He was a do-it-yourselfer with a workshop in their backyard shed. I don't remember the details, but she rigged one of his tools to short out."

"Did it work?"

"Fortunately, not the way she'd hoped. He only got a slight shock, noticed it had been tampered with and called the police. She got her divorce, but also a prison term." My mother chuckled ruefully. "I don't know why that case came to mind, though. It's not very similar to the one involving the Fosters."

"On the contrary, Mom, I think it might be," I told her. "Thanks for your input and your good memory!"

I hung up without telling her anything at all about the showdown at Chester Tillman's house. That shock to her system could wait for another day.

When I needed to brainstorm, I preferred to do it on paper rather than electronically. I sat at the front counter, with a notepad and a pen that we kept by the shop phone, and began to jot some of the most recent clues regarding the fire at the Foster house.

Gillian nagged Donald to finish electrical work in basement, without help from Nick. Just impatient, or—?

She gave her maid Monday off, unusual.

Alone in house, she locked all doors—so no one would disturb her?—and went down to cellar.

She wore Whitney's thick-soled sneakers. To insulate her, when she fiddled with electricity?

Had Gillian damaged the wiring and generated the spark that started the fire in the basement? Was she trying to do some of the work herself, or to do damage? Burning to death certainly would be a roundabout and ghastly way to commit suicide; anyway, her daughter didn't think Gillian even knew about the nearly odorless gas behind the walls. So exactly what was she trying to accomplish?

My already smoldering suspicions had been fanned to a blaze by Mom's ironic legal anecdote. I punched Bonelli's number on my phone, hoping the detective would finally be willing to confirm them.

Dawn's dining room was as unique as every other space of her apartment, which occupied the whole second floor above her shop. Tall, arched windows faced the street, and she dressed them only with white gauze curtains pinned back at the sides. In front of these, retro macramé hangers held pots of various ferns, vines and succulents, thriving in the muted light. The back wall displayed a large, freeform tapestry created by Dawn's mother, a professional fiber artist.

Next to this hung a masterpiece I'd never seen before—an oversized Pop portrait of Dawn herself as a hippie princess. Obviously based on a photo, it zeroed in on just the left half of her face, the one eye shut and the rosy lips smiling. A string of beads draped across her forehead anchored her wavy russet hair as it lifted in the breeze.

"This is stunning!" I told her when I first set foot in the room. "Don't tell me . . . Keith?"

She nodded, blushing a little. "He dropped it off last week, called it an early birthday present. I feel kind of funny, looking at myself in close-up while I'm eating, but if I didn't hang it somewhere prominent, I'd hurt his feelings."

"It's perfect here." I'd known her longtime boyfriend was a sought-after commercial artist, but this suggested an even more serious level of talent. "It's a painting, right?"

"Airbrushed, yes. He's got a few more in his studio—not all of me—and I told him he should try to get into a gallery show."

I thought instantly of Chadwick's own storefront art gallery. "He should show them to Nidra at Eye of the Beholder," I said. "She likes modern, unusual things, and he could play the 'local artist' card."

Dawn had draped her rustic dining table in a cloth with a Southwestern pattern; the half-dozen mismatched chairs had been painted in coordinating colors. She brought out a kind of tureen and ladled vegetarian chili onto plates for the two of us—the pieces all handmade pottery glazed in earth tones and freeform designs.

The recipe blended tomatoes, squash, zucchini, broccoli, chickpeas and corn; the spices also mixed well, with just a hint of South-of-the-Border fire. Dawn served it with chunky, organic sourdough bread.

As we tucked in, she reminded me, "So, you told me on the phone that you solved Gillian Foster's murder."

"Not exactly," I corrected her. "Between me and Bonelli, I think we figured out how and why Gillian *died*. And it might have involved an *attempted* murder."

While doing justice to the chili, I summarized for my friend the clues I'd tallied up. "Whitney told me Gillian saw a therapist in the past, and Donald mentioned that she'd also been on medication for her 'anxiety.' But Bonelli said that, with their latest move, Gillian decided she didn't need either the shrink or the meds anymore, and that's when her mood swings got more extreme. She also got more possessive of Whitney, complaining that the girl would rather spend time with her father, or even her horse, than with her own mother. Donald said he tried to tolerate these tantrums, and to persuade Gillian to go back to her therapist. But she just accused him of trying to sedate her so he'd be free to play around with Linda, the designer."

"There was nothing between those two?" Dawn asked.

"They both deny it, and Bonelli believes them."

"Seems strange that Gillian would become so obsessed with that idea, would almost *want* to believe Donald was unfaithful and out to kill her, with so little evidence. You studied psychology, Cassie. Any theories?"

I had given the question some thought since Gillian's death. "Maybe those are the things *she* would have done, in her husband's shoes. Or maybe she knew, on some level, how difficult she was to live with."

With a baffled shake of her head, Dawn offered me more chili and took a couple additional spoonfuls herself.

"Anyway," I continued, "our intrepid detective also checked out the wills of both the Fosters. Gillian had a decent income and savings from her work as an efficiency consultant, but the real money was Donald's. If she divorced him, she might get a share of it, but more if he was unfaithful and she could claim emotional damages."

"Sounds like she was trying to prove that," Dawn said. "Not only accusing him to his face, but in front of their daughter and even outsiders, like Nick."

"Yes, it could've been a cold-blooded plan . . . except Gillian may have even convinced herself. She probably didn't need his money that badly, but I think she grew paranoid.

Nick heard Gillian tell Donald that the only way he'd ever leave her was over her dead body. Maybe she even thought he planned to do away with her."

"Is there any evidence of that?"

"Not much," I admitted. "But Bonelli checked the recent activity on Gillian's phone, and found that *she* visited several sites that explained electrical work on an old house, including the risks of electrocution. So you might ask, was she worried about Donald's safety? Or planning to do him in? The fire investigator said the wall and part of the ceiling had been opened up in the area where the fire started. Nick said he did that, to check out the gas pipes. But some of the old knob-and-tube had been pulled through the gap, and both Nick and Donald denied touching that."

"Gillian did hear them talking about that stuff, right? So she knew it was hazardous."

"She did. The cloth covering on some wires was badly frayed, and those fibers also were found on the wire cutters. Nick and Donald knew the gas behind the walls was dangerous, so they'd never have exposed themselves by risking a spark."

"But Gillian didn't understand that risk," Dawn offered.

"And finally, Nick had warned Donald that the old wires weren't color-coded the same as they would be today. So even if he turned a circuit off, he should still assume a particular wire could be live until he tested it. Whoever stripped those wires on Monday apparently didn't have that information, either."

"Had to be Gillian, right?"

I nodded. "Our theory is that she intended to sabotage the job. The next time Donald turned the circuit on and touched a wire, at the very least he'd suffer a bad shock. If he just got injured, maybe Gillian would consider that his punishment for cheating on her. But if he died accidentally, she'd inherit everything. Including the complete attention and devotion of her daughter."

Dawn tilted her head, bemused. "I guess because she always planned things so carefully, with such attention to detail, she believed she could pull off the perfect crime."

A good insight, I thought. "She never learned what most of us come to accept, early on: Nothing in life is ever perfect."

Chapter 24

In spite of both of our speculations, Bonelli decided there really was no point in trying to prove that Gillian had accidentally killed herself while trying to do away with her husband. It would only hurt Donald and Whitney, who already had been through enough. So the official report by the Chadwick PD concluded that Ms. Foster may have tried to finish the electrical work in the cellar herself, unaware of some serious hazards, and sparked the fire. Based on that theory, the case was declared closed.

This allowed her husband and her daughter to bury Gillian with a dignified funeral, attended by friends, family and a few business associates. Whether or not Donald or Whitney nurtured any lingering suspicions as to what she'd been up to in the cellar that Saturday, others accepted Gillian's death as simply a tragic accident.

Donald hired a contractor who specialized in older homes to finish the cellar quickly and simply, with an eye to safety rather than period detail. As soon as the repairs were finished, he put the Ramsford-Cooper house on the market. In the meantime, the Chadwick Historical Society finally added the home to its official register; possibly that would blunt the negative impact of the previous owner having died there. The real estate ad stated that historically minded buyers were welcome to also purchase any of the antique furnishings.

When I last heard from Donald Foster, he and Whitney had moved to a new-build condo in a neighboring town. He said they badly needed a place with "no maintenance, no history . . . and no painful memories."

Over Fourth of July weekend, as part of Chadwick's annual outdoor celebration, several area bands were scheduled to perform in the quaint gazebo of Riverside Park. Quintessence got a slot on Saturday afternoon and invited Mark to sit in with them for three numbers, his first public gig as a jazz guitarist. I rallied as many people as I could to come with me, so that afternoon the audience included Sarah, Robin, Dawn and Keith.

It was a lovely, clear day. At least a hundred people sat in lawn or camp chairs, or sprawled on blankets, covering the swath of grass between the gazebo and the nearby river. I knew Mark worked some Saturday mornings, but as I listened to Quintessence's first few numbers, I kept wondering when he would show up. About five minutes before he was due go on, he texted me to say he was running late. He must also have contacted Stan, because shortly afterward the group went ahead and played "Summertime," one of the arrangements I knew Mark had rehearsed with them.

Tracy did a good job on the song, her style less breathy than usual. Her outfit today also was more family-friendly, though still forties flamboyant—a "patriotic" combo of red shorts and a snug blue sailor top over a red-and-white-striped tee.

Eventually Mark came hiking up from the parking lot with his guitar, his dark hair a bit tousled and his demeanor sheepish. As he took to the stage, Stan introduced him and added, "Dr. Coccia apologizes for his late arrival, but at least he had an original excuse—he was spaying a rabbit."

Many in the crowd chuckled, as did the other band members, and the drummer heckled Mark, "C'mon, man, you expect us to buy *that* old line?"

They went into a peppy rendition of "Blue Skies," and Stan stepped aside to let Mark demonstrate how much his chops had improved over the past month or so. He diverged more confidently from the basic melody and rhythm, injecting just enough surprises to keep things fresh. The rousing applause at the end of the song seemed to recognize not only his musical skill, but his courage to step out of his customary role as hardworking veterinarian.

Before they began his second number, Tracy dedicated it to "a *very* special guy. I wasn't sure he'd be able to make it here this afternoon, because he's got an important job—life and death, really—and deals with a lot of emergencies. But I know he really wanted to come and I'm so glad he's here!"

Lounging in a lawn chair among my friends, I started to fume, and Dawn glanced toward me in sympathy. If Tracy embarrassed both me and Mark in front of everyone in this park, I'd hunt her down some night and pepper-spray her so bad, she'd never sing another note again.

"Freddy," she finished, in her vampiest tone, "you've started a five-alarmer in my heart!"

Everyone turned to stare at a muscular young man who blushed to the roots of his blond crew cut—one of the Chadwick firefighters who had responded to my 911 call at the Foster house.

I exhaled with a laugh, and Dawn grinned, too. We both probably shared the same thought: If Tracy had publicly declared her devotion to this guy, I shouldn't have to worry about her bugging *my* boyfriend anymore.

I didn't mind her sultry delivery of "Body and Soul," because she obviously aimed it at the hunky fireman. Instead, I could relax and go on appreciating Mark's inventive guitar work. He embellished this number with countermelodies that wove subtly in and out of Tracy's notes. Once again, the group's performance earned hearty applause.

When at last Mark joined us in the audience, Sarah, Robin, Dawn and Keith all praised his playing, and scolded him for keeping it a secret from them until now.

"Did Stan make up that story about the rabbit?" I asked him.

"Nope, absolutely true. I thought it would be a quick job, but after the surgery she had a bad reaction to the anesthesia. I couldn't leave until we got her stabilized."

Keith needled him, "Well, once you're a famous jazz guitarist, you won't have such *hare*-raising problems anymore."

Though Mark grinned, he insisted, "Stan has no serious competition from me. I've enjoyed improving my guitar skills, but that will always be a hobby. If I'd had to choose between saving an animal's life or getting to this gig, it would have been no contest. I knew a five-year-old boy was worried that his bunny might not make it, so seeing her EKG waves go back to normal was the bigger rush."

I put my arm through his. "Good to know you have your priorities straight."

By late July, the Tillman house also had gone on the market.

Bernice's murder and Chester's close call finally shamed his son and daughter into paying more attention to his living conditions. They hired a service to clean out his home, though they spared a few mementoes and collections that meant a lot to their father. They also vowed that under no circumstances would they ever sell the place to Dan Pressley.

Meanwhile, because complaints about Officer Brewer and Chief Hill came to the attention of the county prosecutor, the Dalton Police Department also had gone through some serious "housecleaning."

Swayed by pressure from Sarah and Robin, Chester's adult children did move him into Mountainview, just outside of Dalton. It allowed each resident to keep up to two small pets, so Chester brought both his indoor cats—his "girls"—Candy and Minnie. Becky and Chris talked Mountainview's administrators into letting them bring their shelter kittens to visit one day each month, and also added Sugarman to their program. They told me the dementia patients especially benefited from this experience, often reminiscing fondly about pets they'd had in their younger days.

The doctors at the community did not consider Chester's memory problems too severe, so he was allowed a fair amount of independence. Every Sunday morning, Robin drove him to services at the First Baptist Church, where the parishioners welcomed him back warmly.

His new one-bedroom apartment included a good-size living/dining area with a kitchenette. (The residents could get more substantial meals in a larger, common dining room.) A housekeeper tidied it regularly, but the community's staff knew better than to change things around too much, or store them out of sight, without the residents' permission. Chester would always have a tendency to clutter and misplace things, but with fewer possessions it did not get out of control.

He'd kept a dozen tapes of his radio interviews with famous sports figures, along with an old-school cassette player. These helped him make friends among the other men. They sometimes gathered at Chester's place to listen to his conversations, recorded in the 1970s and early '80s, with Jersey-born greats such as Joe Theismann, Dennis Rodman and Drew Pearson.

At Smiley's house, the police had found the Nintendo games that Philip Russell had rejected as not worth much, as well as a few Star Trek toys for which Bob had not yet found a buyer on eBay. Chester didn't care much about getting any of those things back. It angered him more to hear that Smiley had sold the American Girl doll online for a good price, and he grumbled, "Just hope it went to somebody who appreciated it more than my daughter did."

Though the cops also searched online for the Roger Maris baseball, it never resurfaced—whoever had bought that treasure would not be giving it back. We also never recovered Chester's stolen Blue Note albums, but since I'd made a list of them, Sarah, Robin and I purchased several that had been remastered on CD.

One evening in mid-August, on his eighty-first birthday, we visited Chester to present him with these. I threw in a compact, easy-to-operate CD player so he could listen to the albums on his own or share them with his new friends.

Chester thanked us with a tear in his eye, not only for the gifts, but for helping to prove the plot against him and to nail those responsible. All three of us assured him that we were just glad we'd been able to help him get justice, for Bernice and himself.

The community had made him a birthday cake, and he offered us slices of what remained. With Robin's help, he chose a CD to play—*Moanin'*, with Art Blakey and the Jazz Messengers, first released on vinyl in 1958. The restoration had a clean, vibrant sound, and we all enjoyed the music. I made a mental note that Mark would probably love this album, too.

During the slow, romantic tune "Contemplation," Chester leaned back in his easy chair and shut his eyes. "This was Bernice's favorite," he told us in a soft voice. "I just know she's up there now, eavesdropping." He sounded more nostalgic, though, than sad.

Candy, the pretty calico, responded to this mood by jumping onto Chester's lap; the older man smiled and cuddled her. Minnie-Mouse, the tuxedo cat, balanced with queenly poise on the back of the sofa behind Sarah, Robin and me. The living room's deep windows offered a lovely, twilight view of the community's landscaped gardens, shadowed by mature trees. Here Chester could leave his curtains parted and his blinds open, with no worries about predatory neighbors or rogue cops who might be out to harm him.

The windowsill held an electronic picture frame, a birthday gift from his son, James. Chester already had shown us the pictures loaded into it—various shots of both James and Sylvia with their spouses and Chester's grandkids. Next to this stood a large vase filled with tiger lilies and other late-summer flowers, from the congregation at First Baptist.

After baking all day in the hot sun of the window, the flowers had begun to wilt a little. Birthday cards from Chester's new friends and notices of community activities cluttered his coffee table. His new tan sofa held both black hairs shed by Minnie and mostly white hairs from Candy, and one arm already showed claw marks. Our empty dessert plates teetered in a pile on the dining table, and some crumbs had fallen on the carpet.

The mismatched furniture came from all different decades. It would have given Gillian Foster apoplexy.

But even though it wasn't the same house where Chester and Bernice had raised their children, and it might be far from perfect, he looked content.

Already, to Chester, it was home.

Connect with U(s)

Visit us online at
KensingtonBooks.com
to read more from your favorite authors, see books
by series, view reading group guides, and more.

for sneak peeks, chances to win books and prize packs,
and to share your thoughts with other readers.

facebook.com/kensingtonpublishing
twitter.com/kensingtonbooks

Tell us what you think!

To share your thoughts, submit a review,
or sign up for our eNewsletters, please visit:
KensingtonBooks.com/TellUs.